2nd Chance

2nd Chance

A NOVEL BY

JAMES PATTERSON

WITH ANDREW GROSS

LITTLE, BROWN AND COMPANY

LARGE PRINT

First Large Print Edition

This Large Print Edition published in accord with the standards of the N.A.V.H.

ISBN 0-316-69597-1
LCCN 2001038725

10 9 8 7 6 5 4 3 2 1

Q-FF

Printed in the United States of America

Acknowledgments

A SPECIAL THANKS to Inspector / Sergeant Holly Pera of the SFPD's Homicide Detail. To her partner, Inspector / Sergeant Joe Toomey. And Pete Ogten, Captain, Ret., SFPD. And again, to Dr. Greg Zorman of Fort Lauderdale.

But most of all, this is for Lynn and Sue.

Prologue

THE CHOIR KIDS

AARON WINSLOW would never forget the next few minutes. He recognized the terrifying sounds the instant they *cracked* through the night. His body went cold all over. He couldn't believe that someone was shooting a high-powered rifle in this neighborhood.

K-pow, k-pow, k-pow . . . k-pow, k-pow, k-pow.

His choir was just leaving the La Salle Heights Church. Forty-eight young kids were streaming past him toward the sidewalk. They had just finished their final rehearsal before the San Francisco Sing-Off, and they had been excellent.

Then came the gunfire. Lots of it. Not just a single shot. A strafing. An *attack.*

K-pow, k-pow, k-pow . . . k-pow, k-pow, k-pow.

"Get down!" he screamed at the top of his voice. "Everybody down on the ground! Cover your heads. Cover up!" He almost couldn't believe the words as they left his mouth.

At first, no one seemed to hear him. To the kids, in their dress white blouses and shirts, the shots must have sounded like firecrackers. Then a volley of shots rained through the church's beautiful stained-glass window. The depiction of Christ's blessing over a child at Capernaum shattered, glass splintering everywhere, some of it falling on the heads of the children.

"Someone's shooting!" Winslow screamed. Maybe more than one person. *How could that be?* He ran wildly through the kids, shouting, waving his arms, pushing as many as he could down to the grass.

As the kids finally crouched low or dove for the ground, Winslow spotted two of his choir girls, Chantal and Tamara, frozen on the lawn as bullets streaked past them. "Get down, Chantal, Tamara!" he yelled, but they remained there, hugging each other, emitting frantic wails. They were best friends. He had known them since they were little kids, playing four-square on blacktop.

4

There was never any doubt in his mind. He sprinted toward the two girls, grasped their arms firmly, and tumbled them to the ground. Then he lay on top of them, pressing their bodies tightly.

Bullets whined over his head, just inches away. His eardrums hurt. His body was trembling and so were the girls shielded beneath him. He was almost sure he was about to die. "It's all right, babies," he whispered.

Then, as suddenly as it had begun, the firing stopped. A hush of silence hung in the air. So strange and eerie, as if the whole world had stopped to listen.

As he raised himself, his eyes fell on an incredible sight. Slowly, everywhere, the children struggled to their feet. There was some crying, but he didn't see any blood, no one seemed to be hurt.

"Everyone okay?" Winslow called out. He made his way through the crowd. "Is anyone hurt?"

"I'm okay. . . . I'm okay" came back to him. He looked around in disbelief. This was a miracle.

Then he heard the sound of a single child whimpering.

He turned and spotted Maria Parker, only twelve years old. Maria was standing on the whitewashed wooden steps of the church entrance. She seemed lost. Choking sobs poured from her open mouth.

Then Aaron Winslow's eyes came to rest on what had made the girl hysterical. He felt his heart sink. Even in war, even growing up on the streets of Oakland, he had never felt anything so horrible, so sad and senseless.

"Oh, God. Oh, no. How could you let this happen?"

Tasha Catchings, just eleven years old, lay in a heap in a flowerbed near the foundation of the church. Her white school blouse was soaked with blood.

Finally, Reverend Aaron Winslow began to cry himself.

Part I

THE WOMEN'S MURDER CLUB — AGAIN

Chapter 1

ON A TUESDAY NIGHT, I found myself playing a game of crazy eights with three residents of the Hope Street Teen House. I was loving it.

On the beat-up couch across from me sat Hector, a barrio kid two days out of Juvenile; Alysha, quiet and pretty, but with a family history you wouldn't want to know; and Michelle, who at fourteen had already spent a year selling herself on the streets of San Francisco.

"Hearts," I declared, flipping down an eight and changing the suit just as Hector was about to lay out.

"Damn, badge lady," he whined. "How come each time I'm 'bout to go down, you stick your knife in me?"

"Teach *you* to ever trust a cop, fool."

Michelle laughed, tossing a conspiratorial smile my way.

For the past month, I'd been spending a night or two a week at the Hope Street House. For so long after the terrible bride and groom case that summer, I'd felt completely lost. I took a month off from Homicide, ran down by the marina, gazed out at the bay from the safety of my Potrero Hill flat.

Nothing helped. Not counseling, not the total support of my girls — Claire, Cindy, Jill. Not even going back to the job. I had watched, unable to help, as the life leaked out of the person I loved. I still felt responsible for my partner's death in the line of duty. Nothing seemed to fill the void.

So I came here . . . to Hope Street.

And the good news was, it was working a little.

I peered up from my cards at Angela, a new arrival who sat in a metal chair across the room cuddling her three-month-old daughter. The poor kid, maybe sixteen, hadn't said much all night. I would try to talk to Angela before I left.

The door opened and Dee Collins, one of the house's head counselors, came in. She was followed by a stiff-looking black woman in a conservative gray suit. She had Department of Children and Families written all over her.

"Angela, your social worker's here." Dee knelt down beside her.

"I ain't blind," the teenager said.

"We're going to have to take the baby now," the social worker interrupted, as if completing this assignment was all that kept her from catching the next Caltrain.

"No!" Angela pulled the infant even closer. "You can keep me in this hole, you can send me back to Claymore, but you're not taking my baby."

"Please, honey, only for a few days," Dee Collins tried to assure her.

The teenage girl drew her arms protectively around her baby, who, sensing some harm, began to cry.

"Don't you make a scene, Angela," the social worker warned. "You know how this is done."

As she came toward her, I watched as Angela jumped out of the chair. She was clutching the baby in one arm and a glass of juice she'd been drinking in the opposite hand.

In one swift motion, she cracked the glass against a table. It created a jagged shard.

"Angela." I jumped up from the card table. "Put that down. No one's going to take your baby anywhere unless you let her go."

"*This bitch* is trying to ruin my life." She glared. "First she lets me sit in Claymore three days past my date, then she won't let me go home to my mom. Now she's trying to take my baby girl."

I nodded, peering into the teenager's eyes. "First, you gotta lay down the glass," I said. "You *know* that, Angela."

The DCF worker took a step, but I held her back. I moved slowly toward Angela. I took hold of the glass, then I gently eased the child out of her arms.

"She's all I have," the girl whispered, and then she started to sob.

"*I know.*" I nodded. "That's why you'll change some things in your life and get her back."

Dee Collins had her arms around Angela, a cloth wrapped around the girl's bleeding hand. The DCF worker was trying unsuccessfully to hush the crying infant.

I went up and said to her, "That baby gets placed somewhere nearby with daily visitation rights. And by the way, I didn't see anything going on here that was worth putting on file. . . . *You?*" The caseworker gave me a disgruntled look and turned away.

Suddenly, my beeper sounded, three dissonant beeps punctuating the tense air. I pulled it out and read the number. *Jacobi, my ex-partner in Homicide. What did he want?*

I excused myself and moved into the staff office. I was able to reach him in his car.

"Something bad's happened, Lindsay," he said glumly. "I thought you'd want to know."

He clued me in about a horrible drive-by shooting at the La Salle Heights Church. An eleven-year-old girl had been killed.

"Jesus . . ." I sighed as my heart sank.

"I thought you might want in on it," Jacobi said.

I took in a breath. It had been over three months since I'd been on the scene at a homicide. Not since the day the bride and groom case ended.

"So, I didn't hear," Jacobi pressed. "You want in, *Lieutenant?*" It was the first time he had called me by my new rank.

I realized my honeymoon had come to an end. "Yeah," I muttered. "I want in."

Chapter 2

A COLD RAIN STARTED TO FALL as I pulled my Explorer up to the La Salle Heights Church on Harrow Street, in the predominantly black section of Bay View. An angry, anxious crowd had formed — a combination of saddened neighborhood mothers and the usual sullen homeboys huddled in their bright Tommys — all pushing against a handful of uniformed cops.

"This ain't goddamn Mississippi," someone shouted as I forced my way through the throng.

"How many more?" an older woman wailed. *"How many more?"*

I badged my way past a couple of nervous patrolmen to the front. What I saw next absolutely took my breath away.

The facade of the white clapboard church was slashed with a grotesque pattern of bullet holes and lead-colored chinks. A huge hole gaped in a wall where a large stained-glass window had been shot out. Jagged edges of colored glass teetered like hanging ice. Kids were still scattered all over the lawn, obviously in shock, some being attended to by EMS teams.

"Oh, Jesus," I whispered under my breath.

I spotted medical techs in black windbreakers huddled over the body of a young girl by the front steps. A couple of plainclothesmen were nearby. One of them was my ex-partner, Warren Jacobi.

I found myself hesitating. I had done this a hundred times. Only months ago I had solved the biggest murder case in the city since Harvey Milk, but so much had happened since then. I felt weird, like I was new at this. Balling my fists, I took a deep breath and went over to Jacobi.

"Welcome back to the world, Lieutenant," Jacobi said with a roll of the tongue on my new rank.

The sound of that word still sent electricity surging through me. Heading Homicide had been the goal I had pursued throughout my career: the first female homicide detective in

San Francisco, now the department's first female lieutenant. After my old L.T., Sam Roth, opted for a cushy stint up in Bodega Bay, Chief Mercer had called me in. *I can do one of two things,* he'd said to me. *I can keep you on long-term administrative leave and you can see if you find the heart to do this job again. Or I can give you these, Lindsay.* He pushed a gold shield with two bars on it across the table. Until that moment, I don't think I had ever seen Mercer smile.

"The lieutenant's shield doesn't make it any easier, does it, Lindsay?" Jacobi said, emphasizing that our three-year relationship as partners had now changed.

"What do we have?" I asked him.

"Looks like a single gunman, from out in those bushes." He pointed to a dense thicket beside the church, maybe fifty yards away. "Asshole caught the kids just as they came out. Opened fire with everything he had."

I took a breath, staring at the weeping, shell-shocked kids scattered all over the lawn. "Anybody see the guy? Somebody did, right?"

He shook his head. "Everyone hit the deck."

Near the fallen child, a distraught black woman sobbed into the shoulder of a comforting friend. Jacobi saw my eyes fix on the dead girl.

"Name's Tasha Catchings," he muttered. "In the fifth grade, over at St. Anne's. Good girl. Youngest kid in the choir."

I moved in closer and knelt over the blood-soaked body. No matter how many times you do this, it's a wrenching sight. Tasha's school blouse was soaked with blood, mixed with falling rain. Just a few feet away, a rainbow-colored knapsack lay on the grass.

"She's it?" I asked incredulously. I surveyed the scene. "She's the only one who got hit?"

Bullet holes were everywhere, splintered glass and wood. Dozens of kids had been streaming out to the street. . . . *All those shots, and only one victim.*

"Our lucky day, huh?" Jacobi snorted.

Chapter 3

PAUL CHIN, one of my Homicide crew, was interviewing a tall, handsome black man dressed in a black turtleneck and jeans on the steps of the church. I'd seen him before, on the news. I even knew his name, Aaron Winslow.

Even in shock and dismay, Winslow carried himself with a graceful bearing — a smooth face, jet-black hair cut flat on top, and a football running back's build. Everyone in San Francisco knew what he was doing for this neighborhood. He was supposed to be a real-life hero, and I must say he looked the part.

I walked over.

"This is Reverend Aaron Winslow," Chin said, introducing us.

"Lindsay Boxer," I said, extending my hand.

"*Lieutenant* Boxer," said Chin. "She'll be overseeing the case."

"I'm familiar with your work," I said. "You've given a lot to this neighborhood. I'm so sorry for this. I don't have any words for it."

His eyes shifted toward the murdered girl. He spoke in the softest voice imaginable. "I've known her since she was a child. These are good, responsible people. Her mother . . . she brought up Tasha and her brother on her own. These were all young kids. Choir practice, Lieutenant."

I didn't want to intrude, but I had to. "Can I ask a few questions? Please."

He nodded blankly. "Of course."

"You see anyone? Someone fleeing? A shape, a glimpse?"

"I saw where the shots came from," Winslow said, and he pointed to the same thicket of bushes where Jacobi had gone. "I saw the trailer fire. I was busy trying to get everyone down. It was madness."

"Has anyone made any threats recently against you or your church?" I asked.

"Threats?" Winslow screwed up his face. "Maybe years ago, when we first got funding to rebuild some of these houses."

A short distance away, a haunting wail came from Tasha Catchings's mother as the girl's body was lifted onto a gurney. This was so sad. The surrounding crowd was growing edgy. Taunts and accusations began to ring out. "Why are you all standing around? Go find her killer!"

"I better get over there," Winslow said, "before this thing goes the wrong way." He started to move, then turned with tight-lipped resignation on his face. "I could have saved that poor baby. I heard the shots."

"You couldn't save them all," I said. "You did what you could."

He finally nodded. Then he said something that totally shocked me. "It was an M Sixteen, Lieutenant. Thirty-round clip. The bastard reloaded twice. "

"How would you know that?" I asked, surprised.

"Desert Storm," he answered. "I was a field chaplain. No way I would ever forget that awful sound. No one ever does."

Chapter 4

I HEARD MY NAME CALLED OUT over the din of the crowd. It was Jacobi. He was in the woods behind the church. "Hey, Lieutenant, come check this out."

Heading over, I wondered what kind of person could do such a terrible thing. I had worked on a hundred homicides; usually drugs, money, or sex was at the heart of them. But *this . . . this was meant to shock.*

"Check it out," Jacobi said, bending down over a spot. He'd found a bullet casing.

"M Sixteen, I bet," I replied.

Jacobi nodded. "Little lady's been brushing up during her time off? Shell's a Remington two twenty-three."

"*Lieutenant* Little Lady to you." I smirked. Then I told him how I knew.

Dozens of empty shells were scattered all around. We were deep in the brush and trees, hidden from the church. The casings were strewn in two distinct clusters about five yards apart.

"You can see where he started firing," Jacobi said. "I figure here. He must've moved around."

From the first cluster of shells, there was a clear line of sight to the side of the church. That stained-glass window in full view . . . all those kids streaming toward the street . . . I could see why no one had spotted him. His hiding place was totally protected.

"When he reloaded, he must've moved over there." Jacobi pointed.

I made my way over and crouched near the second cluster of shells. Something wasn't making sense. The facade of the church was in view, the front steps where Tasha Catchings had lain. But only barely.

I squinted through an imaginary sight, leveling my gaze at where Tasha must've been when she was hit. You could barely even fix it into sight. There was no way he could've intentionally been aiming for her. She had been struck from a totally improbable angle.

"Lucky shot," Jacobi muttered. "What do you think, a ricochet?"

"What's back here?" I asked. I looked around, pushing my way through the thick bushes leading away from the church. No one had seen the shooter escape, so he obviously hadn't made his way along Harrow Street. The brush was about twenty feet deep.

At the end was a five-foot-high chain-link fence dividing the church grounds from the surrounding neighborhood. The fence wasn't high. I planted my flats and hoisted myself over.

I found myself facing penned-in backyards and tiny row houses. A few people had gathered, watching the show. To the right, the playgrounds of the Whitney Young projects.

Jacobi finally caught up with me. "Take it easy, Loo," he huffed. "There's an audience. You're making me look bad."

"This is how he must've made his way out, Warren." We looked in both directions. One way led toward an alley, the other toward a row of homes.

I shouted to a group of onlookers who had gathered on a back porch, "Anyone see anything?" No one responded.

"Someone was shooting at the church," I shouted. "A little girl's been killed. Help us out. We need your help."

Everyone stood around with the unconfiding silence of people who don't talk to the police.

Then slowly a woman of about thirty came forward. She was nudging a young boy ahead of her. "Bernard saw something," she said in a muffled voice.

Bernard appeared to be about six, with cautious, round eyes, wearing a gold-and-purple Kobe Bryant sweatshirt.

"It was a van," Bernard blurted. "Like Uncle Reggie's." He pointed to the dirt road leading to the alley. "It was parked down *there*."

I knelt down, gently smiling into the scared boy's eyes. "What color van, Bernard?"

The kid replied, "White."

"My brother's got a white Dodge minivan," Bernard's mother said.

"Was it like your uncle's, Bernard?" I asked.

"Sorta. Not really, though."

"Did you see the man who was driving it?"

He shook his head. "I was bringing out the garbage. I only saw it drive away."

"Do you think you would recognize it again if you saw it?" I asked.

Bernard nodded.

"Because it looked like your uncle's?"

He hesitated. "No, because it had a picture on the back."

"A picture? You mean like an insignia? Or some kind of advertising?"

"Uh-uh." He shook his head; his moonlike eyes were searching around. Then they lit up. "I mean like that." He pointed toward a pickup truck in a neighbor's driveway. There was a sticker of a Cal Golden Bear on the rear bumper.

"You mean a decal?" I confirmed.

"On the door."

I held the boy softly by the shoulders. "What did this decal look like, Bernard?"

"Like Mufasa," the boy said, "from *The Lion King.*"

"A lion?" My mind raced through anything that seemed likely. Sports teams, college logos, corporations . . .

"Yeah, like Mufasa," Bernard repeated. "Except it had two heads."

Chapter 5

LESS THAN AN HOUR LATER, I was pushing through a surging crowd that had built up on the steps of the Hall of Justice. I felt hollowed out and terribly sad, but knew I couldn't show it here.

The lobby of the tomblike granite building where I worked was packed with reporters and news crews, shoving their microphones at anyone who came in wearing a badge. Most of the crime reporters knew me, but I waved them off until I could get upstairs.

Then a set of hands grasped my shoulders and a familiar voice chimed, "Linds, we need to talk. . . ."

I spun to face Cindy Thomas, one of my closest friends, though it also happened she was the lead crime reporter at the *Chronicle*. "I won't bother you now," she said above the din. "But it's important. How about Susie's, at ten?"

It had been Cindy who, as a stringer buried on the paper's Metro desk, had sneaked into the heart of the bride and groom case and helped blow it wide open. Cindy who, as much as any of us, was responsible for the gold on my shield today.

I managed a smile. "I'll see you there."

Upstairs on three, I strode into the cramped fluorescent-lit room that the twelve inspectors who managed Homicide for the city called home. Lorraine Stafford was waiting for me there. She had been my first appointment, after six successful years in Sex Crimes. And Cappy McNeil had come in, too.

Lorraine asked, "What can I do?"

"You can check with Sacramento for any stolen white vans. Any model. In-state plates. And put out an APB along with it for a bumper sticker of some sort of lion on the rear." She nodded and started away.

"Lorraine." I stopped her. "Make that a *two-*headed lion."

Cappy walked with me while I made myself a cup of tea. He'd been in Homicide for fifteen years, and I knew he had supported me when Chief Mercer consulted him about offering me the lieutenant job. He looked sad, thoroughly depressed. "I know Aaron Winslow. I played ball with him in Oakland. He's devoted his life to those kids. He really is one of the good guys, Lieutenant."

All of a sudden Frank Barnes from Auto Theft stuck his head into our office. "Heads up, Lieutenant. Weight's on the floor."

Weight, in the lexicon of the SFPD, meant Chief of Police Earl Mercer.

Chapter 6

MERCER STRODE IN, all two hundred fifty pounds of him, trailed by Gabe Carr, a mean little weasel who was the department's press liaison, and Fred Dix, who managed community relations.

The chief was still dressed in his trademark dark gray suit, blue shirt, and shiny gold cuff links. I'd watched Mercer manage a number of tense scenes — transit bombings, Internal Affairs stings, serial killers — but I'd never seen his face so tight. He motioned me into my office and, with barely a word, pulled the door shut. Fred Dix and Gabe Carr were already inside.

"I just got off the phone with Winston Gray and Vernon Jones" — two of the city's most outspoken leaders. "They've assured me they'll plead for restraint, give us some time to find out just what the fuck is going on. Just so I'm clear: By *restraint,* what they mean is, deliver the person or group who's responsible for this or they'll have two thousand outraged citizens at City Hall."

He barely relaxed his face when he stared at me. "So I'm hoping, Lieutenant, you got something you want to share . . . ?"

I took him through what I had found at the church, along with Bernard Smith's sighting of the white getaway van.

"Van or not," the mayor's man, Fred Dix, cut in, "you know where you have to start on this. Mayor Fernandez is going to come down hard on anyone operating in the area espousing a racist or antidiversity message. We need some heat to fall their way."

"You seem pretty sure that's what we're looking at," I said with a noncommittal glance. "Your garden-variety hate crime?"

"Shooting up a church, murdering an eleven-year-old child? Where would you start, *Lieutenant?*"

"That girl's face is going to be on every news report in the country," Carr, the press liaison, pitched in. "The effort in the Bay View neighborhood is one of the mayor's proudest accomplishments."

I nodded. "Does the mayor mind if I finish my eyewitness interviews first?"

"Don't worry yourself with the mayor," Mercer cut in. "Right now, all you have to be concerned with is me. I grew up on these streets. My folks still live in West Portal. I don't need a TV sound bite to see that kid's face in my mind. You run the investigation wherever it leads. Just run it fast. And Lindsay . . . nothing gets in the way, you understand?"

He was about to get up. "And most importantly, I want total containment on this. I don't want to see this investigation being run on the front page."

Everyone nodded, and Mercer, followed by Dix and Carr, stood up. He let out a deep blast of air. "Right now, we have one hell of a press conference to muck our way through."

The others filed out of the room, but Mercer stayed behind. He leaned his thick hands on the edge of my desk, his hulking shape towering over me.

"Lindsay, I know you left a lot on the table after that last case. But all that's done. It's history now. I need everything you have on this case. One of the things you left behind when you took that shield was the freedom to let personal pain interfere with the job."

"You don't have to worry about me." I gave him a solid stare. I'd had my differences with the man over the years, but now I was ready to give him everything I had. I had seen the dead little girl. I had seen the church torn up. My blood was on fire. I hadn't felt this way since I left the job.

Chief Mercer flashed me a smile of understanding. "It's good to have you back, Lieutenant."

Chapter 7

AFTER A HIGHLY CHARGED news conference conducted on the steps of the Hall, I met Cindy at Susie's as we had arranged. After the frenzied scene at the Hall, the relaxed, laid-back atmosphere at our favorite meeting place was a relief. She was already sipping a Corona as I arrived.

A lot had happened here — at this very table. Cindy; Jill Bernhardt, the assistant district attorney; and Claire Washburn, the chief medical examiner, my closest friend. We had started to meet last summer, when it seemed that fate had pulled us together with links to the bride and groom case. In the process, we had evolved into the closest of friends.

I signaled our waitress, Loretta, for a beer, then planted myself across from Cindy with a worn-out smile. "Hey . . ."

"Hey, yourself." She smiled back. "Good to see you."

"Good to be seen."

A TV blared above the bar, a broadcast of Chief Mercer's news conference. "We believe it was a single gunman," Mercer announced to a flash of photographers' bulbs.

"You stay for that?" I asked Cindy, taking a welcome swig of my ice-cold beer.

"I was there," she replied. "Stone and Fitzpatrick were there, too. They filed the report."

I gave her a startled look. Tom Stone and Suzie Fitzpatrick were her competition on the crime desk. "You losing your touch? Six months ago, I would've found you coming out of the church as soon as we arrived."

"I'm going at it from another angle." She shrugged.

A handful of people crowded around the bar, trying to catch the breaking news. I took another chug of beer. "You should've seen this poor little girl, Cindy. All of eleven years old. She sang in the choir. There was this rainbow-colored knapsack with all her books on the ground nearby."

"You know this stuff, Lindsay." She gave me a bolstering smile. "You know how it is. It sucks."

"Yeah." I nodded. "But just once, it'd be nice to pick one of them up . . . you know, brush them off, send them home. Just once, I'd like to hand one back their book bag."

Cindy tapped her fist affectionately on the back of my hand. Then she brightened. "I saw Jill today. She's got some news for us. She's excited. Maybe Bennett's retiring and she's getting the big chair. We should get together and see what's up with her."

"For sure." I nodded. "That what you wanted to tell me tonight, Cindy . . . ?"

She shook her head. In the background, all hell was breaking loose in the news conference on the screen — Mercer promising a swift and effective response. "You've got a problem, Linds. . . ."

I shook my head. "I *can't* give you anything, Cindy. Mercer's handling everything. I've never seen him so worked up. I'm sorry."

"I didn't ask you here to get something, Lindsay. . . ."

"Cindy, if you know something, tell me."

35

"I know that boss of yours better be careful what he's committing to."

I glanced at the screen. *"Mercer . . . ?"*

In the background, I heard his voice asserting that the shooting was an isolated incident, that we already had tangible leads, that every available cop would be on the case until we tracked the killer down.

"He's telling the world you're gonna nail this guy *before* it happens again . . . ?"

"So . . . ?"

Our eyes met solidly. "I think it already has."

Chapter 8

THE KILLER WAS PLAYING Desert Command and he was a master.

Phffft, phffft, phffft . . . phffft, phffft.

Impassively, he squinted through the illuminated infrared sight as hooded figures darted into view. As if by an extension of his finger, the darkened, mazelike chambers of the terrorist bunker exploded in balls of orange flame. Shadowy figures burst into narrow halls, *phffft, phffft, phffft.*

He was a champion at this. Great hand-eye coordination. No one could touch him.

His finger twitched on the trigger. *Ghouls, sand mites, towel-heads.* Come at me, baby. . . . *Phffft, phffft . . .* Up through the dark corridors . . . He smashed through an iron door, came upon a whole nest of them, sucking on tabbouleh, playing cards. His weapon spit a steady orange death. *Blessed are the peacemakers.* He smirked.

He squinted one more time through the sight, replaying the scene at the church in his mind, imagining her face. That little Jemima, with her braided hair, the rainbow-colored knapsack on her back.

Phfft, phfft. An onscreen figure's chest exploded. This next kill was for the record. *Got it!* His eye flashed toward the score. *Two hundred seventy-six enemy dead.*

He took a tug on his Corona and grinned. A new personal record. This score was worth keeping. He punched in his initials: *F.C.*

He stood at the machine in the Playtime arcade in West Oakland, flicking the trigger long after the game had ended. He was the only white guy in the room. The only one. In fact, that was why he chose to be here.

Suddenly, the four large television sets overhead were blaring the same face. It sent a chill down his back and made him furious.

It was Mercer, the pompous ass who ran the San Francisco cops. He was acting like he had everything figured out.

"We believe this was the act of a single gunman . . . ," he was saying. "An isolated crime . . ."

If you only knew. He laughed.

Wait until tomorrow. . . . You'll see. Just you wait, Chief Asshole.

"What I want to stress," the chief of police declared, "is that under no circumstance will we permit this city to be terrorized by racial attack. . . ."

This city. He spat. *What do you know about this city? You don't belong here.*

He clutched at a C-1 grenade in his jacket pocket. If he wanted to, he could blow everything open right here. *Right now.*

But there was work to do.

Tomorrow.

He was going for another personal record.

Chapter 9

THE NEXT MORNING Jacobi and I were back examining the grounds of the La Salle Heights Church.

All night long, I had fretted over what Cindy had told me about a case that had come across her desk. It involved an elderly black woman who lived alone in the Gustave White projects in West Oakland. Three days ago, the Oakland police had found her hanging from a pipe in the basement laundry room, an electrical cord tightly wound around her neck.

At first, the police assumed it was a suicide. No abrasions or defensive wounds were found on her body. But the next day, during the autopsy, a flaky residue was found packed under her nails. It turned out to be human skin with microscopic specks of dried blood. *The poor woman had been desperately digging in to someone.*

She hadn't hung herself after all, Cindy said.

The woman had been lynched.

As I went back over the crime scene at the church, I felt uneasy. Cindy could be right. This might not be the first, but *the second* in an onset of racially driven murders.

Jacobi walked up. He was holding a curled-up *Chronicle.* "You see this, boss?"

The front page rocked with the blaring headline, "POLICE STUMPED AS GIRL, 11, IS KILLED IN CHURCH ASSAULT."

The article was written by Tom Stone and Suzie Fitzpatrick, whose careers had been nudged aside by Cindy's work on the bride and groom case. With the newspapers stoking the fire, and the activists Gray and Jones railing on the air, soon the public would be accusing us of sitting on our hands while the terror suspect was running free.

"*Your* buddies . . ." Jacobi huffed. "They always make it about us."

"Uh-uh, Warren." I shook my head. "My buddies don't take cheap shots."

Behind us in the woods, Charlie Clapper's Crime Scene Unit team was going over the ground around the sniper's position. They'd turned up a couple of foot imprints, but nothing identifiable. They would fingerprint the shell casings, grid-search the ground, pick up every piece of lint or dust where the supposed getaway vehicle had been parked.

"Any more sightings on that white van?" I asked Jacobi. In a strange way it was good to be working with him again.

He grumbled and shook his head. "Got a lead on a couple of winos who hold a coffee klatch on that corner at night. So far, all we have is this." He unfolded an artist's rendering of Bernard Smith's description — a two-headed lion, the sticker on the rear door of the van.

Jacobi sucked in his cheeks. "Who are we after, Lieutenant, the *Pokémon killer?*"

Across the grass, I spotted Aaron Winslow coming out of the church. A knot of protestors approached him from a police barrier some fifty yards away. As he saw me, his face tensed.

"People want to help any way they can. Paint over the bullet holes, build a new facade," he said. "They don't like to look at this."

"I'm sorry," I said. "I'm afraid there's still an active investigation going on."

He took in a breath. "I keep playing it over in my mind. Whoever did this had a clear shot. I was standing right *there,* Lieutenant. More in the line of fire than Tasha. If someone was trying to hurt someone, *why didn't they hurt me?*"

Winslow knelt down and picked up a pink butterfly hair clip from the ground. "I read somewhere, Lieutenant, that 'courage abounds where guilt and rage run free.'"

Winslow was taking this hard. I felt sorry for him; I liked him. He managed a tight smile. "It'll take more than this bastard to ruin our work. We won't fold. We'll have Tasha's service here, in this church."

"We were headed to pay our respects," I said.

"They live over there. Building A." He pointed toward the projects. "I guess you'll find a warm reception, given that there's some of your own."

I looked at him, puzzled. "I'm sorry? What was that?"

"Didn't you know, Lieutenant? Tasha Catchings's uncle is a city cop."

Chapter 10

I VISITED THE CATCHINGS'S apartment, paid my respects, then I headed back to the Hall. This whole thing was incredibly depressing.

"Mercer's looking for you," hollered Karen, our longtime civilian secretary, as I got into the office. "He sounds mad. Of course, he always sounds mad."

I could imagine the folds under the chief's jaw getting even deeper with the afternoon headline. In fact, the entire Hall was buzzing with the news that the La Salle Heights murder victim had been related to one of our own.

There were several other messages waiting for me on my desk. At the bottom of the pile I came across Claire's name. Tasha Catchings's autopsy should be finished by now. I wanted to hold off on Mercer until I had something concrete to report, so I called Claire.

Claire Washburn was the sharpest, brightest, most thorough M.E. the city ever had, notwithstanding the fact that she also happened to be my closest friend. Everyone associated with law enforcement knew it, and that she ran the department without a hitch while Chief Coroner Righetti, the mayor's stiff-suited appointee, traveled around the country to forensic conferences working on his political résumé. You wanted something done in the M.E.'s office, you called Claire.

And when I needed someone to set me straight, make me laugh, or just be there to listen, that's where I went, too.

"Where you been hiding, baby?" Claire greeted me with her always upbeat voice, which had the ring of polished brass.

"Normal routine." I shrugged. "Staff appraisals, case write-ups . . . city-dividing, racially motivated homicides . . ."

"Just my region of expertise." She chuckled. "I knew I'd be hearing from you. My spies tell me you've got yourself a bitch of a case out there."

"Any of those spies maybe work for the *Chronicle* and drive a beat-up silver Mazda?"

"Or the D.A.'s office, and a BMW five-thirty-five. How the hell do you think information ever gets down here, anyway?"

"Well, here's one, Claire. Turns out the dead little girl's uncle is in uniform. He's at Northern. And the poor kid ends up being a poster child for the La Salle Heights project in action. Top-of-the-line student, never once in trouble. Some justice, huh? This bastard leaves a hundred slugs in the church and the one that hits finds its way into her."

"Uh-uh, honey." Claire cut me off. "There were *two* of them in there."

"*Two* . . . ? She was hit twice?" EMS had been all over the body. How could we have failed to catch that?

"If I'm hearing you right, my guess is you think this shot was some kind of accident."

"What are you saying?"

"Honey," Claire said soberly, "I think you better come on down for a visit."

Chapter 11

THE MORGUE was on the ground floor of the Hall, out a back entrance and accessible from an asphalt path that led from the lobby. It took me no more than three minutes to rush down two flights of stairs.

Claire met me in the reception area outside her office. Her bright and usually cheery face bore a look of professional concern, but as soon as she saw me, she eased into a smile and gave me a hug.

"How you been, stranger?" she asked, as if the case were a million miles away.

Claire always had a way of defusing the tension in even the most critical of situations. I'd always admired how she could relax my single-minded focus with just a smile.

"I've been good, Claire. Just swamped since I got the job."

"I don't get to see you much now that you're Mercer's pet butt-boy."

"Very funny."

She smiled that coy, wide-eyed smirk of hers that was partly, *Hey, I know what you mean,* but maybe a lot more, *You gotta make the time, girl, for those who love you.* But without as much as a reproving word, she led me down an antiseptic, linoleum-tiled hall-way toward the morgue's operating room, called the Vault.

She glanced behind and said, "You made it sound like you were sure Tasha Catchings was killed by a stray bullet."

"That's what I thought. The gunman fired three clips at the church and she was the only one hit. I even went and cased the area where the shots came from. There was no way he had anything even close to a clean shot. But you said *two. . . .*"

"Uh-huh." She nodded. We burst through a closed compression door into the dry, cold air of the Vault. The icy chill and chemical smell always made my skin crawl.

And it was no different now. A single inhabited gurney was visible from its refrigerated vault. A small mound was on it, covered by a white sheet. It barely filled half the length of the gurney.

"Hold on," Claire warned. Naked post-op victims, rigid and terrifyingly pale, were never an easy sight.

She pulled down the sheet. The child's face shot into my view. *God, she was young. . . .*

I looked at her soft ebony skin, so innocent, so out of place against the cold, clinical surroundings. Part of me wanted to just reach out and lay a hand against her cheek. She had such a lovable face.

A large puncture wound, freshly cleaned of blood, tore up the flesh around the child's right chest. "*Two* bullets," Claire explained, "basically right on top of each other, in rapid succession. I could see why EMS might've missed it. They almost tore through the same hole."

I sucked in a horrific double take. A fit of nausea gripped at my gut.

"The first one exited right through her scapula," Claire went on, easing the tiny body over on its side. "The second bounced off the fourth vertebra and lodged in her spine."

Claire reached over and picked up a glass petri dish resting on a nearby counter. With a tweezer, she held up a flattened lead disk about the size of a quarter. "*Two* shots, Linds . . . The first tore through the right ventricle, doing the trick. She was probably dead before this one even struck."

Two shots . . . two one-in-a-million ricochets? I replayed the likely position of Tasha as she exited the church and the killer's line of fire in the woods. One seemed plausible, but *two* . . .

"Did Charlie Clapper's crew find any bullet nicks in the church above where the girl was positioned?" Claire inquired.

"I don't know." It was standard procedure in all homicides to painstakingly match up all bullets with their marks. "I'll check."

"What was the church constructed of where she was hit? Wood or stone?"

"Wood," I said, realizing where she was heading. No way wood on its own would deflect a bullet from an M16.

Claire pushed her operating glasses high on her forehead. She had a cheery, amiable face, but when she was certain, as she was now, it had a glow of conviction that admitted no doubt. "Lindsay, the angle of entry is frontal and clean for both shots. A ricocheting shell would likely have come in from a different trajectory."

"I went over every inch of the shooter's position, Claire. The way he was firing, he'd have to be a goddamn sharpshooter to set up that shot."

"You say the fire was sprayed irregularly across the side of the church."

"In a steady pattern, right to left. And Claire, no one else was struck. A hundred shots, *she was the only one hit.*"

"So you assumed this was a tragic accident, right?" Claire peeled off her plastic medical gloves and tossed them deftly into a waste receptacle. "Well, these two were no accident at all. They didn't ricochet off of anything. They were straight and perfectly placed. Killed her instantly. You willing to consider the possibility that maybe your gunman hit exactly what he was aiming at?"

I brought back the scene in my mind. "He would have only had an instant to line up such a shot, Claire. And only a foot or two of clearance from the wall to squeeze it in."

"Then either God didn't smile on that poor girl last night," Claire said with a sympathetic sigh, "or you better start looking for one hell of a shooter."

Chapter 12

THE SHOCKING POSSIBILITY that Tasha Catchings might not have been a random victim after all dogged me all the way back to the office. Upstairs, I ran into a wall of detectives anxiously awaiting me. Lorraine Stafford informed me there was a positive from the auto search, a '94 Dodge Caravan reported stolen three days ago down the peninsula in Mountain View. I told her to see if any of the characteristics matched.

I grabbed Jacobi and told him to wrap up his bagel and come with me.

"Where we headed?" he groaned.

"Across the bay. Oakland."

"Mercer's still looking for you," Karen shouted as we hit the hall. "Whaddaya want me to say?"

"Tell him I'm investigating a murder."

Twenty minutes later, we had crossed the

Bay Bridge, woven through the drab, antiquated skyline that was downtown Oakland, and pulled up in front of the Police Administration Building on Seventh. Oakland's police headquarters was a short gray panel-and-glass building in the impersonal style of the early sixties. On the second floor was Homicide, a cramped, dreary office no larger than our own. Over the years, I'd been here a few times.

Lieutenant Ron Vandervellen stood up to greet us as we were led into his office. "Hey, I hear congratulations are in order, Boxer. Welcome to the world of sedentary life."

"I wish, Ron," I replied.

"What brings you here? You looking to check out how the real world works?"

For years, the San Francisco and Oakland homicide departments had maintained a kind of friendly rivalry, they believing all we dealt with across the bay was the occasional computer parts salesman found naked and dead in his hotel room.

"I saw you on the news last night." Vandervellen cackled. "Very photogenic. I mean *her*. . . ." He grinned at Jacobi. "What brings you celebrities out here?"

"A little bird named Chipman," I replied. Estelle Chipman was the elderly black woman Cindy told me had been found hung in her basement.

He shrugged. "I got a hundred unsolved murders if you guys don't have enough to keep you busy."

I was used to the Vandervellen barbs, but this time he sounded particularly edgy. "No agenda, Ron. I just want to look at the crime scene, if that's okay."

"Sure, but I think it's gonna be tough to tie it into your church shooting."

"Why's that?" I asked.

The Oakland lieutenant got up, went out into the outer office, and came back with a case file. "I guess I'm having a hard time putting together how a homicide as obviously racially motivated as yours could be committed by *one of their own.*"

"What are you saying?" I asked. "Estelle Chipman's killer was *black?*"

He donned a pair of reading glasses, leafed through the file until he came to an official document marked "Alameda County Coroner's Report."

"Read it and weep," he muttered. "If you'd called, I could've saved you the toll. . . . 'Dermal specimens found under the victim's fingernails suggest a hyperpigmented dermis consistent with a *non-Caucasian.*' Slides are out being tested as we speak."

"You still want to check out the site?" Vandervellen asked, seemingly enjoying the moment.

"You mind? We're already here."

"Sure, yeah, be my guest. It's Krimpman's case, but he's out. I can take you through. I don't get out to the Gus White projects much anymore. Who knows? Riding with you two supercops, I might pick something up along the way."

Chapter 13

THE GUSTAVE WHITE PROJECTS were six identical redbrick high-rises on Redmond Street in West Oakland. As we pulled up, Vandervellen said, "Didn't make much sense. . . . The poor woman wasn't ill, seemed to have okay finances, even went to church twice a week. But sometimes people just give up. Until the autopsy, it looked legit."

I recalled the case file: There were no witnesses, no one had heard any screams, no one saw anybody running away. Only an elderly woman who kept to herself, found hanging from a steam pipe in the basement, her neck at a right angle and her tongue protruding.

At the projects, we walked right into Building C. "Elevator's on the fritz," Vandervellen said. We took the stairs down. In the graffiti-marked basement, we came upon a hand-painted sign that read, "Laundry Room — Boiler Room."

"Found her in here."

The basement room was still criss-crossed with yellow crime scene tape. A pungent, rancid odor filled the air. Graffiti was everywhere. Anything that had been here — the body, the electrical wire she was hung with — had already been taken to the morgue or entered into evidence.

"I don't know what you're looking to find," Vandervellen said with a shrug.

"I don't know either." I swallowed. "It happened late last Saturday night?"

"Coroner figures around ten. We thought maybe the old lady came down to do her laundry, that someone surprised her. Janitor found her the next morning."

"What about security cameras?" Jacobi asked. "They were all over the lobby and the halls."

"Same as the elevator — broken." Vandervellen shrugged again.

It was clear Vandervellen and Jacobi wanted to head out as quickly as possible, but something pulled at me to stay. *For what?* I had no idea. But my senses were buzzing. *Find me . . . over here.*

"The race thing aside," Vandervellen said, "if you're looking for a connection, I'm sure you know how unusual it is for a killer to switch methods in the midst of a spree."

"Thanks," I snapped back. I had scanned the room; nothing jumped at me. Just the feeling. "Guess we'll have to solve *this* one on our own. Who knows? By now maybe something's popped up on our side of the pond."

As Vandervellen was about to flick off the light, something caught my eye. "Hold it," I said.

As if pulled by gravity, I was drawn to the far side of the room, to the wall behind the spot where Chipman had been found hanging. I knelt, tracing my fingers over the concrete wall. If I hadn't seen it before it would've passed right by my sight.

A primitive drawing, like a child's, in bright orange chalk. It was a lion. Like Bernard Smith's drawing but more fierce. The lion's body led into a coiled tail, but it was the tail of something else . . . a reptile? *A serpent?*

And that wasn't all.

The lion had two heads: one a lion, the other possibly a goat.

I felt a knot in my chest, a tremor of revulsion, and recognition, too.

Jacobi came up behind me. "Find something, Lieutenant?"

I drew a long breath. *"Pokémon."*

Chapter 14

SO NOW I KNEW. . . .

These cases were probably related. Bernard Smith's sighting of the fleeing van had been on the mark. We had our getaway car. We might have a double killer.

It didn't surprise me that when I finally got back to the Hall, an angry Chief Mercer insisted he be buzzed the minute I walked in.

I closed the door to my office, dialed his extension, and waited for the barrage.

"You know what's going on here," he said, the sting of authority rippling through his voice. "You think you can stay out in the field all day and ignore my calls? You're *Lieutenant* Boxer now. Your job is to manage your squad. And keep me informed."

"I'm sorry, Chief, it's just that —"

"A child has been killed. A neighborhood terrorized. We've got some psycho a brick short out there who's trying to turn this place into an inferno. By tomorrow, every African American leader in this town will be demanding to know what we're going to do."

"It's gotten deeper than that, Chief."

Mercer stopped short. "Deeper than what?"

I told him what I had found in the basement in Oakland. The lionlike symbol that had been at both crimes.

I heard him suck in a deep breath. "You're saying these two killings are related?"

"I'm saying that before we jump to any fast conclusions, that possibility exists."

The air seemed to seep right out of Mercer's lungs. "You get a photo of what you found on that wall over to the lab. And the sketch of what that kid in Bay View saw. I want to know what those drawings mean."

"It's already in the works," I replied.

"And the getaway van? Anything back on it yet?"

"Negative."

A troubling possibility seemed to be forming in Mercer's mind. "If there's some kind of conspiracy taking place here, we're not going to sit back while this city is held hostage to a terror campaign."

"We're running the van. Let me have some time on that symbol." I didn't want to tell him my worst fear. If Vandervellen was right, that Estelle Chipman's killer was black, and Claire was right, that Tasha Catchings was an intended target, this might not be a racial-terror campaign at all.

Even on the phone, I could sense the creases underneath Mercer's jaw deepening. I was asking him to take a risk, a big one. Finally I heard him exhale. "Don't let me down, Lieutenant. Solve your case."

As I hung up the phone, I could feel the pressure intensifying. The world was going to expect me to bust down the door of every hate group operating west of Montana, and already I had real doubts.

On my desk, I spotted a message from Jill. "How about a drink? Six o'clock," it read. *All of us.*

One full day into the case . . . If there was anything that would calm my fears, it was Jill, and Claire and Cindy, and a pitcher of margaritas at Susie's.

I left a message on Jill's voice mail that I'd be there.

I glanced at a faded blue baseball cap hanging on a wooden coatrack in the corner of my office, with the words "It's *Heavenly* . . ." embroidered on the brim. The cap had belonged to Chris Raleigh. He'd given it to me during a beautiful weekend up at Heavenly Valley, where the outside world had seemed to disappear for a while and both of us had opened up to what was starting to take place between us.

"Don't let me mess up," I whispered. I felt my eyes begin to sting with tears. *God, I wished he was here.* "You sonofabitch . . ." I shook my head at the hat. "I miss you."

Chapter 15

IT TOOK NO MORE THAN A MINUTE of settling back in our old booth at Susie's to feel the magic begin to spark, and to realize it was happening all over again.

A troublesome case that was getting worse. A pitcher full of high-octane margaritas. My three best friends, all at the top of law enforcement. I was afraid that our murder club was back in business.

"Just like old times?" Claire smiled, scooting her large frame over to make room for me.

"In more ways than you know." I sighed. Then, pouring myself a frothy drink, "Jesus, do I need one of these."

"Tough day?" Jill inquired.

"No," I shook my head. "Routine. Piece of cake."

"That paperwork, it'll drive anyone to drink." Claire shrugged, taking a sip of her margarita. "Cheers. Great to see you wenches."

There was an obvious level of anticipation buzzing through the group. As I took a sip myself, I scanned around. All eyes were focused on me.

"Uh-uh." I almost spit into my drink. "I can't get into it. Don't even start."

"I told you," Jill croaked with a confirming smile. "Things have changed. Lindsay's management now."

"That's not it, Jill. There's a gag order. Mercer's got this thing shut down. Besides, I thought we were here for you."

Jill's sharp blue eyes twinkled. "The representative from the district attorney's office is willing to cede the floor to her esteemed colleague from the third floor."

"Jesus, guys, I've been on this case for *two days.*"

"What the hell else is anybody in the city talking about?" said Claire. "You want to hear about my day? I did a full frontal at ten, then a talk at SFU on the pathology of —"

"We could talk about global warming," Cindy said, "or this book I'm reading, *The Death of Vishnu.*"

"It's not that I don't want to talk about it," I protested. "It's just that it's sealed, confidential."

"*Confidential,* like what I turned you on to in Oakland?" Cindy asked.

"We have to talk about that," I said. *"After."*

"I'll make you a deal," Jill said. "You share it with us. Like *always.* Then I'll share something. You judge which is juicier. Winner pays the check."

I knew it was only a matter of time before I gave in. How could I keep secrets from my girls? It was all over the news — at least part of it. And there weren't three sharper minds anywhere in the Hall.

I let out an expectant sigh. "This all stays here."

"Of course," Jill and Claire said. "Duh."

I turned to Cindy. "And that means you don't go to press. With any of it. Until I say so."

"Why do I get the sense I'm always being blackmailed by you?" She shook her head, then acquiesced. "Fine. Deal."

Jill filled up my glass. "I knew we'd eventually break you down."

I took a sip. "Nah. I decided to tell you when you said, 'Tough day?' "

Piece by piece, I took them through the case so far. The decal Bernard Smith had seen on the getaway van. The identical drawing I had found in Oakland. The possibility that Estelle Chipman might have been murdered. Claire's thought that Tasha Catchings may not have been an accidental target after all.

"I knew it," Cindy shouted with a triumphant beam.

"You've got to find out what that lion image represents," insisted Claire.

I nodded. "I'm on it. Big-time."

Jill, the A.D.A., inquired, "Anything out there that actually ties these two victims together?"

"Nothing so far."

"What about motive?" she pressed.

"Everyone's reading them as hate crimes, Jill."

She nodded cautiously. "And you?"

"I'm starting to read them differently. I think we have to consider the possibility that someone's using the hate crime scenario as a smoke screen."

There was a long silence at the table.

"A racial serial killer," Claire said.

Chapter 16

I HAD SHARED MY NEWS, all of it bad. Everyone ran it over glumly.

I nodded to Jill. "Now you . . ."

Cindy jumped the gun. "Bennett's not going to run again, is he?" In her eight years in the prosecutor's office, Jill had shot up to be his number two in command. If the old man decided to step down, she was the logical choice to be appointed San Francisco's next D.A.

Jill laughed and shook her head. "He'll be propped up at that oak desk the day he dies. That's the truth."

"Well, you've got *something* to tell us," pressed Claire.

"You're right," she admitted. "I do. . . ."

One by one, Jill met each one of our gazes as if to ratchet up the suspense. Those normally piercing cobalt eyes had never looked so serene. At last, a crooked little smile crept across her face. She let out a sigh, then said, *"I'm pregnant."*

We sat there, waiting for her to admit that she was just putting us on. But she didn't. She just kept those sharp eyes blinking right in our faces, until thirty seconds must have gone by.

"Y-you're joking," I stammered. Jill was the most driven woman I knew. You could catch her at her desk most any night until after eight. Her husband, Steve, ran a venture fund for Bank America. They were fast-track achievers: They mountain-biked in Moab, windsurfed on the Columbia River in Oregon. *A baby* . . .

"People *do* it," she exclaimed at our amazement.

"I knew it," Claire exclaimed, slapping the table. "I just knew it. I saw the look in your eyes. I saw that sheen on your face. I said, something's toasting in that oven. You're talking to an expert, you know. How long?"

"Eight weeks. I'm due the end of May." Jill's eyes sparkled like a young girl's. "Other than our families, you're the first people I've told. *Of course."*

"Bennett's gonna shit graham crackers." Cindy cackled.

"He's got three of his own. And it's not like I'm trading it in to go off and grow grapes in Petaluma. I'm just having a baby."

I found myself smiling. Part of me was so pleased for her, I almost wanted to cry. Part of me was even a little jealous. Most of me still couldn't believe it. "This kid better know what he's in for." I grinned. "He'll be rocked to sleep by tapes of California case law."

"No way." Jill laughed defiantly. "I won't do it. I promise I won't do it. I'm gonna be a really good mom."

I stood up and leaned across the table to her. "This is so great, Jill." For a moment, we just stared at each other, our eyes glistening. I was so damned happy for her. I remembered when I was scared shitless because of a blood disease I had, and Jill had bared her arms to us and showed us her terrible scars; she explained how she had cut herself in high school and college, how the challenge to always go to the top had so deeply ruled her life that she could only take it out on herself.

We threw our arms around each other, and I squeezed her.

"Was this something you've been thinking about?" Claire asked.

"We'd been trying for a couple of months," Jill answered, sitting back down. "I'm not sure it was any conscious decision, other than the timing seemed right." She looked at Claire. "The first time I met you, when Lindsay asked me into your group and you talked about *your* kids . . . it just sort of set off a spark in me. I remember thinking, 'She runs the M.E.'s office. She's one of the most capable women I know, at the top of her profession, yet this is what she talks about.'"

"When you start out working," Claire explained, "you have all this drive and focus. As a woman, you feel you have to prove everything. But when you have kids, it's different, natural. You realize it's no longer about you at all. You realize . . . you no longer have to prove anything. You already have."

"So, hey . . . ," Jill said with glistening eyes, "I want a little of that, too.

"I never told this to you guys," she went on, "but I was pregnant once before. Five years ago." She took a sip of water and shook the dark hair off the back of her neck. "My career was in overdrive — you remember, there was that La Frade hearing — and Steve had just started running his own fund."

"It just wasn't the right time for you then, honey," Claire said.

"That wasn't it," Jill answered quickly. "I wanted it. It was just that everything was so intense. I was pulling stints at the office until ten. It seemed like Steve was always away. . . ." She paused, a remote cloudiness in her eyes. "I had some bleeding. The doctor warned me to cut back. I tried, but everyone was pushing on this case, and I was always alone. One day, I just felt my insides explode. I lost it . . . in the fourth month."

"Oh, Jesus." Claire gasped. "Oh, Jill."

Jill sucked in a breath, and a hushed silence fell over the table.

"So how *are* you feeling?" I asked.

"Ecstatic . . . ," she replied. "Physically, strong as ever . . ." Then she blinked remotely for a moment and faced us again. "Truth is, I'm a total wreck."

I reached for her hand. "What does your doctor say?"

"He says we'll keep a close watch and keep the sensationalist cases down to a minimum. Run it in low gear."

"Do you have that gear?" I asked.

"I do now." She sniffed.

"Wow." Cindy chuckled. "Jill's suddenly got *drag*," referring to the dot-com term for anything that could keep you from your job 24 / 7.

In Jill's eyes, I saw a glorious transformation taking place, something I had never seen before. Jill was always successful. She had that beautiful face, that hard-charging drive. Now I could see at last that she was happy.

Beautiful tears welled up in her eyes. I had seen this woman stand up in court against some of the toughest bastards in the city; I had seen her go after murderers with an undeterred conviction. I had even seen the scars of self-doubt on the insides of her arms.

But until that moment, I had never seen Jill cry.

"Dammit . . ." I smiled. I reached for the check. "I guess I pay."

Chapter 17

AFTER A FEW MORE GIDDY HUGS with Jill, I made my way home to my apartment on Potrero Hill.

It was the second floor of a renovated blue Victorian. Cozy and bright, with an alcove of wide windows overlooking the bay. Martha, my affectionate Border collie, met me at the door.

"Hey, sweetie," I said. She wagged up to greet me and threw her paws against my leg.

"So, how was *your* day?" I nuzzled close, smooching her happy face.

I went into the bedroom and peeled off my work clothes, pulled up my hair, putting on the oversize Giants sweatshirt and flannel pajama pants I lived in when the weather turned cool. I fed Martha, made myself a cup of Orange Zinger, and sat in the cushioned alcove.

74

I took a sip of tea, Martha perched in my lap. Out in the distance, a grid of blinking airplane lights descending into SFI came into view. I found myself thinking about the unbelievable image of Jill as a mom . . . Her thin, fit figure with a bulging belly . . . a shower with just us girls. It made me chuckle. I smiled at Martha. "Jilly-bean's gonna be a mommy."

I had never seen Jill look so complete. It was only a few months ago when my own thoughts had run to how much I would have loved to have a baby. As Jill said, *I wanted some of that, too.* It just wasn't meant to be. . . .

Parenting just didn't seem like the natural occupation in my family.

My mother had died eleven years before, when I was twenty-four and just entering the Police Academy. She had been diagnosed with breast cancer, and my last two years of college, I helped take care of her, rushing back from class to pick her up at the Emporium, where she worked, preparing her meals, watching over my younger sister, Cat.

My father, a San Francisco cop, disappeared on us when I was thirteen. To this day, I didn't know why. I had grown up hearing all the stories — that he handed his paycheck over to the bookies, that he had a secret life away from Mom, that the bastard could charm the pants off of anyone, that one day he lost heart and just couldn't put the uniform back on.

Last I heard from Cat, he was down in Redondo Beach, doing his own thing, private security. Old-timers down in the Central district still asked me how Marty Boxer was. They still told stories about him, and maybe it was good someone could think about him with a laugh. Marty, who once nabbed three perps with the same set of handcuffs . . . Marty Boxer, who stopped off to lay a bet with the suspect still in the car. All I could think about was that the bastard let me tend and nurse my mother while she was dying and never came back.

I hadn't seen my father for almost ten years. Since the day I became a cop. I'd spotted him in the audience when I graduated from the police academy, but we hadn't spoken. I didn't even miss him anymore.

God, it had been ages since I had examined these old scars. Mom had been gone for eleven years. I'd been married, divorced. I had made it into Homicide. Now I was running it.

Somewhere along the way, I had met the man of my dreams. . . .

I was right when I told Mercer the old fire was back.

But I was lying when I told myself I had put Chris Raleigh in the past.

Chapter 18

IT WAS ALWAYS THE EYES that got him. Naked on his bed, in the stark, cell-like room, he sat staring at the old black-and-white photographs he had looked at a thousand times.

It was always the eyes . . . that deadened, hopeless resignation.

How they *posed,* even knowing that their lives were about to end. Even with the nooses wrapped around their necks.

In the loosely bound album, he had forty-seven photos and postcards arranged in chronological order. He had collected them over the years. The first, an old photograph, dated June 9, 1901, his father had given him. *Dez Jones, lynched in Great River, Indiana.* On the border, someone had written in faded script: "This was that dance I went to the other night. We sure *played* afterwards. Your son, Sam." In the foreground, a crowd in suit coats and bowler hats, and behind them the limply hanging corpse.

He flipped the page. *Frank Taylor, Mason, Georgia, 1911.* It had cost him $500 to get the photo, but it was worth every penny. From the back of a buggy parked under an oak, the condemned man stared, seconds before his death. On his face, neither resistance nor fear. A small crowd of properly dressed men and women grinned toward the camera as if they were witnessing Lindbergh arriving in Paris. Dressed up as if it were a family portrait.

Their eyes conveyed that the hanging was something proper and natural. Taylor's, simply that there wasn't a damn thing he could do about it anyway.

He got off the bed and dragged his slick, muscular frame to the mirror. He had always been strong. He had lifted weights for ten years now. He flinched as he drew blood and mass into his swollen pecs. He massaged a scratch. That old bitch had dug her nails into his chest as he wrapped the coil around the ceiling pipes. It had barely drawn blood, but he looked at the scratch with contempt. He didn't like anything that disturbed the surface of his skin.

He posed in front of the mirror, looking at the seething lion-goat tattooed across his chest.

Soon, all the stupid assholes would see that it wasn't just about hate. They would read his pattern. The guilty had to be punished. Reputations needed to be restored. He had no particular antipathy for any of them. It wasn't hate. He climbed back on the bed and masturbated to the photo of Missy Preston, whose tiny neck was snapped by a rope in Childers County, Tennessee, in August of 1931.

Without even a groan, he ejaculated. The forceful rush made his knees quake. That old lady, she had deserved to die. The choir girl, too. He was pumped up!

He massaged the tattoo on his chest. *Pretty soon, I will let you free, my pet. . . .*

He opened his photo scrapbook and flipped to the last blank page, just after Morris Tulo and Sweet Brown, in Longbow, Kansas, 1956.

He had been saving this spot for the right picture. And now he had it.

He took a tube of roll-on glue and dabbed all over the back of the photo. Then he pressed it onto the blank page.

Here's where it belonged.

He remembered her staring up at him, that sad inevitability etched all over her face. *The eyes* . . .

He admired the new addition: Estelle Chipman, eyes stretched wide, looking at the camera just before he kicked the chair out from under her feet.

They always posed.

Chapter 19

FIRST THING the following morning, I called Stu Kirkwood, who ran a hate crimes desk assigned to the police department. I asked him, *personally,* for any leads on these types of groups that might be operating in the Bay Area. My people had talked to Stu earlier, but I needed action fast.

So far, Clapper's CSU team had scoured the area around the church with nothing to show for it, and the only thing we came back with on Aaron Winslow was that no one had a negative thing to say about him.

Kirkwood informed me over the phone that a few organized supremacist groups operated out of Northern California, offshoots of the Klan or some crazy neo-Nazi skinheads. He said that maybe the best thing would be to contact the local chapter of the

FBI, who kept a much more active eye on them. Gay bashing was more his thing.

Bringing in the FBI at this stage didn't fill me with enthusiasm. I asked Kirkwood to give me what he had, and an hour later he came up, carrying a plastic bin crammed with blue and red folders. "Background reading." He winked, dropping the bin heavily on my desk.

At the sight of the mass of files, my hopes sank. "You got any ideas about this, Stu?"

He shrugged sympathetically. "San Francisco's not exactly a hotbed for these groups. Most of what I gave you here seems pretty benign. They seem to spend most of their time hoisting back a few beers and shooting off ammo."

I ordered up a salad, figuring I'd spend the next couple of hours at my desk with a bunch of nutcases railing against blacks and Jews. I pulled out a handful of files and opened one at random.

Some sort of militia group, operating up in Greenview, near the Oregon border. *The California Patriots*. Some summary information supplied by the FBI: *Activity Type:* Militia, sixteen to twenty members. *Weapons Assessment:* Minor, small to semi-automatic arms, over-the-counter. On the bottom it had: *Threat:* Low / Moderate.

I skimmed through the file. Some printed materials with logos of crossed guns, detailing everything from population shifts from "the white, European majority," to media cover-ups on government programs to promote test-tube fertilization of minorities.

I couldn't imagine my killer buying into this claptrap. I didn't see him on the same wavelength at all. Our guy was organized and bold, not some pumped-up backwoods bozo. He had gone to elaborate lengths to hide the murders in the MO of a hate crime. And he had signed them.

Like most serials, *he wanted us to know.*

And to know there would be more.

I leafed through a few more files. Nothing jumped out at me. I was starting to have the feeling this was a waste of time.

Suddenly, Lorraine burst into my office. "We caught a break, Lieutenant. We found the white van."

Chapter 20

I STRAPPED ON MY GLOCK and grabbed Cappy and Jacobi on the way out before Lorraine had even finished filling me in. "I want a SWAT team out there," I yelled.

Ten minutes later, we all screeched up to a makeshift roadblock on San Jacinto, a quiet residential street.

A radio car on routine patrol had spotted a Dodge Caravan parked outside a house in tony Forest Hills. What made him sure this was the car we were looking for was the decal of a two-headed lion on the rear bumper.

Vasquez, the young patrolman who had called in the van, pointed toward a tree-shaded Tudor halfway down the block, the white minivan parked at the end of the driveway. It seemed crazy. This was an affluent neighborhood, not a likely haven for criminals or murderers.

But there it was.

Our white van.

And Bernard Smith's Mufasa.

Moments later, an unmarked SWAT vehicle rigged to look like a cable TV repair truck pulled onto the street. The team was headed by Lieutenant Skip Arbichaut. I didn't know what the situation entailed, whether we would have a siege or possibly have to break our way in.

"Cappy, Jacobi, and I will go in first," I said.

This was a homicide operation and I wasn't letting anyone else take the risk. I had Arbichaut deploy his men, two around back, three manning the front, and one with a sledge with us in case we had to bust in.

We strapped on protective vests and donned black nylon jackets identifying us as police. I clicked my 9mm off safety. There wasn't much time to get nervous.

The SWAT truck started down the street, three black-vested snipers hugging its opposite side.

Cappy, Jacobi, and I followed the truck as cover until it pulled to a stop in front of a mailbox marked 610. Vasquez was right. *The van was a match.*

My heart was racing now. I had been in many forced entries before, but none with more at stake. We cautiously wove our way to the front of the house.

There were lights on inside, some noise from a TV.

At my nod, Cappy pounded the door with his gun. *"San Francisco Police."* Jacobi and I crouched with our guns ready.

No one answered.

After a few tense seconds, I signaled Arbichaut for a ram.

Suddenly, the front door cracked open.

"Freeze," Cappy boomed, swinging his gun into a shooting position. "San Francisco Police."

A wide-eyed woman in powder blue exercise clothes stood frozen in the door. "Oh, my God," she screeched, eyes fastened on our weapons.

Cappy yanked her out the front door as Arbichaut's SWAT team rushed the house. He barked, "Is anyone else at home?"

"Just my daughter," the frightened woman shrieked. "She's two."

The black-vested SWAT team barged past

her into the house as if they were searching for Elian Gonzalez.

"Is that your van?" Jacobi barked.

The woman's eyes darted toward the street. "What is this about?"

"Is that your van?" Jacobi's voice boomed again.

"No," she said, trembling. "No . . ."

"Do you know who it belongs to?"

She looked again, terrified, and shook her head. "I've never seen it before in my life."

It was all wrong; I could see that. The neighborhood, the plastic kid's slide on the lawn, the spooked mom in the workout clothes. A disappointed sigh was expelled from my chest. The van had been dumped here.

All of a sudden, a green Audi knifed its way up to the curb, followed by two police cars. The Audi must have gone right through our roadblock. A well-dressed man in a suit and tortoiseshell glasses jumped out and ran toward the house. "Kathy, what the hell's going on?"

"*Steve* . . ." The woman hugged him with a sigh of relief. "This is my husband. I called him when I saw all the police outside our house."

The man looked around at the eight cop cars, SWAT backup, and the SFPD inspectors standing around with weapons drawn. "What are you doing at my house? This is insane! This is nuts!"

"We believe that van was the vehicle used in the commission of a homicide," I said. "We have every right to be here."

"A homicide . . . ?"

Two of Arbichaut's men emerged from the house, indicating that there wasn't anyone else inside. Across the street, people were starting to file outdoors. "That van's been our number one priority for two days. I'm sorry to have upset you. There was no way to be sure."

The husband's indignation rose. His face and neck were beet red. "You're thinking *we* had something to do with this? With a homicide?"

I figured I had upset their lives enough. "The La Salle Heights shooting."

"Have you people lost your minds? You suspected us in the strafing of a church?" His jaw dropped, and he fixed on me incredulously. "Do you idiots have any idea what I do?"

My eyes fell on his pinstriped gray suit, his blue button-down-collar shirt. I had the humiliating feeling I had just been made a fool of.

"I'm chief counsel for the Northern California chapter of the Anti-Defamation League."

Chapter 21

WE *HAD* BEEN made fools of by the killer. No one on the block knew anything about or had any connection to the stolen van. It had been dumped there, purposely, to show us up. Even as Clapper's CSU went over it inch by inch, I knew it wouldn't yield shit. I studied the decal and I was sure it was the same thing I had seen in Oakland. One head was a lion's, one seemed to be a goat's, the tail suggested a reptile. But what the hell did it mean?

"One thing we learned." Jacobi smirked. "The SOB's got a sense of humor."

"I'm glad you're a fan," I said.

Back at the Hall, I said to Lorraine, "I want to know where that van came from; I want to know who it belonged to, who had access to it, every contact the owner had a month prior to its theft."

I was fuming mad. We had a vicious killer out there but not a single clue as to what made him tick. Was it a hate crime or a killing spree? An organized group or a lone wolf? We knew the guy was fairly intelligent. His strikes had been well planned, and if irony was part of his MO, dumping the getaway car where he had was a real *beaut.*

Karen buzzed in, informing me that Ron Vandervellen was on the line. The Oakland cop came on chuckling. "Word is you managed to subdue a dangerous threat to our society masquerading as a legal watchdog in the Anti-Defamation League."

"I guess that makes our investigations about equal, Ron," I retorted.

"Relax, Lindsay, I didn't call to rub it in," he said, shifting his tone. "Actually, I thought I would make your day."

"I won't argue, Ron. I could use anything about now. What do you have for us?"

"You knew Estelle Chipman was a widow, right?"

"I think you mentioned that."

"Well, we were doing some standard background on her. We found a son in Chicago. He's coming to claim the body. Given what's been going on, I thought what he told us was too coincidental to ignore."

"What, Ron?"

"Her husband died five years ago. Heart attack. Want to guess what the dude did for a living?"

I had the rising feeling Vandervellen was about to blow this thing wide open.

"Estelle Chipman's husband was a San Francisco cop."

Chapter 22

CINDY THOMAS parked her Mazda across from the La Salle Heights Church and let out a long sigh. The church's white clapboard front had been defaced by a pattern of ugly chinks and bullet holes. A gaping hole where the beautiful stained-glass window had been was sealed with a black canvas tarp.

She remembered seeing it the day the window was first unveiled, on her old beat at the paper. The mayor, some local dignitaries, Aaron Winslow, all made speeches about how the beautiful scene had been paid for through community work. A symbol. She remembered interviewing Winslow and being impressed with his passion, and also his unexpected humbleness.

Cindy ducked under the yellow police tape and stepped closer to the bullet-ridden wall. On her job at the *Chronicle*, she'd been assigned to other stories where people had died. But this was the first one where she felt the human race had died a little, too.

She was startled by a voice. "You can stare for as long as you want, but it doesn't get any prettier."

Cindy spun and found herself facing a man with a smooth and very handsome face. Kind eyes. She knew him. She nodded. "I was here when the window was unveiled. It carried a lot of hope."

"Still does," Winslow said. "We didn't lose our hope. Don't worry about that."

She smiled, staring into his deep brown eyes.

"I'm Aaron Winslow," he said, shifting a stack of children's textbooks to extend his hand.

"Cindy Thomas," she replied. His grip was warm and gentle.

"Don't tell me they've put our church as one of the scenic sights on the Forty-nine Mile Drive." Winslow started to walk toward the rear of the church, and she followed along.

"I'm not a tourist," Cindy said. "I just wanted to see this. Listen." She swallowed. "I'd like to pretend I just came by to pay my respects . . . which I did. But I'm also with the *Chronicle*. On the crime desk."

"A reporter." Winslow exhaled. "It makes sense now. For years, everything that *really* goes on here — tutoring, literacy training, a nationally recognized choir — doesn't crank up a story. But one madman acts, and now *Nightline* wants to do a town meeting. What do you want to know, Ms. Thomas? What does the *Chronicle* want?"

His words had stung her a little, but she kind of liked that. He was right.

"Actually, I did a story here once before, when that window was unveiled. It was a special day."

He stopped walking. He focused his eyes on her, then smiled. "It was a special day. And actually, Ms. Thomas, I knew who you were when I walked up. I remember you. You interviewed me back then."

Someone called Winslow's name from inside the church, and a woman came out. She reminded him that he had an eleven o'clock meeting.

"So, have you seen all you came to see, Ms.

Thomas? Should we expect you back in another couple of years?"

"No. I want to know how you deal with this. This violence in the face of all you've done, how the neighborhood feels about it."

Winslow let himself smile. "Let me clue you in on something. I don't deal in innocence. I've spent too much time in the real world."

She remembered that Aaron Winslow wasn't someone whose faith had been formed through a life of detachment. He'd come up from the streets. He'd been an army chaplain. Only days before, he'd put himself in the line of fire and possibly saved lives.

"You came here to see how this neighborhood is responding to the attack? Come see for yourself. Tasha Catchings is being memorialized tomorrow."

Chapter 23

VANDERVELLEN'S stunning disclosure drummed in my head for the rest of the day.

Both murder victims had been related to San Francisco cops.

It could add up to nothing. They could be two random and unrelated victims. People in different cities, separated by sixty years.

Or it could mean everything.

I picked up the phone and called Claire. "I need a big favor," I said.

"Just how big?" I could feel her grin.

"I need you to take a look at the autopsy of that woman who was hung in Oakland."

"I can do that. Send it over. I'll take a look."

"This is where it gets huge, Claire. It's still at the Oakland M.E.'s office. It hasn't been released."

I waited expectantly as she sighed. "You must be kidding, Lindsay. You want me to stick my nose into an investigation that's still in progress?"

"Listen, Claire, I know this isn't exactly procedure, but they've made some pretty important assumptions that could determine this case."

"Want to tell me what type of assumptions I'd be stepping all over a respected M.E.'s toes to review?"

"Claire, these cases are related. There's a pattern here. Estelle Chipman was married to a cop. Tasha Catchings's uncle is a cop, too. My whole investigation hinges on whether we're dealing with one killer. Oakland believes there's a black man involved, Claire."

"A black man?" She gasped. "Why would a black want to do these things?"

"I don't know. But there's starting to be a lot of circumstantial evidence linking both crimes. I have to know."

She hesitated. "Precisely what the hell would I be looking for?"

I told her about the skin specimens they had found under the victim's nails and their M.E.'s conclusion.

"Teitleman's a good man," Claire responded. "I'd trust his findings like I would my own."

"I know, Claire, but he's not you. Please. This is important."

"I want you to know," she shot back, "that if Art Teitleman asked to poke his nose into one of my preliminary investigations, I'd have his parking ticket stamped and politely tell him to go back to his side of the bay. I wouldn't do this for anyone else, Lindsay."

"I know that, Claire," I said with a grateful tone. "Why do you think I've been working this friendship all these years?"

Chapter 24

LATE THAT AFTERNOON, I sat at my desk as one by one my staff called it quits for the day. I couldn't leave with them.

My mind tried over and over to put together the parts. Everything I had was based on assumptions. Was the killer black or white? Was Claire right, that Tasha Catchings was intentionally killed? But the lion symbol had definitely been there. *Link the victims*, my instincts said. *There's a connection. But what the hell is it?*

I glanced at my watch and placed a call to Simone Clark in personnel, catching her just as she was preparing to leave. "Simone, I need you to pull a file for me tomorrow."

"Sure, whose do you need?"

"A cop who retired maybe eight, ten years ago. His name was Edward Chipman."

"That's a while back. It would be out on the docks." The department outsourced its old records to a document storage company. "Early afternoon, okay?"

"Sure, Simone. Best you can do."

I was still bristling with nervous energy. I took out another stack of Kirkwood's hate files and plopped them on my desk.

I opened one at random. Americans for Constitutional Action . . . Ploughs and Fifes, another hayseed militia group. All these ass-holes, they seemed like such a bunch of right-wing jerk-offs. Was I wasting my time? Nothing jumped out. Nothing gave me any hope that this was the right track.

Go home, Lindsay, a voice urged. *Tomorrow new leads might develop. There's the van, Chipman's file . . . Call it a night. Take Martha for a run.*

Go home . . .

I stacked the files, about to give in, when the top one caught my eye. *The Templars.* A Hells Angels offshoot out of Vallejo. The original Templars were Christian knights from the Crusades. Immediately, I noticed the FBI's assessment of threat. Their rating was *High.*

I took the file off the pile and leafed further

in. There was an FBI report outlining a series of unsolved felonies the Templars had been suspected of involvement in, bank robberies, hits for hire against Latino and black gangs.

I leafed on, case files, prison records, surveillance photos of the group. Suddenly, the breath emptied out of my lungs.

My eyes fixed on a surveillance shot: a bunch of heavy, muscled, tattoo-covered bikers huddled outside a Vallejo bar they used as a headquarters. One of them hunched over his bike, back to the camera. He had a shaved head, a bandanna, and a sleeveless denim jacket over massive arms.

It was the embroidery on the back of the denim jacket that caught my eye.

I was staring at a two-headed lion with the tail of a snake.

Chapter 25

SOUTH OF MARKET, in a run-down warehouse section of the city, a man in a green windbreaker ducked along a shadowy curb. The killer.

This time of night, in this decrepit neighborhood, no one was around, only a couple of scum-bums huddled over a blazing trash can. Abandoned warehouses, daytime businesses with shorted-out electrical signs: CHECKS CASHED TODAY . . . METAL WORKS . . . EARL KING, CITY'S MOST TRUSTED BAIL BONDSMAN.

His eyes drifted across the street, toward Seventh, to the dilapidated shell of an abandoned residential hotel: *303*. He had carefully staked the place out over the past three weeks. Half the apartments were vacant, the other half the nightly resting place for homeless bums with nowhere else to go.

Spitting onto the trash-littered street, he threw a black Adidas sport bag over his shoulder and headed around the block onto Sixth and Townsend. He crossed the dingy street toward a boarded-up warehouse marked only by a scratched-out sign: AGUELLO'S . . . COMIDAS ESPANOL.

Making sure he was alone, the killer pushed in the paint-chipped metal door, then he ducked inside. His heart was starting to pump pretty good now. He was addicted to the feeling, actually.

A foul odor met him in the lobby, a firetrap that was littered with old newspapers and oily corrugated boxes. He hit the stairs, hoping not to run into any of the homeless scum camped out in the halls.

He climbed all the way to five, where he quickly made his way to the end of the hall. He pushed through a grating and stepped out onto the fire escape. From there, it was only a quick flight up to the roof.

Up here, the desolate streets gave way to the luminous aura of the city's skyline. His position was in the shadow of the Bay Bridge, which loomed over him like a hulking ship.

He rested the black sport bag on an air-conditioning vent, unzipped it, and carefully removed the parts of a customized PSG-1 sniper rifle.

At the church, I needed maximum saturation. Here I only get one shot.

As traffic rumbled over him on the Bay Bridge freeway, he screwed the long barrel of the rifle to the shaft and locked it in place. Handling guns was like handling a fork and knife to him. He could do this in his sleep.

He fastened on the infrared sight. He squinted through it, amber-colored shapes coming into focus.

He was so much smarter than them. While they were looking for white vans and silly-ass symbols, he was here, about to blow the lid wide open. Tonight, they would finally begin to understand.

His heart slowed as he aimed across the street, at the rear of the transient hotel marked 303. On the fourth floor, a dimly lit apartment shone through the window.

This was it. The moment of truth.

He calmed his breath to a whisper and licked his dry lips. He aimed at a picture in his mind he had held for so long. He *feathered* the sight.

Then, when it was just right, he squeezed.

Click . . .

This time he wouldn't even have to sign it. They'd know from the shot. From the target.

Tomorrow, every person in San Francisco would know his name.

Chimera.

Part II

JUSTICE WILL BE SERVED

Chapter 26

I KNOCKED on Stu Kirkwood's glass office door, interrupting his morning coffee and bagel. I tossed the surveillance shot of the biker wearing the lion with the tail of a snake in front of him. "I need to know what this is. I need it ASAP, Stu."

I followed the shot up with two other versions of the same image: the decal on the rear of the white van and a Polaroid of the basement wall where Estelle Chipman had been killed. *Lion, goat, tail of a snake or lizard.*

Kirkwood stiffened. "I don't have any idea," he looked up and said.

"This is *our killer,* Stu. So how do we find him? I thought this was your specialty."

"I told you, gay bashing's more my bag. We could e-mail the pictures to Quantico."

"Okay." I nodded. "How long will it take?"

Kirkwood straightened up. "I know a chief

researcher down there I took a seminar with. Let me put in the call."

"Do it quick, Stu, *then* finish your bagel. And let me know as soon as you get something back. The minute you hear something."

Upstairs, I nudged Jacobi and Cappy into my office. I slid Kirkwood's Templar file and a copy of the biker photo across my desk. "You recognize the artist, guys?"

Cappy studied the photo and glanced up. "You're thinking these dust mites have something to do with the case?"

"I want to know where these guys are," I said. "And I want you to be careful. This crew's been implicated in stuff that makes La Salle Heights seem like a paintball outing. Weapons traffic, aggravated violence, murder for hire. According to the file, they operate out of a bar over in Vallejo called the Blue Parrot. I don't want you busting in there like you're razzing a pimp down on Geary. And remember, *it's not our jurisdiction.*"

"We hear you, Loo," Cappy said. "No thumping. Just a little R and R. It'll be nice to spend the day out of town." He picked up the file and tapped Jacobi on the shoulder. "Your clubs in the trunk?"

"Guys. *Careful*," I reminded them. "Our killer's a shooter."

After they left, I leafed through a handful of messages and opened the morning *Chronicle* on my desk. There was a headline, with Cindy's attribution, reading, "POLICE WIDEN CHURCH SHOOTING PROBE, OAKLAND WOMAN'S DEATH THOUGHT TO BE BROUGHT IN."

Quoting "sources close to the investigation" and "unnamed police contacts," she outlined the possibility that we had widened our investigation, citing the murder in Oakland. I had given her the green light to go that far.

I speed-dialed Cindy. "This is Source Close to the Investigation calling," I said.

"No way. You're Unnamed Contact. Source Close to the Investigation is Jacobi."

"Oh, shit." I chuckled.

"I'm glad you have your sense of humor. Listen, I have something important I need to show you. Are you going to Tasha Catchings's funeral?"

I looked at my watch. It was scheduled in less than an hour. "Yeah. I'll be there."

"Look for me," Cindy said.

Chapter 27

A BITING DRIZZLE was coming down as I arrived at the La Salle Heights Church.

Hundreds of black-clad mourners were jammed into the bullet-scarred church. A canvas was draped over the gaping hole where the stained-glass window had been. It flapped like a somber flag whipped by the breeze.

Mayor Fernandez was there, along with other important faces I recognized from city government. Vernon Jones, the activist, was stationed an arm's length from the family. Chief Mercer was there, too. This little girl was getting the biggest funeral the city had seen in years. It made her death seem even sadder.

Standing in the rear of the chapel, in a short black suit, I spotted Cindy. We both nodded as we caught each other's eye.

I took a seat near Mercer among a delegation from the department. Soon, the famous

La Salle Heights choir began a haunting rendition of "I'll Fly Away." There is nothing more stirring than uplifting hymns resonating through a filled church. I have my own private credo, and it starts not far from what I've seen on the streets: Nothing in life ever breaks down simply into good or bad, judgment or redemption. But when the swell of voices lifted up the church, it didn't seem wrong to privately ask for mercy to shine down on this innocent soul.

After the choir finished, Aaron Winslow stepped up to a microphone. He looked very elegant in a black suit. He spoke about Tasha Catchings as someone who had known her most of her life could: her little-girl's giggle; the poise she showed being the youngest in the choir; how she wanted to be a diva, or an architect who would rebuild this neighborhood; how, now, only the angels would get to hear her beautiful voice.

He didn't speak like some gentle minister exhorting people to turn the other cheek. He kept it hopeful, very emotional, but real. I couldn't watch him without thinking that this handsome man had been on the battlefields of Desert Storm, and that only the other day he had put his life at risk to protect his children.

He said, his voice soft but powerful, that he could not forgive, and he could not help but judge. "Only saints don't judge," he said, "and believe me, I'm no saint. I'm like all of you, just someone who has grown tired of having to make peace with injustice." He looked toward Chief Mercer. "Find the killer. Let judgment be in the courts. This isn't about politics, or faith, or even race. It's about the right to be free from hate. I am convinced that the world doesn't break in the face of its worst possible deed. The world mends itself."

People rose up, and they clapped and they cried. I stood with them. My eyes were wet. Aaron Winslow brought such dignity to these proceedings. It was over within an hour. No blazing sermons, only a smattering of amens. But a sadness none of us would ever forget.

Tasha's mother looked so strong as she followed the casket out, her young daughter being carried to her final rest.

I walked out to a chorus of "Will the Circle Be Unbroken," feeling numb, and broken.

Chapter 28

OUTSIDE, I WAITED FOR CINDY, and I watched Aaron Winslow mingle among mourners and weeping schoolmates. There was something about him I liked. He seemed genuine to me and he definitely had a passion for his work, and these people.

"Now, there's a man I could share a foxhole with," said Cindy, coming up to me.

"And just how do you mean *that?*" I asked.

"I'm not sure. . . . All I can say is I came out here yesterday to talk with him, and I left with the hairs on my arms standing up at attention. I felt like I was interviewing Denzel Washington, or maybe that new guy on *NYPD Blue*."

"You know, ministers aren't the same as priests," I said.

"Meaning what?"

"Meaning it's okay to go in foxholes with them. Just to get out of the line of fire, of course."

"Of course." She nodded. Then she mimicked an exploding mortar shot, *"Pow!"*

"He is impressive. His speech made me cry. Is that what you meant to show me?"

"No," she said with a sigh, coming back to the matter at hand. She dug in her black shoulder bag and pulled out a folded piece of paper. "I know you told me to butt out. . . . I guess I've just gotten used to covering your ass."

"Right," I said. "So what do you have for me? We're a team, right?"

As I unfolded the paper, to my shock I found myself staring at the same lion, goat, and snake rendering I had just given Kirkwood to identify. Professional restraint couldn't keep my eyes from opening wide. "Where did you get this?"

"You *know* what you're looking at, Lindsay."

"My guess is that it's not Tyco's new toy craze."

She didn't laugh. "What it is, is a hate group symbol. A white supremacist thing. A colleague at the paper did research on these groups. I couldn't help looking into it after our meeting the other night. This is used by a small, elite group. That's why it was hard to find out about."

I stared at the image that I had seen over and over again since Tasha Catchings had been killed. "This thing has a name, doesn't it?"

"It's called a chimera, Lindsay. It's from Greek mythology. According to my source, the lion represents courage, the body of the goat stubbornness and will, and the serpent's tail stealth and cunning. It means that whatever you do to crush it, it will always prevail."

I stared at the symbol, the chimera, the bile roiling in my gut. "Not this time."

"I haven't run with it," Cindy said. "But it's out there. Everybody thinks these murders are connected. This symbol is the key, right? Let me give you a second definition I found: *'a grotesque product of the imagination.'* That fits, right?"

I found myself nodding. *Back to square one. Hate groups.* Maybe even the Templars. Once Mercer found out, we'd be busting the doors down on every hate group we could find. But how the hell could the killer be black? It didn't make sense to me.

"You're not mad at me, are you?" Cindy asked.

I shook my head. "Of course I'm not mad. So that source of yours, did he tell you just how they killed this chimera back then?"

"He said they called in some big hero who rode a winged horse and cut off its head. Nice to have dudes, or dudesses, like that around in a pinch, huh?" She looked at me seriously. "You have a winged horse, Lindsay?"

"No." I shook my head again. "I've got a Border collie."

Chapter 29

CLAIRE MET ME in the lobby of the Hall just as I returned with a salad. "Where you heading?" I asked.

She kept my eye coyly, dressed in an attractive purple coatdress, a Tumi leather briefcase slung over her shoulder. "Actually, I was coming to see you."

Claire had a look on her face that I had learned to recognize. You wouldn't call it smugness or self-importance; Claire didn't run that way. It was more of a *twinkle* that read, *I found something.* Or more like, *Sometimes I even amaze myself.*

"You had lunch?" I asked.

She snickered. "Lunch? Who has time for lunch? Since ten-thirty, I've been under a microscope across the bay covering for you." She peeked into my bag and caught a glimpse of my curried-chicken salad. "That looks tempting."

I pulled it back. "That depends. On what you came up with."

She pushed me into the elevator.

"I had to promise Teitleman parterre box seats to the symphony to calm him down," Claire said as we got to my office. "You can consider it Edmund's treat." Edmund was her husband, who for the past six years had played kettle drums for the San Francisco Symphony.

"I'll send him a note," I said as we sat around my desk. "Maybe I can get Giants tickets." I set out my lunch.

"You mind?" she asked, dangling a plastic fork over the salad. "Saving your ass is tiring work."

I pulled the container away. "Like I said. Depends on what you have."

Without hesitating, Claire speared a piece of chicken. "Didn't make sense, did it, why a black man would be acting out hate crimes against his own race?"

"All right," I said, pushing the container her way. "What did you find out?"

She nodded. "Mostly, it was pretty much like you told me. None of the normal abrasions or lacerations you would connect with forced submission. But then there were those unusual dermal specimens from under the subject's nails. So we scoped it. They did reveal a hyperpigmented skin type. As the report said, 'normally consistent with a non-Caucasian.' Samples are out being histopathologied as we speak."

"So what are you saying?" I pressed. "The person who killed that woman was black?"

Claire leaned over, lifting the last piece of chicken out from under my fork. "At first blush, I could see how someone might feel that way. If not African American, then a dark Latino, or Asian. Teitleman was inclined to agree, until I asked him to perform one last test.

"I ever tell you" — she mooned her wide brown eyes — "I did my residency at Moffitt in dermapathology?"

"No, Claire." I found myself shaking my head and smiling. She was so good at what she did.

She shrugged. "No, huh? I don't know how we overlooked that. Anyway, basically, what a lab is going to be looking for is whether that hyperpigmentation is *intra*cellular, as in melanocytes, which are the dark, pigmented cells that are much more concentrated in non-Caucasians, or *inter*cellular . . . *in* the tissue, more on the surface of the skin."

"English, Claire. Is the subject white or black?"

"Melanocytes," she continued as if I hadn't asked, "are the dark skin cells concentrated in people of color." She pushed up her sleeve. "You're looking at Melanocyte Central here. Trouble is, the sampling found under the Chipman lady's nails didn't have a one. All that pigment was *inter*cellular . . . surface coloration. On top of that, it was a bluish hue, atypical for naturally occurring melanin. Any self-respecting dermapathologist would've caught that."

"Caught *what*, Claire?" I asked, fixing on her smug grin.

"*Caught* that it wasn't a black man who did that terrible thing," she said emphatically, "but a white man with some topical pigmentation. *Ink*, Lindsay. What that poor woman dug her nails into was the killer's tattoo."

Chapter 30

AFTER CLAIRE LEFT, I was buoyed by her discovery. This was good stuff. Karen knocked and handed me a manila folder. "From Simone Clark." It was the file from personnel I had requested. *Edward R. Chipman.*

I slid the file out of the envelope and began to read.

Chipman had been a career street patrolman out of Central who retired in 1994 with the rank of sergeant. He had twice received a Captain's Commendation for bravery on the job.

I stopped at his photo. A narrow, chiseled face with one of those bushy Afros popular in the sixties. It was probably taken the day he joined the force. I looked through the rest of the contents. What would make someone want to kill this man's widow? There wasn't a single censure on his record. For excessive force or anything else. In his thirty-year career, the officer never fired his gun. He was part of the Police Outreach Unit in the Potrero Hill projects and a member of a minority action group called the Officers for Justice, which lobbied for and promoted the interests of black officers. Chipman, like most cops, had one of those proud, uneventful careers, never in trouble, never under review, never in the public's eye. Nothing in there drew the slightest connection to Tasha Catchings or to her uncle, Kevin Smith.

Had I read more into the whole thing than was there? Was this even a serial thing? My antennae were crackling. *I know there's something. C'mon, Lindsay.*

Suddenly, I was hammered back to reality by Lorraine Stafford knocking at my door. "You got a minute, Lieutenant?"

I asked her in. The stolen vehicle, she informed me, belonged to a Ronald Stasic. He taught anthropology at a community college down in Mountain View. "Apparently the van was stolen from the parking lot outside where he works. The reason it was late being reported missing was that he went to Seattle for a night. Job interview."

"Who knew he was going to be away?"

She flipped through her notes. "His wife. The college administrator. He teaches two classes at the college and tutors students from other schools in the area."

"Any of these students show an interest in his van or in where he parked?"

She snickered. "He said half these kids come to class in BMWs and Saabs. Why would they be interested in a six-year-old van?"

"What about that sticker on the back?" I had no idea if Stasic had anything to do with these killings, but his van did have the same symbol on it that had turned up in the Oakland basement.

Lorraine shrugged. "Said he never saw it before. I said I'd check his story and asked if he'd take a lie detector on that. He told me to go right ahead."

"You better check if any of his friends, or his students, have any weird political leanings."

Lorraine nodded. "I will, but this guy's totally legit, Lindsay. He acted like he was jerked out of his skin."

As the afternoon wound down, I had the shaky feeling we were nowhere on this case. I was sure it was a serial, but maybe our best chance was this guy with the chimera embroidered on his jacket.

My phone rang, startling me. It was Jacobi. "Bad information, L.T. We've been outside this damned Blue Parrot place all day. *Nothing.* So we managed to find out from the bartender the dudes you're looking for are history. They split, five, six months ago. Toughest guy we've seen was some weight lifter wearing a 'Rock Rules' T-shirt."

"What do you mean by *split*, Warren?"

"Vamoose, moved on. Somewhere south. According to the dude, one or two guys who used to hang around with them still come in from time to time. Some big redheaded dude. But basically they hit the road. *Permanentmente . . .*"

"Keep on it. Find me the redheaded dude." Now that the van led nowhere and I had no connection between the victims, that lion-and-snake symbol was all we had.

"Keep on it?" Jacobi whined. "How long? We could be out here for days!"

"I'll send out a change of underwear," I said, and hung up.

For a while I just sat there, rocking back in my chair with a mounting feeling of dread. It had been three days since Tasha Catchings was killed, and three days before that, Estelle Chipman.

I had nothing. No significant clues. Only what the killer had left us. This damned chimera.

And the knowledge . . . *serials kill. Serials don't stop until you catch them.*

Chapter 31

PATROLMAN SERGEANT ART DAVIDSON responded to the 1-6-0 the minute he heard the call. *"Disturbance, domestic violence. Three oh three Seventh Street, upstairs. Available units respond."*

He and his partner, Gil Herrera, were only four blocks away on Bryant. It was almost eight; their shift was over in ten minutes.

"You want to take it, Gil?" said Davidson, glancing at his watch.

His partner shrugged. "Your call, Artie. You're the one with the wild party to go to."

Some wild party. It was his seven-year-old's birthday. Audra. He had called in on break, and Carol had said if he got home by nine-thirty, she'd keep her up for him so that he could give her the Britney Spears makeup mirror he had picked out. Davidson had five kids, and they were his life.

"What the hell." Davidson shrugged. "It's what we get paid the big bucks for, right?"

They hit the siren, and in less than a minute, Mobile 2-4 pulled up in front of the dismal and dilapidated entrance to 303 Seventh, the tilted sign of the defunct *Driscoll Hotel* hanging over the front door.

"People still camping out in this dump?" Herrera sighed. "Who the hell would live here?"

The two cops grabbed their nightsticks and a large flashlight, and stepped up to the front door. Davidson pulled it open. Inside, the place smelled of feces, urine, probably rats. "Hey, anybody here?" Davidson called out "Police."

Suddenly, from above, they heard the sound of shouting. Some kind of argument.

"On it," Herrera said, bounding up the first flight.

Davidson followed.

On the second floor, Gil Herrera went down the hall, banging his flashlight on doors. *"Police, police . . ."*

In the stairwell, Davidson suddenly heard the sounds again — loud, frantic voices. A crash, as if something had broken. The noise came from over his head. He headed up two flights of stairs on his own.

The noises grew even louder. He stopped in front of a shut door. Apartment 42. *"Bitch . . . ,"* someone yelled. The sound of a plate shattering. A woman seemed to beg, "Stop him, he's going to kill me. Stop him, please. . . . Somebody help me. Please."

"Police," Art Davidson responded, and drew his gun. He yelled, "Herrera, up here. *Now!*"

He threw all his weight against the door. It opened. The inside was dimly lit, but from an interior room, more light and the arguing voices . . . closer . . . screaming.

Art Davidson clicked his gun off safety. Then he barged through the open door into the room. To his amazement, no one was in there.

There was dim yellow light angling from an exposed bulb. A metal chair with a large boom box on it. Loud voices coming from the speakers.

The words were the same ones he'd heard earlier. "Stop him, he's going to kill me!"

"What the hell?" Davidson squinted in disbelief.

He walked over to the stereo, knelt down, and turned off the power. The loud, blaring argument came to a halt.

"What the fuck . . . ?" Davidson muttered. "Somebody playing games."

He looked around. The pitiful room looked as if it hadn't been occupied in a while. His eyes were drawn to the window, then beyond it, across an alley, to a facing building. He thought he saw something. What was it?

Ping . . .

His eye caught the tiniest pinprick of a yellow spark, so quick it was like the snap of a finger, the blink of a firefly on a dark night.

Then the window splintered and a blunt force slammed into Art Davidson's right eye. He was dead before he hit the floor.

Chapter 32

I HAD JUST ABOUT GOTTEN HOME when the distress call crackled in: "Available units, proceed to three oh three Seventh, near Townsend."

1-0-6 . . . officer in trouble.

I pulled my Explorer to the curb. Listened to the call. *EMS's to the scene, the district captain called in.* The quick, urgent exchanges convinced me the situation was critical.

The hairs on my arms were standing up. It was an ambush, a long-distance shot. Like La Salle Heights. I threw my car in gear and executed a quick U-turn down Potrero, slamming onto Third Street and heading for downtown.

When I pulled up four blocks from Townsend and Seventh, bedlam reigned. Barricades of blue-and-whites, flashing lights, uniforms everywhere, radios crackling in the night.

I drove ahead, holding my police ID out the window, until I couldn't go any farther. Then I left my car and ran toward the center of the commotion. I grabbed the first patrolman I could find. "Who is it? Do you know?"

"Patrol cop," he said. "Out of Central. Davidson."

"*Oh, shit . . .* " My heart sank. I felt nauseated. I knew Art Davidson. We had gone through the academy at the same time. He was a good cop, a good guy. Did it mean anything that I knew him?

Then a second wave of fear and nausea. *Art Davidson was black.*

I pushed my way through the crowd toward a run-down tenement where a ring of EMS trucks were parked. I ran into Chief of Detectives Sam Ryan coming out of the building, holding a radio to his ear.

I pulled him aside, "Sam, I heard it was Art Davidson. . . . Any chance . . . ?"

Ryan shook his head. "*Chance?* He was lured here, Lindsay. Rifle shot to the head. Single shot, we think. He's already been pronounced."

I stood to the side, a whirring wail growing louder and louder inside my skull, as if some private, unknowable fear had revealed itself only to me. I was sure it was *him*. Chimera. Murder number three. He only needed one shot this time.

I brandished my badge to the uniformed cops at the entrance and hurried into the run-down building. Some EMS techs were coming down the stairs. I kept going past them. My legs felt heavy, and I could hardly breathe.

On the third-floor landing, a uniformed cop barreled past me, shouting, "Coming down. Everybody get out of the way."

A couple of medical techs appeared — and two more cops carrying a gurney. I couldn't turn my head away. "Hold it here," I said.

It was Davidson. His eyes still and open. A crimson dime-sized peephole above his right eye. Every nerve in my body seemed to go slack. I remembered that he had children. *Did these murders have something to do with kids?*

"Oh, Jesus, Art," I whispered. I forced myself to study his body, the bullet wound. I finally touched the side of his forehead. "You can take him down now," I said. *Fuck.*

I made my way to the next floor somehow. A crowd of angry plainclothesmen was gathered outside an open apartment. I saw Pete Starcher, an ex-homicide detective who worked with IAB, coming out.

I went up to him. "Pete, what the hell happened?"

Starcher had always had an edge for me. He was one of those cynical old-timers. "You got business here, Lieutenant?"

"I knew Art Davidson. We went through school together." I didn't want to give him any inkling of why I was here.

Starcher sniffed, but he filled me in. The two patrolmen were responding to a 911 in the building. There was only this tape recorder there. It was all set up, orchestrated. "He was suckered. Some sonofabitch wanted to kill a cop."

My body grew numb. I was sure it was him. "I'm going to look around."

Inside, it was just like Starcher had said. Spooky, weird, unreal. The living room was empty. Walls stripped of paint, and cracks in the plaster. As I wandered into the adjoining room, I froze. There was a pool of blood soaked into the floor; blood had splattered on the wall where the bullet had probably lodged. *Poor Davidson.* A portable tape deck sat on a folding chair in the center of the room.

I looked to the window, a hanging pane of splintered glass.

Suddenly, everything was clear to me. There was a cold spot at the center of my chest.

I went to the open window. I leaned out, looked across the street. There was no sign of Chimera, or anybody. But I knew. . . . I knew because he had told me — the shot, the victim. *He wanted us to know it was him.*

Chapter 33

"IT WAS HIM, LINDSAY, WASN'T IT?"

Cindy was on the phone. It was after eleven. I was trying to pull my wits together at the end of an insane, horrible night. I had just come in from taking Martha on a late walk. All I wanted was to take a hot shower and wash the image of Art Davidson's body out of my mind.

"You *have* to tell me. It was the same guy, *Chimera*. Wasn't it?"

I threw myself onto my bed. "We don't know. There was nothing at the scene."

"You *know*, Lindsay. I know you know. We both know it was him."

I just wanted her to let me be and curl up in bed. "I don't know," I said wearily. "It could be."

"What caliber was the gun? Did it match Catchings?"

"Please, Cindy, don't try to play detective on

me. I knew the guy. His partner said it was his kid's seventh birthday. He had five children."

"I'm sorry, Lindsay," Cindy finally came back in a softer, gentler voice. "It's just that it's like the first murder, Lindsay. The shot that no one else could make."

We sat awhile on the phone without talking. She was right. I knew she was right. Then Cindy said, "You've got another one, don't you, Lindsay?"

I didn't answer, but I knew what she meant.

"Another pattern killer. A cold-blooded marksman. And he's targeting blacks."

"Not just blacks." I sighed.

"Not just blacks . . . ?" Cindy hesitated, then she came back in a rush. "The Oakland crime reporter got a rumor out of Homicide there. About the Chipman widow. Her husband was a cop. First Tasha's uncle. Then her. Now Davidson makes three. Oh, Jesus, Lindsay."

"This stays with us," I insisted. "Please, Cindy. I need to sleep now. You don't realize how hard this is for us."

"Let us help, Lindsay. All of us. We want to help you."

"I will, Cindy. I need your help. I need all of your help."

Chapter 34

I THOUGHT OF SOMETHING during the night. *The killer had called 911.*

I got right on it in the morning. Lila Mc-Kendree ran Dispatch. She had been on the board when the Davidson call came in.

Lila was plump, rosy cheeked, and quick to smile, but no one was more professional, and she could coolly juggle serious situations like an air-traffic controller.

She set up the tape of the actual 911 call in the squad room. The entire detail huddled around. Cappy and Jacobi had come in before heading back out to Vallejo.

"It's on a three-loop reel," Lila explained. She pressed the playback key.

In a few seconds, we were going to hear the killer's voice for the first time.

"San Francisco Police, nine one one hot-line," a dispatcher's voice said.

There wasn't another sound in the squad room.

An agitated male voice shot back, "I need to call in a disturbance. . . . Some guy's doing an O. J. on his wife."

"Okay . . . ," the operator replied. "I'll need to start with your location. Where is this disturbance taking place?"

There was an interfering background noise like a TV or traffic, making it difficult to hear. "Three oh three Seventh. Fourth floor. You better send someone out. It's starting to sound real bad."

"You said the address was three oh three Seventh?"

"That's right," the killer said.

"And who am I speaking with?" the operator asked.

"My name's Billy. Billy Reffon. I live down the hall. You better hurry."

We all looked around, surprised. *The killer gave a name? Jesus.*

"Listen, sir," the dispatcher asked, "are you able to hear what's going on as I'm talking to you?"

"What I can hear," he said, "is some spook getting the living shit beat out of her."

The dispatcher hesitated. "Yes, sir. Can you determine if there's been any physical injury so far?"

"I'm no doctor, lady, I'm just trying to do the right thing. Just send someone!"

"Okay, Mr. Reffon, I'm calling a patrol car now. What I want you to do is exit the building and wait for the officers. They're on the way."

"You better move quick," the killer said. *"Sounds like someone's about to get hurt."*

After the transmission ended, there was the follow-up recording of the outgoing dispatch call.

"The call came from a mobile phone," Lila said, shrugging her broad shoulders. "No doubt cloned. Here, it's starting up again on a three-cycle loop." In a moment the tape came on a second time. This time, I listened closely for what the voice could tell me.

I need to call in a disturbance. . . . It was a worried voice, panicked but cool.

"The guy's a good fucking actor," Jacobi huffed.

My name's Billy. Billy Reffon. . . .

I clenched the edges of my wooden chair as I listened to the dispatcher's well-intended instructions. "Exit the building and wait for the officers. They're on the way." All the while, he was sitting behind a rifle scope, waiting for his prey to show up.

You better move quick, he said. *Someone's about to get hurt.*

We listened to the recording one more time.

This time, I heard the mocking indifference in his voice. Not even the slightest tone of compunction for what he was about to do. In the last warning, I even detected a hint of a cold chuckle: *Quick . . . Someone's about to get hurt.*

"That's all I have," Lila McKendree said. "The killer's voice."

Chapter 35

THE DAVIDSON MURDER changed everything.

A bold headline in the *Chronicle* shouted, "MURDERED COP THOUGHT TO BE THIRD IN TERROR SPREE." The front-page article, with Cindy's byline, cited the accurate, long-range rifle shots and also the symbol used by active hate groups that had been found at the scenes.

I headed down to the CSU lab and found Charlie Clapper curled up behind a metal desk, wearing a lab coat, munching on a breakfast of Doritos chips. His salt-and-pepper hair was oily and tousled, and his eyes sagged like heavy bags. "I've slept at this desk twice this week." He scowled. "Doesn't anyone get killed during the day anymore?"

"In case you didn't notice, I haven't been getting my normal beauty rest the last week either." I shrugged. "C'mon, Charlie, I need something on this Davidson thing. He's killing our own guys."

"I know he is." The rotund CSU man sighed. He hoisted himself up and shuffled over to a counter. He picked up a small zip-lock sandwich bag with a dark, flattened bullet in it.

"Here's your slug, Lindsay. Took it out of the wall behind where Art Davidson got dropped. One shot. Lights out. Check with Claire if you like. The sonofabitch can definitely shoot."

I lifted up the shell and tried to pull a reading.

"Forty caliber," Clapper said. "My first read is that it's from a PSG-One."

I frowned. "You're sure about this, Charlie?" Tasha Catchings had been killed with an M16.

He pointed toward a scope. "Be my guest, Lieutenant. I figure ballistics must be a life-long study of yours."

"I didn't mean that, Charlie. I was just hoping for a match on the Catchings girl."

"Reese is still working on it," he said, grabbing a chip out of the Doritos bag. "But don't bet on it. This guy was clean, Lindsay. Just like at the church. No prints, nothing left behind. The tape machine's standard, could've been bought anywhere. Set off by a long-distance remote control. We even traced what we thought to be his route up there through the building and dusted everything from the railings to the window locks. We did turn up one thing. . . ."

"What's that?" I pressed.

He walked me over to a lab counter. "Partial sneaker print. Off the tar on the roof where the shots came from. Looks like a standard shoe. But we did take out some traces of a fine white powder. No guarantees it even came from him."

"Powder?"

"Chalk," Charlie said. "That narrows it down to about fifty million possibilities. If this guy's signing his pictures, Lindsay, he's making it tough to find."

"He *signed* it, Charlie," I said with conviction. "It was the shot."

"We're sending the nine-one-one tape out for a voice reading. I'll let you know when we get it back."

I patted him appreciatively. "Get some sleep, Charlie."

He lifted the Doritos bag. "Sure, I will. After breakfast."

Chapter 36

I WENT BACK to the office and sank disappointedly back behind my desk. I had to know more about that chimera. I was about to dial Stu Kirkwood at the hate crimes desk when a cadre of three men in dark suits came into the squad room.

One of them was Mercer. No surprise. He had been on the morning talk shows, pushing for calm. I knew facing tough questions without concrete results didn't sit well with him.

But the other, accompanied by his press liaison, was a man I had never seen on the floor in seven years in Homicide.

It was the mayor of San Francisco.

"I don't want the slightest bit of bullshit," Art Fernandez, San Francisco's two-term mayor, said. "I don't want the standard protecting the ranks, and I don't want any misplaced reflex to control the situation." He shifted his eyes on a narrow track between Mercer and me. "What I want is an honest answer. Do we have a read on this situation?"

We were crammed into my tiny glass-enclosed office. Outside, I could see staffers standing around, watching the circus.

I fumbled under my desk to get my pumps back on. "We do not," I admitted.

"So Vernon Jones is right." The mayor exhaled, sinking into a chair across from my desk. "What we have is an out-of-control spree of hate-driven killings on which the police have no handle, but the FBI may."

"No, that's not it," I replied.

"That's not it?" he arched his eyebrows. He looked at Mercer and frowned. "What is it I don't understand? You've got a recognized hate group symbol, this chimera, at two of the three crime scenes. Our own M.E. believes the Catchings girl was the intended target of this madman."

"What the lieutenant is saying," Mercer cut in, "is that this may not be simply a hate crime issue."

My mouth was a little cottony, and I swallowed. "I think it's deeper than a hate crime spree."

"Deeper, Lieutenant Boxer? Just what is it you believe we have?"

I stared straight at Fernandez. "What I think we have is someone with a personal vendetta. Possibly a single assailant. He's couching his murders in the MO of a hate crime."

"A vendetta, you say," Carr, the mayor's man, chimed in. "A vendetta against blacks, but not a hate crime. Against black children and widows . . . *but not a hate crime?*"

"Against black *cops,*" I said.

The mayor's eyes narrowed. "Go on."

I explained that Tasha Catchings and Estelle Chipman had been related to cops. "There has to be some further relationship, though we don't know what it is yet. The killer is organized, haughty in the way he's leaving his clues. I do *not* believe a hate crime killer would leave their mark on the hits. The getaway van, the little drawing in Chipman's basement, that cocky nine-one-one tape. I don't think this is a hate crime spree. It's a vendetta — calculated, *personal.*"

The mayor looked at Mercer. "You go along with this, Earl?"

"Protecting the ranks aside . . ." Mercer smiled tightly. "I do."

"Well, I don't," Carr said. "Everything points to a hate crime."

There was silence in the cramped room; the temperature suddenly felt like 120 degrees.

"So it seems I have two choices," the mayor said. "Under the Hate Crimes Legislation, Article Four, I can call in the FBI, who, I believe, keep a close watch on these groups . . ."

"They have no fucking idea how to run a homicide investigation," Mercer protested.

"Or . . . I can let the lieutenant do her job. Tell the Feds we got it all handled ourselves," the mayor said.

I met his eyes. "I went to the academy with Art Davidson. You think you want to catch his killer any more than I do?"

"Then catch him," the mayor said and rose. "Just so we know what's at stake," he added.

I was nodding glumly when Lorraine burst through my door. "Sorry to interrupt, Lieutenant, but it's urgent. Jacobi called in from Vallejo. He said make the place up nice and neat for an important guest. They found the biker from the Blue Parrot.

"They found Red."

Chapter 37

ABOUT AN HOUR LATER, Jacobi and Cappy entered the squad room. They were pushing a large redheaded biker type, his hands cuffed behind his back.

"Look who decided to drop in." Jacobi smirked.

Red jerked his arms defiantly out of Cappy's grip as the policeman shoved him into Interrogation Room 1, where he tripped over a wooden chair and crashed to the floor.

"Sorry, big fella." Cappy shrugged. "Thought I warned you about that first step."

"Richard Earl Evans," Jacobi announced. "AKA Red, Boomer, Duke. Don't feel insulted if he doesn't stand up and shake hands."

"This is what you thought I meant by no contact?" I said, looking cross but inside delighted that they had brought him in.

"The guy's got a CCI sheet so long it begins with 'Call me Ishmael.' " Jacobi grinned. "Theft, aggravated mischief, attempted murder, two weapons charges."

"Behold," exclaimed Cappy, producing a dime bag of marijuana, a five-inch hunter's blade, and a palm-sized Beretta .22-caliber pistol out of a Nordstrom's shopping bag.

"He know why he's here?" I asked.

"Nah," Cappy grunted. "We busted him on the gun charge. Let him cool his jets in the backseat."

The three of us crowded into the small interrogation room facing Richard Earl Evans. The creep leered up at us with a smug grin, sleeves of tattoos covering both arms. He wore a black T-shirt with block letters on the back: "If You Can *Read* This . . . the Bitch Must've Fallen Off!"

I nodded, and Cappy freed him from the cuffs. "You know why you're here, Mr. Evans?"

"I know you guys are in deep shit if you think I'm talking to you." Evans sniffed a mixture of mucus and blood. "You got no teeth in Vallejo."

I raised the bag of dope. "Santa seems to have brought you a lot of naughty toys. Two felonies . . . still on parole for a weapons charge. Time at Folsom, Quentin. My sense is you must like it there, 'cause next time up, you qualify for the thirty-year lease."

"One thing I do know" — Evans rolled his eyes — "is you didn't drag me all this way for some two-bit weapons rap. The sign on the door says *Homicide*."

"No, big fella, you're right," Cappy injected. "Tossing your sorry ass in jail on a gun charge is only a hobby for us. But depending on how you answer a few questions, that weapons rap could determine where you spend the next thirty years."

"Pupshit," the biker grunted, leveling his cold, hard eyes in his face. "That's all you ass-holes got on me."

Cappy shrugged, then brought the flat end of an unopened soda can down hard on the biker's hand.

Evans yelped in pain.

"Damn, I thought you said you were thirsty," Cappy said contritely.

Red leered at Cappy, no doubt imagining running over the cop's face with his bike.

"But you're right, Mr. Evans," I said. "We didn't ask you down here to go over your current possessions, though it wouldn't take much to hand your sorry ass right over to the Vallejo police. But today could work out lucky for you. Cappy, ask Mr. Evans if he'd like another drink."

Cappy feinted, and Evans jerked his hand off the table.

Then the big cop opened the can and placed it in front of him, grinning widely. "This all right, or would you prefer a glass?"

"See," I assured him, "we can be nice. Truth is, we don't give a shit about you. All you have to do is answer a few questions and you'll be headed home, compliments of the SFPD. You never have to see us again. Or we can lock your three-time-loser ass on the tenth floor for a few days until we remember we got you here and notify the Vallejo police. And, when it comes to a third felony offense, we'll see about just how much teeth we really have."

Evans ran his hand across the bridge of his nose, dabbing at the blood. "Maybe I will take a swig of that soda, if you're still offering."

"Congratulations, son," Jacobi said. "That's the first thing you've done that makes sense since we set eyes on you."

Chapter 38

I LAID OUT A BLACK-AND-WHITE surveillance photo of the Templars in front of Red's startled face. "First thing we need to know is where can we find your buddies?"

Evans looked up grinning. "So that's what this is all about?"

"C'mon, sharp-as-nails," pressed Jacobi, "the lieutenant asked a question."

One by one, I spread on the table three more photos showing various members.

Evans shook his head. "Never ran with those guys."

The last photo I put down was a surveillance shot of *him*.

Cappy reached out, all two hundred fifty pounds of him, and raised the biker by the shirt, lifting him out of his seat. "Listen, codshit, you're only lucky we're not concerned here with what you sorry bunch of losers got off doing. So act smart and you'll be outta here, and we can go on to what we do give a shit about."

Evans shrugged. "Maybe I did run a bit with them. But no more. Club's disbanded. Too much heat. I ain't seen these guys around here in months. They split. You wanna find them, start with *Five South.*"

I looked at the two inspectors. As much as I doubted whether Evans would actually turn over on his buddies, I believed him.

"One more question," I said. "A big one." I laid down the photo of the biker with the chimera jacket. "What does this mean to you?"

Evans sniffed. "The dude's got bogus taste in attire?"

Cappy leaned forward.

Evans recoiled. "It's a symbol, man. Means he's in the movement. A patriot."

"A patriot?" I asked him. "What the hell is that supposed to mean?"

"An advocate of the white race, the self-determination of a free and orderly society." He smiled at Cappy. "Present company excluded, of course. Course, none of this shit necessarily reflects my personal views."

"Did this guy head off to the Sun Belt, too?" Jacobi asked.

"Him? Why? What do you think he's done?"

"There he goes" — Cappy stood over him — "answering questions with questions again."

"Look." Evans swallowed. "The brother only hung with us a short while. I don't even know his real name. Mac . . . McMillan, McArthur? What'd he do?"

I figured there was no reason not to tell him what we thought. "What's the word about what happened in La Salle Heights?"

Red finally flinched. His pupils widened. All of a sudden, it was falling into place. "You think my old dudes lit up that church? *This guy . . . Mac?*"

"You know how we could talk to him?" I said.

Evans grinned. "That's a tough order. Even for you."

"Try us," I said. "We're resourceful."

"I'm sure you are, but this fucker's dead. Back in June. He and a partner blew themselves up, in Oregon. Sonofabitch must've read somewhere you could turn cowshit into a bomb."

Chapter 39

IN THE SMALL BLACKTOP PARKING LOT adjacent to the La Salle Heights Church, Cindy Thomas climbed out of her Mazda. Her stomach growled, telling her that it didn't quite know what she was doing here.

She took a breath and opened the large oak door into the main chapel. Just yesterday it had been filled with the choir's resonating sound. Now it was eerily quiet, the pews empty. She walked through the chapel and into a connecting building.

A carpeted hallway led to a row of offices. A black woman, glancing up from a copy machine, asked, "Can I help you? What do you want?"

"I'm here to see Reverend Winslow."

"He's not seeing visitors now," the woman said.

Winslow's voice rang out from one of the offices. "It's all right, Carol."

Cindy was led to his office. It was small, crowded with books. He was wearing a black T-shirt and khakis, and didn't look like any minister she'd ever known.

"So, we managed to get you back after all," he said. Then finally, he smiled.

He had her take a seat on a small couch and he sat in a well-worn red leather chair. A pair of glasses was resting on a book nearby, and she instinctively sneaked a peek. *A Heartbreaking Work of Staggering Genius*. Not what she would have expected.

"You mending?" she asked.

"Trying to. I read your story today. It was terrible about that policeman. It's true? Tasha's murder might be tied up with two others?"

"The police think so," Cindy answered. "The M.E. believes she was deliberately shot."

Winslow grimaced and then shook his head. "I don't understand. Tasha was just a little girl. What possible connection could there be?"

"It wasn't so much Tasha" — Cindy held eye contact with Aaron Winslow — "as what she represented. All the victims apparently have a link to San Francisco cops."

Winslow's eyes narrowed. "So tell me, what brings you back so soon? Your soul aching? Why are you here?"

Cindy lowered her eyes. "The service yesterday. It was moving. I felt chills. It's been a long time for me. Actually, I think my soul has been aching. I just haven't bothered to notice."

Winslow's look softened. She'd told him a small truth, and it had touched him. "Well, good. I'm glad to hear you were moved."

Cindy smiled. Incredibly, he made her feel at ease. He seemed centered, genuine, and she'd heard nothing but good things about him. She wanted to do a story on him, and she knew it would be a good one, maybe a great story.

"I bet I know what you're thinking," Aaron Winslow said.

"Okay," she said, "shoot."

"You're wondering . . . the man seems together enough, not completely weirded out. He doesn't seem like a minister. So what is he doing making his living working like this?"

Cindy flashed an embarrassed smile. "I admit, something like that did cross my mind.

I'd like to do a story about you and the Bay View neighborhood."

He seemed to be thinking it over. But then he changed the subject on her.

"What is it you like to do, Cindy?"

"Do . . . ?"

"In the big, bad world of San Francisco you cover out there. After you call in your story. What moves you besides your job at the *Chronicle*? What are your passions?"

She found herself smiling. "Hey, I ask the questions. I want to do a story on *you*. Not the other way around," she said. "All right. I like yoga. I take a class twice a week on Chestnut Street. You ever do yoga?"

"No, but I meditate every day."

Cindy smiled some more. She wasn't even sure why. "I'm in a women's book club. Two women's clubs, actually. I like jazz."

Winslow's eyes lit. "What kind of jazz? I like jazz myself."

Cindy laughed. "Okay, now we're getting somewhere. What kind of jazz do you like?"

"Progressive. Interpretive. Anything from Pinetop Perkins to Coltrane."

"You know the Blue Door? On Geary?" she asked.

"Of course I know the Blue Door. I go there Saturday nights, whenever Carlos Reyes is in town. Maybe we could go sometime. As part of your story. You don't have to answer right now."

"Then you agree to let me do a piece on you?" Cindy said.

"I agree . . . to let you do a piece on the neighborhood. I'll help you with it."

A half hour later, in her car, Cindy sat letting the engine run, almost too astonished to put it in gear. *I don't believe what I just did. . . .* Lindsay would rap her in the head. Question whether her gadgets were properly working.

But they were *working.* They were *humming* a little, actually. The tiny hairs on her arms were standing straight up.

She had the beginnings of what she thought might be a good story, maybe a prizewinner.

She'd also just accepted a date from Tasha Catchings's pastor, and she couldn't wait to see him again.

Maybe my soul has been aching, Cindy thought as she finally drove away from the church.

Chapter 40

IT WAS CLOSE TO SEVEN on Saturday. The end of a long, insane, incredibly stressful week. Three people had died. My only good leads had come and gone.

I needed to talk to somebody, so I went up to eight, where the D.A.'s staff was located. Two doors down from the big man himself was Jill's corner office.

The executive corner was dark, offices empty, staff scattered for the weekend. In a way, though I needed to vent, I was sort of hoping Jill — the *new* Jill — would be at home, maybe picking through swatch books for her baby's room.

But as I approached, I heard the sound of classical music coming from within. Jill's door was cracked half open.

I knocked gently and pushed it in. There

was Jill, in her favorite easy chair, knees tucked to her chest and a yellow legal pad resting on them. Her desk was piled high with briefs.

"Why are you here?" I asked.

"Snagged." She sighed, raising her hands in mock surrender. "It's just this goddamn Perrone thing. Closing arguments Monday morning." Jill was at the end of a high-profile case in which a derelict landlord was being charged with manslaughter after a faulty ceiling caved in on an eight-year-old child.

"You're pregnant, Jill. It's after seven o'clock."

"So is Connie Sperling, for the defense. They're calling it the Battle of the Bulge."

"Whatever they're calling it, so much for the shift of gears."

Jill turned down the CD player and extended her long legs. "Anyway, Steve's out of town. What else is new? I'd only be doing the same thing if I were at home." She cocked her head and smiled. "You're checking up on me."

"No, but maybe someone should."

"Good lord, Lindsay, I'm just preparing notes, not running a ten-k. I'm doing fine.

Anyway" — she glanced at her watch — "since when did you turn into the poster girl for keeping everything in perspective?"

"I'm not pregnant, Jill. All right, all right — I'll stop lecturing."

I stepped inside her office — eyed her women's final four soccer photo from Stanford, framed diplomas, and pictures of her and Steve rock climbing and running with their black Lab, Snake Eyes.

"I still have a beer in the fridge if you want to sit," she said, tossing her legal pad on the desk. "Pull a Buckler out for me."

I did just that. Then I shifted the black Max Mara suit jacket hastily thrown over a cushion and sank back in the leather couch. We tilted our bottles, and both of us blurted in the same breath, "So . . . how's your case?"

"You first." Jill laughed.

I spread my thumb and index finger barely a half inch apart to indicate basically zip. I took her through the maze of dead ends: the van, the chimera sketch, the surveillance photo of the Templars, that CSU had come up with nothing on the Davidson ambush.

Jill came over and sat beside me on the couch. "You want to talk, Linds? Like you said, you didn't come up here to make sure I was behaving myself."

I smiled guiltily, then placed my beer on the coffee table. "I need to shift the investigation, Jill."

"Okay," she said. "I'm listening. . . . This is just between us."

Piece by piece, I laid out my theory that the killer was not some reckless, hate-mongering maniac but a bold, plotting pattern killer acting out a vendetta.

"Maybe you're overreaching," Jill replied. "What you *do* have is three terror crimes aimed at African Americans."

"So why these victims, Jill? An eleven-year-old girl? A decorated cop? Estelle Chipman, whose husband has been dead for five years?"

"I don't know, honey. I just nail 'em to the wall when you turn them over."

I smiled. Then I leaned forward. "Jill, I need you to help me. I need to find some connection between these victims. I know it's there. I need to check out past cases in which a white plaintiff was victimized by a black police officer. That's where my gut leads me. It's where I think these killings might start. It has something to do with revenge."

"What happens when the next victim never had anything to do with a police officer? What are you gonna do then?"

I looked at her imploringly. "Are you going to help me?"

"Of course I'm going to help you." She shook her head at me. "Duh . . . Anything you can give me that will help me narrow it down?"

I nodded. "Male, white. Maybe a tattoo or three."

"That oughtta do it." She rolled her eyes.

I reached out and squeezed her hand. I knew I could count on her. I looked at my watch. Seven-thirty. "I better let you finish up while you're still in your first trimester."

"Don't go, Lindsay." Jill held my arm. "Stick around."

I could see something on her face. That clear, professional intensity suddenly weakened into a thousand-yard stare.

"Something wrong, Jill? Did the doctor tell you something?"

In her sleeveless vest, with her dark hair curled around her ears, she looked every bit the power lawyer, number two in the city's legal department. But there was a tremor in her breath. "I'm fine. Really, physically, I'm fine. I should be happy, right? I'm gonna have a baby. I should be riding the air."

"You should be feeling whatever you're feeling, Jill." I took her hand.

She nodded glassily. Then she curled her knees up to her chest. "When I was a kid, I would sometimes wake up in the night. I always had this little terror, this feeling that the whole world was asleep, that around this whole, huge planet, I was the only one left awake in the world. Sometimes my father would come in and try to rock me to sleep. He'd be downstairs in his study, preparing his cases, and he'd always check on me before he turned in. He called me his second chair. *But even with him there,* I still felt so alone."

She shook her head at me, tears glistening in her eyes. "Look at me. Steve's away for two nights and I turn into a fucking idiot," she said.

"I don't think you're an idiot," I said, stroking her pretty face.

"I can't lose this baby, Lindsay. I know it seems stupid. I'm carrying a life. It's *here,* always in me, right next to me. How is it I feel so alone?"

I held her tightly by the shoulders. My father had never been there to rock me to sleep. Even before he left us, he worked the third shift and would always head to McGoey's for a beer afterward. Sometimes I felt like the heartbeat that was closest to me was the pulse of the bastards I had to track down.

"I know what you mean," I heard myself whisper. I held Jill. "Sometimes I feel that way, too."

Chapter 41

ON THE CORNER of Ocean and Victoria, a man in a green fatigue windbreaker hunched chewing a burrito as the black Lincoln slowly made its way down the block. He had waited here dozens of nights, stalked his next prey for weeks.

The person he had watched for so long lived in a pleasant stucco house inside Ingleside Heights, just a short walk away. He had a family, two girls in Catholic school; his wife was a registered nurse. He had a black Lab; sometimes it bounded out to greet him as his car pulled up. The Lab was named Bullitt, like the old movie.

Usually, the car drove by around seven-thirty. A couple of times a week, the man got out to walk. It was always at the same spot, on Victoria. He liked to stop at the

Korean market, chat with the owner as he picked out a melon or a cabbage. Playing the big man walking among his people.

Then he might mosey into Tiny's News, stuff his arms with a few magazines: *Car and Driver, PC World, Sports Illustrated.* Once, he had even stood behind him in the line as he waited to pay for his reading material.

He could have taken him out. Many times. One dazzling shot from a distance.

But no, this one had to be up close. Eye to eye. This murder would blow the lid off everything, the entire city of San Francisco. This would take the case international, and not many got that big.

His heart sprung alive as he huddled in the damp drizzle, but this time the black Lincoln merely passed by.

So it won't be tonight. He exhaled. *Go home to your little wife and dog. . . . But soon . . . You've grown forgetful,* he thought, balling his burrito in the wrapper and tossing it in a trash bin. *Forgetful of the past.* But it always finds you.

I live with the past every day.

He watched as the black Lincoln, its windows dark, made its customary left turn onto Cerritos and disappeared into Ingleside Heights.

You stole my life. Now I'm going to take yours.

Chapter 42

I TOOK SUNDAY MORNING OFF to run Martha by the bay and do my tai chi on the Marina Green. By noon I was in jeans and a sweatshirt, back at my desk. By Monday, the investigation was listing toward the dead zone, no new angles to work. We were putting out releases just to keep the press off our tail. Each stalled line of questioning, each frustrating dead end only narrowed the time to when Chimera would strike again.

I was returning some case files to Jill when the elevator door opened and Chief Mercer ambled in. He looked surprised when he saw me but not displeased.

"Come take a ride with me," he said.

Mercer's car was waiting along the side entrance on Eighth Street. As the police driver leaned back, Mercer told him, "West Portal, Sam."

West Portal was a diverse middle-class neighborhood out of the center of the city. I didn't know why Mercer would be dragging me out there in the middle of the day.

As we rode, Mercer asked a few questions but stayed mostly silent. A tremor shot through me: *He's gonna take me off the case.*

The driver pulled onto a residential street I had never been on before. He parked in front of a small blue Victorian across from a high school playground. A pickup basketball game was going on.

I blinked first. "What was it you wanted to talk about, Chief?"

Mercer turned to me. "You have any personal heroes, Lindsay?"

"You mean like Amelia Earhart or Margaret Thatcher?" I shook my head. I had never grown up with those. "Maybe Claire Washburn." I grinned.

Mercer nodded. "Arthur Ashe was always one of mine. Someone asked him if it was hard to cope with AIDS, and he answered, 'Not nearly as hard as it was to deal with growing up black in the United States.'"

His expression deepened. "Vernon Jones tells the mayor that I've lost sight of what's

175

really at stake in this case." He pointed toward the blue Victorian across the street. "You see that house? My parents' house. I was raised there.

"My father was a mechanic in the transit yards, and my mother did the books for an electrical contractor. They worked their whole lives to send me and my sister to school. She's a trial litigator now, in Atlanta. But this is where we're from."

"My father worked for the city, too." I nodded.

"I know I never told you, Lindsay, but I knew your father."

"You knew him?"

"Yeah, we started out together. Radio cops, out of Central. Even shifted together a few times. *Marty Boxer* . . . Your father was a bit of a legend, Lindsay, and not necessarily for exemplary duty."

"Tell me something I don't know."

"All right . . ." He paused. "He was a good cop then. A damned good cop. A lot of us looked up to him."

"Before he bagged out."

Mercer looked at me. "You must know by now, things happen in a cop's life that don't always break down so easily into choices the rest of us can understand."

I shook my head. "I haven't spoken to him in twenty-two years."

Mercer nodded. "I can't speak for him as a father, or as a husband, but is there a chance that as a man, or at least a cop, you've judged him without knowing all the facts?"

"He never stuck around long enough to present the facts," I said.

"I'm sorry," Mercer said. "I'll tell you some things about Marty Boxer, but another time."

"Tell me what? When?"

He drew down the privacy barrier and instructed his driver that it was time to head back to the Hall. "When you find Chimera."

Chapter 43

LATER THAT NIGHT, as his Town Car slowed in the evening traffic near his home, Chief Mercer spoke up from the backseat. "Why don't I get out here, Sam."

His driver, Sam Mendez, glanced back. The mandate from the Hall was no unnecessary risks.

Mercer was firm on the matter. "Sam, there's more cops on patrol in a five-block radius here than there are back at the Hall." There was usually a patrol car or two cruising on Ocean and one stationed across from his home.

The car eased to a stop. Mercer opened the door and thrust his heavy shape onto the street. "Pick me up tomorrow, Sam. Have a good night."

As his car pulled away, Mercer lugged his thick briefcase in one hand and threw his tan raincoat over his shoulder with the other. He experienced a surge of freedom and relief. These little after-work excursions were the only times he felt free.

He stopped at Kim's Market and picked out the sweetest-looking basket of strawberries, and some choice plums, too. Then he wandered across the street to the Ingleside Wine Shop. He decided on a Beaujolais that would go with the lamb stew Eunice was making.

On the street, he glanced at his watch and headed toward home. On Cerritos, two stone pillars separated Ocean from the secure enclave of Ingleside Heights. The traffic disappeared behind him.

He passed the low stone house belonging to the Taylors. A noise rustled out from a hedge. "Well, well, Chief . . . ?"

Mercer stopped. His heart was already pounding.

"Don't be shy. I haven't seen you in years," the voice said again. "You probably don't remember."

What the hell was going on?

A tall, muscular man stepped out from behind the hedge. He was wearing a cocky smirk, a green windbreaker wrapped around him.

A vague recognition came over Mercer, a familiarity in the face he couldn't quite place. Then all at once it came back to him. Suddenly, everything made sense, and it took his breath away.

"This is such an honor," the man said. "For *you.*"

He had a gun, heavy and silver. It was extended toward Mercer's chest. Mercer knew he had to do something. Ram him. Get to his own gun somehow. He needed to act like a cop on the street again.

"I wanted you to see my face. I wanted you to know why you were dying."

"Don't do this. There are cops everywhere around here."

"Good. That makes it even better for me. Don't be scared, Chief. Where you're going, you'll be running into a lot of your old friends."

The first shot struck him in the chest, a burning, clothes-searing thud that buckled his knees. Mercer's first thought was to shout. Was it Parks or Vasquez stationed in front of his house? Only precious yards away. But his voice died inaudibly in his chest. *Jesus God, please save me.*

The second shot tore through his throat. He didn't know if he was up or down. He wanted to charge the killer. He wanted to take this bastard down. But his legs felt — paralyzed, inert.

The man with the gun was standing over him now. The bastard was still talking to him, but he couldn't hear a word. His face kept melting in and out of focus. A name flashed in his mind. It seemed impossible. He said it twice just to be sure, his breath pounding in his ears.

"That's right," the killer said, leveling the silvery gun. "You've solved the case. You figured out Chimera. Congratulations."

Mercer thought he should close his eyes — when the next bright orange flash exploded in his face.

Chapter 44

I WILL ALWAYS REMEMBER what I was doing when I heard the news. I was home, tending a pot of farfalle on the stove. "Adia" by Sarah McLachlan was playing on the stereo.

Claire was coming over. I'd lured her for dinner with my famous pasta with asparagus and lemon sauce. Not lured her, actually . . . *begged.* I wanted to talk about something other than the case. Her kids, yoga, the California Senate race, why the Warriors sucked. *Anything . . .*

I will never forget. . . . Martha sat toying with a headless San Francisco Giants mascot bear that she had appropriated to her side of the property list. I was chopping basil; I checked on the pasta. Tasha Catchings and Art Davidson had drifted out of my mind. Thank God.

The phone rang. A selfish thought knifed

through me, hoping that it wasn't Claire bag-
ging out of our date at the last minute.

I cradled the phone in the nape of my neck
and answered, "Yo . . ."

It was Sam Ryan, the department's chief of
detectives. Ryan was my administrative superior in the chain of command. At the sound of
his voice, I knew something had to be seriously wrong.

"Lindsay, something terrible has happened."

My body went numb. It was like someone
had reached inside my chest and squeezed
my heart in their indifferent fist. I listened to
Ryan speak. *Three shots from point-blank
range . . . Only a few yards from his house.
Oh, my God . . . Mercer . . .*

"Where is he, Sam?"

"Moffitt. Emergency surgery. He's fighting."

"I'll be right down. I'm on my way."

"Lindsay, there's nothing you can do here.
Get out to the scene."

"Chin and Lorraine will cover it. I'll be right
down."

The doorbell buzzed. As if in a trance, I
rushed over, opened it.

"Hey," said Claire.

I didn't say a word. In an instant, she recognized the pallor on my face. "What's happened?"

My eyes were wet. "Claire . . . he's shot Chief Mercer."

Chapter 45

WE RACED DOWN THE STEPS, climbed into Claire's Pathfinder, and made the dash from Potrero to the California Medical Center all the way over in Parnassus Heights. The entire ride, my heart pumped madly and hopefully. The streets blurred by — Twenty-fourth, Guerrero, then across the Castro on Seventeenth to the hospital atop Mt. Sutro.

Barely ten minutes after I got the call, Claire spun the Pathfinder into a restricted parking space across from the hospital entrance.

Claire ID'd herself to a nurse at the front desk, asking for an up-to-date report. She looked worried as she charged inside the swinging doors. I ran up to Sam Ryan. "What's the word?"

He shook his head. "He's on the table now. If anyone can take three bullets and make it through, it's him."

I flipped open my cell phone and patched into Lorraine Stafford at the scene. "Things are crazy here," she said. "There's people from Internal Affairs, and some goddamn city *crisis* agency. And the fucking press. I haven't been able to get close to the radio cop who was first on the scene."

"Don't let *anyone* other than you or Chin get close to that scene," I told her. "I'll be out there as soon as I can."

Claire came back out of the ER. Her face was drawn. "They've got him open now, Lindsay. It doesn't look good. His cerebral cortex was penetrated. He's lost a ton of blood. It's a miracle he's hung on as long as he has."

"Claire, I've got to get in there to see him."

She shook her head. "He's barely alive, Lindsay. Besides, he's under anesthesia."

I had this mounting sense that I owed it to Mercer, each unresolved death. That he knew, and if he died the truth would die with him. "I'm going in there."

I pushed through the doors leading to the ER, but Claire held on to me. As I looked into her eyes, the last glimmer of hopefulness drained out of my body. I had always fought with Mercer, battled him. He was someone to whom I felt I always had something to prove, and prove again and again. But in the end, he had believed in me. In the strangest of ways, I felt as if I were losing a father all over again.

Barely a minute later, a doctor in a green smock came out, peeling off latex gloves. He said a few words to one of the mayor's men, then to the assistant chief, Anthony Tracchio.

"The chief's dead," Tracchio uttered.

Everyone stood staring blankly ahead. Claire put an arm around me and hugged.

"I don't know if I can do this," I said, holding tightly on to her shoulder.

"Yes, you can," she said.

I caught Mercer's doctor as he headed back to the ER. I introduced myself. "Did he say anything when he was brought in?"

The doctor shrugged. "He held on for a while, but whatever he said was incoherent. Just reflexive. He was on life support from the moment he came in."

"His brain was still working, wasn't it, Doctor?" He had faced his killer head-on. Taken three shots. I could see Mercer holding on just long enough to say something. "*Anything* you remember?"

His tired eyes searched for something. "I'm sorry, Inspector. We were trying to save his life. You might try the EMS techs who brought him in."

He went back inside. Through the windows in the ER doors, I caught a glimpse of Eunice Mercer and one of their teenage daughters, tearfully hugging in the corridor.

My insides felt as if they were ripping apart, a knot of nausea building.

I ran into the ladies' room. I bent over the sink and splashed cold water all over my face. "Goddamn it! Goddamn it!"

When my body calmed, I looked up in the mirror. My eyes were dark, hollow and blank; voices drummed loudly in my head.

Four murders, they tolled . . . *Four black cops.*

Chapter 46

LORRAINE STAFFORD walked me down from the stone gate on Cerritos. "The chief was on his way home." She bit her bottom lip. "He lived a couple of houses down that way. No witnesses, but his driver's over there."

I went to the spot where Mercer's body had been found. Charlie Clapper's team was already combing all around it. It was a quiet, residential street, the sidewalk guarded by a high hedge that would've blocked anyone from seeing the killer.

The spot had already been chalked off. Blotches of blood soaked the pavement inside the outline of the body. The remains of his last moments, some plastic bags containing magazines, fruit, and a bottle of wine, were scattered around.

"Didn't he have a car stationed in front of his house?" I asked.

Lorraine nodded toward a young uniformed officer leaning against the hood of a blue-and-white. "By the time he got down here, the perp had fled and the chief was bleeding out."

It became clear the killer had been lying in wait. He must've hidden in the bushes until Mercer came by. He must've known. Just like he knew with Davidson.

From up on Ocean, I saw Jacobi and Cappy coming toward us. The sight of them made me exhale with relief.

"Thanks for coming down," I whispered.

Then Jacobi did something totally uncharacteristic. He grasped my shoulder and looked firmly into my eyes. "This is gonna get big, Lindsay; Feds are gonna come in. Anything we can do, anything you need, anytime you need to talk about it. You know I'm here for you."

I turned to Lorraine and Chin. "What do you need to finish up here?"

"I want to check along the escape route," Chin said. "If he had a car parked, someone must've seen it. Otherwise, maybe someone saw him come out on Ocean."

"Fucking chief." Jacobi sighed. "I always *thought* the guy would hold a news conference at his own funeral."

"We still classifying this as a hate crime, Lieutenant?" Cappy sniffed.

"I don't know about you," I said, "but I hate this bastard pretty bad."

Chapter 47

JACOBI WAS RIGHT about one thing. The next morning, everything *had* changed. A feeding frenzy of every news organization in the country was massing on the outside steps of the Hall of Justice, setting up their camera crews, clawing for interviews. Anthony Tracchio was named acting chief. He had been the chief's administrative right hand, but had never come up through the ranks. On the Chimera case, I was now reporting to him. "No leaks," Tracchio brusquely warned. "No contact with the press. All interviews go through me."

A joint task force was set up to handle Mercer's homicide. It wasn't until I got upstairs that I found out precisely what "joint" meant.

When I got back to my office, two tan-suited FBI agents were waiting in the outer room. A polished, preppy black man named

Ruddy in an oxford shirt and yellow tie, who seemed to be in charge, and the typical hard-nosed field agent named Hull.

The first thing out of Ruddy's mouth was how nice it was to be working with the inspector who had solved the bride and groom case. The second thing was a request for the Chimera files. All of them. Tasha. Davidson. Whatever we had on Mercer.

Ten seconds after they left, I was on the phone to my new boss. "Guess I know what you meant by *joint,*" I said.

"Crimes against public officials are a federal offense, Lieutenant. There's not much I can do," said Tracchio.

"Mercer said this was a *city* crime, Chief. He said city personnel ought to see it through."

Tracchio sent my heart into a tailspin. "I'm sorry. Not anymore."

Chapter 48

LATER THAT AFTERNOON, I drove out to Ingleside Heights to talk with Chief Mercer's wife. I felt I needed to do it myself. A line of cars was already stretched along the street around the chief's home. A relative answered the door and told me Mrs. Mercer was upstairs with family.

I stood around, checking out faces I recognized gathered in the living room. After a few minutes, Eunice Mercer came down the stairs. She was accompanied by a pleasant-looking middle-aged woman who turned out to be her sister. She recognized me and walked my way.

"I'm so sorry. I can't believe it," I said, squeezing her hand first, then hugging her.

"I know," she whispered. "I know you've just gone through this yourself."

"I promise you, I know how tough this is.

But I need to ask you a few questions," I finally said to her.

She nodded, and her sister floated back among the guests. Eunice Mercer took me into a private den.

I asked her many of the same questions I had put forth to the relatives of other victims. Had anyone recently threatened her husband? Calls to the house? Anyone suspicious lately watching the house?

She shook her head no. "Earl said this was the only place where he actually felt like he lived in the city, not just ran the police force."

I changed tack. "You ever come across the name Art Davidson before this week?"

Eunice Mercer's face went blank. "You think Earl was killed by the same man who did these other horrible things?"

I took her hand. "I think these murders were all committed by the same man."

She massaged her brow. "Lindsay, *nothing* makes sense to me right now. Earl's murder. That book."

"Book . . . ?" I asked.

"Yes. Earl always read car magazines. He had this dream, when he retired . . . this old GTO he kept in a cousin's garage. He always said he was gonna tear it down and build it up from scratch. But that book he had stuffed in his jacket . . ."

"What book?" I was squinting at her hard.

"A young doctor at the hospital returned it to me, along with his wallet and keys. I never knew he had such an interest in that sort of thing. Those old myths . . ."

Suddenly my pulse was racing. "Can you show me what you're talking about?"

"Of course," Eunice Mercer said. "It's over here." She left the den and in a minute came back. She handed me a paperback copy of a book every schoolkid reads. *Mythology*, by Edith Hamilton.

It was an old dog-eared copy, looked as if it had been leafed through a thousand times. I rifled through the pages and spotted nothing.

I ran down the table of contents. Then I saw it. Halfway down, page 141. It was under-lined. *Bellerophon Kills the Chimera.*

Bellerophon . . . Billy Reffon.

My heart clenched. It was the name he'd used on the 911 call about Art Davidson. He had called himself Billy Reffon.

I flipped to page 141. It was there. With an

illustration. The lion rearing. The goat's body. The serpent's tail.

Chimera.

The bastard was telling us he had killed Chief Mercer.

A surge rippled through me. There was something else on the page. A sharp, edgy script, a few words, scrawled above the illustration in ink:

More to come . . . justice will be served.

Chapter 49

LEAVING MERCER'S HOME, I drove around in a sweat, terror filled at what I knew to be the truth.

All my instincts had been right. This was no random, racist murder spree. This was a cold, calculating killer. He was taunting us, the same way he had with the white van. With that cocky tape. Billy Reffon.

Finally, I said, *Fuck it.* I called the girls. I couldn't hold back any longer. They were three of the sharpest law-enforcement minds in the city. And this bastard had told me there were going to be more killings. We set up a meeting at Susie's.

"I need your help," I said, panning their faces in our usual booth at the restaurant.

"That's why we're here," Claire said. "You call, we come running."

"Finally." Cindy chuckled. "She admits she's nothing without us."

"This Kiss" by Faith Hill was drowning out a basketball game on the TV, but in the corner booth, the four of us were huddled in our own purposeful world. God, it was good to have everybody back together again.

"Everything's screwed up with Mercer gone. The FBI's come in. I don't even know who's in control. All I know is that the longer we wait, the more people are going to be killed."

"This time there have to be some rules," Jill said, tugging on a Buckler nonalcoholic beer. "This isn't a game. That last case, I think I broke every rule I took an oath to uphold. Withholding evidence, using the D.A.'s office for personal use. If anything had gotten out, I'd be doing my cases from the tenth floor."

We laughed. The tenth floor of the Hall was where the holding cells were located.

"Okay," I agreed. It was the same for me. "Anything we find we take to the task force."

"Let's not go overboard," said Cindy with a mischievous laugh. "We're here to help you, not to make the careers of some uptight, bureaucratic men."

"The Margarita Posse lives," joked Jill. "Jesus, I'm glad we're back."

"Don't you *ever* doubt it," said Claire.

I looked around at the girls. The Women's Murder Club. Part of me bristled with apprehension. Four people were dead, including the highest-ranking police officer in the city. The killer had proved he could strike anywhere he wanted to.

"Each murder has become more high profile, and daring," I said, filling them in on the latest, including the book stuffed in Mercer's jacket. "He no longer needs the subterfuge of the racial MO. It's racial, all right. I just don't know why."

Claire took us through the chief's autopsy, which she had finished up that afternoon. He was hit three times at close range with a .38 gun. "My impression is that the three shots were spaced at measured intervals. I could tell by the pattern that the wounds bled out. The last one was to the head. Mercer was already on the ground. It makes me think they may have confronted each other. That he was trying to kill him slowly. Or that they were even talking. I guess where I'm headed is that it's likely Mercer knew his killer."

"You checked into the possibility that all these officers were somehow connected?" Jill cut in. "Of course you have. You're Lindsay Boxer."

"Of course I have. There's no record any of them had even met. Their careers don't seem to have crossed. Tasha Catchings's uncle is younger than the others by twenty years. We can't find anything that puts them together."

"Somebody hates cops. Well, actually, a lot of people do," Cindy said.

"I just can't find the link. This started out in the guise of a hate crime. The killer wanted us to view the murders in a certain way. He wanted us to find his clues. And he wanted us to find the chimera. His fucked-up symbol."

"But if this is a personal vendetta," Jill said, "it doesn't make sense that it would lead back to some organized group."

"Unless he was setting someone up," I said.

"Or unless," Cindy said, chewing her lip, "the chimera doesn't lead back to a hate group at all. Maybe this book is his way of telling us it's something else."

I stared at her. We all did. "We're waiting, Einstein."

She blinked remotely, then shook her head. "I was just thinking out loud."

Jill said she would dig into any grievance cases against a black officer who had wronged or injured a white. Any act of vengeance that might explain the killer's mind-set. Cindy would do the same at the *Chronicle*.

It had been a long day, and I was exhausted. I had a task force meeting at seven-thirty the next morning. I looked each of my friends in the eye. "Thank you, thank you."

"We're gonna solve this sucker with you," Jill said. "We're going to get Chimera."

"We've got to," Claire said. "We need you to keep picking up the bar bill."

For a few more minutes, we chatted about what we all had going on the next day, when we could get together again. We were starting to cook now. Jill and Claire had their cars parked in the lot. I asked Cindy, who lived in the Castro section, near me, if she needed a ride.

"Actually," she said with a smile, "I have a date."

"Good for you. Who is your next victim?" Claire exclaimed. "When do we get to check him out?"

"If you supposedly mature, talented women want to ogle like a bunch of schoolkids, I guess *now*. He's picking me up."

"I'm always up for a good ogle," Claire said.

I snorted out a laugh. "You could be meeting Mel Gibson *and* Russell Crowe, and it wouldn't rock my boat tonight."

As we pushed through the front door, Cindy tugged my arm. "Hold on to your oars, honey."

We all saw him at once. We all ogled, and my boat was rocked.

Waiting outside, looking altogether sexy and handsome, dressed entirely in black, was Aaron Winslow.

Chapter 50

I COULDN'T BELIEVE IT. I stood there gawking. I looked at Cindy, then back at Winslow, my surprise slowly giving way to a blushing smile.

"Lieutenant." Winslow nodded, cutting through the awkward murk. "When Cindy said she was meeting friends, I wasn't expecting to find you here."

"Yeah, me too," I babbled back.

"We're headed to the Blue Door," Cindy said to the crowd, going through the introductions. "Pinetop Perkins is in town."

"Terrific." Claire nodded.

"Beatific," snipped Jill.

"Anybody care to join?" Aaron Winslow asked. "If you haven't heard it, there's nothing like Memphis blues."

"I'm in the office at six tomorrow," said Claire. "You two go along."

I leaned over to Cindy and whispered, "You know, when we were talking foxholes the other day, I was only joking."

"I know you were," Cindy said, looping her arm around mine. "But I wasn't."

Claire, Jill, and I stood with our jaws open and watched the two of them disappear around the corner. Actually, they looked kind of cute together, and it was only a date to hear some music.

"Okay," Jill said, "tell me I wasn't dreaming."

"You weren't dreaming, girl," Claire replied. "I just hope that Cindy realizes what she's getting herself into."

"Uh-uh." I shook my head. "I hope he does."

Getting into my car, I entertained myself with the notion of Cindy and Aaron Winslow. It almost pushed out of my head the reason we had gotten together in the first place.

I turned my Explorer onto Brannan and waved good-bye to Claire, who was heading over to 280. As I made the turn, I caught a glimpse of a white Toyota pulling out down the block behind me.

My mind was wrapped up with what I had just done, getting the girls involved in this horrible case. I had just countermanded a direct order from the mayor *and* my commanding officer. This time, there was no one backing me up. No Roth, or Mercer.

A Mazda with two teenage girls in it pulled up behind me. We had stopped at a light on Seventh. The driver was talking a mile a minute on her cell phone, while her companion obliviously sung along to the stereo.

As we started up, I kept my eye on them for a block, until they veered onto Ninth. A blue minivan took the Mazda's place.

I got onto Potrero under the underpass to 101, heading south. The blue van turned.

To my surprise, I saw that same white Toyota lurking thirty yards behind.

I continued on. A silver BMW sped up in the left lane and pulled up behind me. Behind it, a city bus. It looked as if the mystery car was gone.

Who could blame you for getting a little jumpy, with what's going on? I said to myself. My picture had been in the paper and on the TV news.

I made my usual right on Connecticut and started the climb up the Potrero hill. I was hoping Mrs. Taylor next door had come by to walk Martha. And I was thinking of stopping in the market on Twentieth for some Edy's vanilla twirl.

Two blocks up, I glanced a last time in my rearview mirror. The white Toyota crept into view.

Either the sonofabitch lived on the same block I did, or the bastard was following me.

It had to be Chimera.

Chapter 51

MY HEART WAS POUNDING; the hairs on the back of my neck stood erect. I squinted in the rearview mirror and ran the plate numbers over in my head: California . . . PCV 182. I couldn't make out the person driving. *This was insane. . . .* But I sure wasn't imagining it.

I pulled into an open parking spot in front of my apartment. I waited in the car until I saw the hood of the Toyota rise over the lip of Twentieth Street, then pause at the base of the last hill. My blood ran cold.

I had let the bastard trail me right to my house.

I reached in the glove compartment and took out my Glock. I checked the clip. *Stay calm. You're gonna take this asshole down. You're going to nail Chimera right now.*

I hunched in my car, scrolling through my options. I could call it in. A patrol car could be here in a matter of minutes. But I had to find out who it was. The appearance of a police car would scare him away.

My heart beat madly. I palmed my gun and opened the car door. I slipped out into the night. *Now what?*

On the first floor of my house, there was a back door that led to an alley underneath my terrace. From there, I could wrap around the block near the park at the top of the hill. If the bastard stayed outside, I could double back and maybe surprise him.

I hesitated in the doorway, just long enough to see the Toyota creeping slowly up the street. My hands fumbled in my bag for the key. I jammed it in the lock.

I was inside. Out a small window, I watched the Toyota. I strained to catch a glimpse of the driver, but his interior lights were off.

I undid the bolt to the back door and crept out into the alley behind my building.

I ran behind the cover of the houses to the cul de sac at the top of the hill. From there, I reversed back, hugging the shadows of the buildings along the opposite side of the street.

Behind him . . .

The Toyota had parked across from my building, its lights off.

The driver in the front seat was smoking a cigarette.

I crouched behind a parked Honda Accord, clasping my gun. *This is what it's all about, Lindsay. . . .*

Could I take Chimera in the car? What if the doors were locked?

Suddenly, I saw the car door open, the interior light flash on. The bastard's back was turned to me as he climbed out of his car.

He was wearing a dark weatherproof jacket, a floppy cap pulled over his eyes. He was glancing up at my house. *My apartment.*

Then he headed across the street. No fears. *Take him down. Now.* The bastard had come for me. He'd threatened me in Mercer's book. I moved out from the cover of the line of parked cars.

My heart was racing so fast and loud, I was afraid he would suddenly spin around. *Now. Do it! You've got him!*

I stepped up, the Glock firm in one hand. I wrapped the other around his neck, pulled, kicked his legs out from under him.

He toppled to the ground, landing hard on his front. I pinned him there. I pressed the barrel of my gun to the back of his head.

"Police, asshole! Hands out wide."

A painful groan came from him. He spread his arms. *Was it Chimera?*

"You wanted me, you bastard, well, you got me. Now, turn around."

I relaxed my knee just enough for him to maneuver around. As he did, my heart almost stopped.

I was staring into the face of my father.

Chapter 52

MARTY BOXER rolled onto his back and groaned, the air squeezed out of his lungs. He still had a glimmer of the rugged handsomeness I remembered, but it was different — older, leaner, worn. His hair had thinned and the once-lively blue eyes seemed washed out.

I hadn't seen him in ten years. I hadn't spoken to him in twenty-two years.

"What are you doing here?" I wanted to know.

"Right now," he gasped, rolling onto his side, "having the shit beat out of me by my daughter."

I felt a hard slab jutting out of his jacket pocket. I pulled out an old department-issued Smith & Wesson .40 caliber. "What the hell is this? How you say hello?"

"It's a dangerous world out there." He groaned again.

I rolled off him. The sight of him was an affront, a sudden illumination of memories I'd shut off years ago. I didn't offer to help him up. "What were you doing? Following me?"

Slowly, he edged himself into a sitting position. "I'm gonna pretend you didn't know it was your old man dropping in, Buttercup."

"*Please* don't call me that," I shot back at him.

Buttercup was his pet name for me when I was about seven and he was still at home. My sister, Cat, was Horsefly; I was Buttercup. Hearing that name brought a surge of bitter memories. "You think you can drop in here after all these years, scare the shit out of me, and get away with it by calling me Buttercup? I'm not your little girl. I'm a homicide lieutenant."

"I know that. And you deliver a hell of a takedown, baby."

"Consider yourself lucky," I said, clicking my Glock onto safety.

"Who the hell were you expecting, anyway?" he said as he massaged his ribs. "The Rock?"

"That doesn't matter. What does matter is just what you're doing here."

He sniffed guiltily. "I'm definitely starting to pick up, Buttercup, that you might not be entirely thrilled to see me?"

"I don't know that I am. Are you sick?"

His blue eyes sparkled. "Can't a guy check up on his firstborn without his motives being called into account?"

I studied the lines on his face. "I haven't seen you in ten years, and you act like it's been a week. You want an update? I was married, now I'm divorced. I got into Homicide. Now I'm lieutenant. I know that's a bit sketchy, but it brings you up to date, Dad."

"You think so much time has passed that I can't look at you as a father?"

"I don't know how you look at me," I said.

My father's eyes suddenly warmed, and he smiled. "God, you do look beautiful . . . *Lindsay.*"

His expression was that same twinkling, guiltless mug I had seen a thousand times as a kid. I shook my head in frustration. "Marty, just answer my question."

"Look." He swallowed. "I know sneaking up on you didn't win me any style points, but do you think I could at least talk my way into a cup of coffee?"

I stared incredulously at the man who had left our family when I was thirteen. Who had stayed away all the time my mother was sick. Whom I had thought of as a coward or a cad or even worse for most of my adult life. I hadn't seen my father since he'd sat in the back row on the day I was sworn in as a cop. I didn't know if I wanted to slug him or take him in my arms and give him a hug.

"Just *one* . . . ," I said, holding out a hand and hoisting him up. I brushed some loose gravel from his lapel. "You talked yourself into one cup of coffee, *Buttercup*."

Chapter 53

I MADE A POT OF COFFEE for my father and a cup of Red Zinger for me. I gave him a quick tour, introducing him to Martha, who almost against my silent instructions took a liking to dear old Dad.

We sat on my white canvas couch, Martha curled up at my father's feet. I gave him a damp cloth, and he dabbed at a scratch on his cheek.

"Sorry about the bruise," I said, cradling the hot mug on my knees. *Kind of sorry.*

"I've earned worse." He shrugged with a smile.

"Yeah, you have."

We sat facing each other. Neither of us knew quite where to begin. "So, I guess this is where you bring me up to date on what you've been up to for the last twenty-two years?"

He swallowed and put down his mug. "Sure. I can do that." He took me through his life, which seemed more like a sputtering spiral of bad luck. He had been an assistant chief, which I guess I knew, down in Redondo Beach. Then he left to go into private security. Celebrities. Kevin Costner. Whoopi Goldberg. "Even went to the Oscars." He chuckled. He'd gotten married again, this time for only two years. "Found out I was underqualified for the job," he quipped with a self-effacing wave. Now he was back in security, no celebrities, doing odd jobs.

"Still gambling?" I asked.

"Only mind bets. In my head," he replied. "Had to give it up when I ran out of funds."

"Still root for the Giants?" When I was a kid, he used to take me after his shift to this bar called the Alibi on Sunset. He'd prop me up on the counter where he and his buddies would watch the afternoon games from Candlestick. I loved being with him back then.

He shook his head. "Nah, gave them up when they traded away Will Clark. I'm a Dodger fan now. I would like to go to the new park, though." Then he looked at me for a long time.

It was my turn now. How to relate the past twenty-two years of my life to my father?

I took him through as much as I could handle, leaving out anything related to Mom. I told him about my ex, Tom, how it hadn't worked out. ("Chip off the old block." He snickered. "Yeah, but at least I stayed," I replied.) How I pushed for Homicide and finally got it.

He nodded glumly. "I read about that big case you worked on. Even down south, it was all over the news."

"A real résumé launcher." I told him how, a month after, I'd been offered the job as lieutenant.

My father leaned forward and placed a hand on my knee. "I wanted to see you, Lindsay. A hundred times . . . I don't know why I didn't. I'm proud of you. Homicide's top of the line. When I look at you . . . you're so . . . strong, in control. So beautiful. I only wish I could take a little of the credit."

"You can. You taught me I had no one to rely on but myself."

I got up, refilled his cup, and sat down again facing him. "Look, I'm sorry things haven't worked out for you. I really am. But it's been twenty-two years. Why are you here?"

"I called Cat, to see if you'd want to hear from me. She told me you'd been sick."

I didn't need to relive that. It was hard enough, just looking at him. "I was sick." I nodded. "I'm better now. Hopefully, I'll stay that way."

My heart was tight against my chest. This was starting to get uncomfortable. "So, how long have you been following me?"

"Since yesterday. I sat across from the Hall in my car for three hours, trying to figure out the way to approach you. I didn't know if you'd want to see me."

"I don't know if I do, Daddy." I tried to find the right words, and I felt the edge of tears welling in my eyes. "You were never there. You ran out on us. I can't just change the way I've felt for all these years."

"I don't expect you to, Lindsay," he said. "I'm becoming an old man. An old man who knows he's made a million mistakes. All I can do now is try and reverse some of them."

I looked at him, half shaking my head in disbelief, half smiling, and dabbing at my eyes.

"Things are crazy here now. You heard about Mercer?"

"Of course." My father exhaled. I waited for him to say something, but he simply shrugged. "I saw you on the news. You *are* stunning. Do you know that, Lindsay?"

"Dad, please. Don't." This case needed everything I had right now. It was madness. Here I was facing my father again. "I don't know if I can handle this now."

"I don't know either," he said, tentatively reaching out for my hand. "What about we try?"

Chapter 54

NINE THE NEXT MORNING, Morris Ruddy, the FBI senior agent, scribbled a point on a yellow legal pad. "Okay, Lieutenant, when did you first determine the chimera symbol pointed toward the white supremacist movement?"

My head was still whirring from the events of the night before. The last place I wanted to be was cooped up in a task force meeting, talking to the Feebies.

"Your office clued us in," I replied, "in Quantico."

It was a bit of a lie, of course. Stu Kirkwood had only confirmed what I had already learned from Cindy.

"Subsequently, since you had that knowledge," the FBI man bored in, "how many of these groups have you checked out?"

I gave him a frustrated look that read, *We might actually start making some progress if we could get out of this goddamn room.*

"You read the files I gave you. We looked into two or three."

"You looked into *one*." He raised an eyebrow.

"Look," I explained, "we don't have a history of these groups operating in this area. The method used in these killings seemed consistent with other cases I had worked. I made a determination that we were dealing with a serial killer. I'll admit, it's a gut call."

"From these four distinct acts," Ruddy said, "you narrowed it down that this was the act of a single UNSUB, right?"

"Yeah. From *that* and seven years working Homicide." I didn't like his tone.

"Look, Agent Ruddy, this isn't a hearing," Sam Ryan, my chief of detectives, finally said.

"I'm merely trying to determine how much of an effort we still have to coordinate in this area," the FBI man replied.

"Look," I insisted, "these chimera clues weren't exactly popping out at us in press releases. The white van was sighted by a six-year-old kid. The second was on a wall of graffiti at the crime scene. Our M.E. suggested that the Catchings shooting might not have been a random bullet."

"But even now," Ruddy said, "after your own chief of police has been murdered, you still believe these killings aren't politically motivated?"

"The killings might be politically motivated. I don't know the killer's total agenda. But it's one guy and he's a nutcase. Where the hell is this going?"

"Where it's *going* is murder number *three*," the other agent, Hull, cut in. "The Davidson shooting." He hoisted his solid frame out of his seat and stepped over to a flip chart on which each separate murder and the pertinent details were listed in neat columns.

"Murders one, two, and four," he explained, "all had ties to this Chimera. Davidson's murder doesn't tie in at all. We want to know what makes you so sure we're dealing with the same guy."

"You didn't see the shot," I said.

"According to what I have" — Hull leafed through his notes — "Davidson was killed with a bullet from a totally different weapon."

"I didn't say ballistics, Hull, I said *the shot.*

223

It was precision, marksman caliber. Just like the one that killed Tasha Catchings."

"I guess my point," Hull continued, "is that we have *no tangible evidence* linking the Davidson murder with the other three. If we stick to simply the facts, not Inspector Boxer's hunch, there's nothing to suggest we're not dealing with a *politically* motivated series of events. Nothing."

At that moment, there was a knock at the conference room door, and Charlie Clapper stuck his head in. Sort of like a shy groundhog peeking out of his burrow.

Clapper nodded toward the FBI guys, then winked at me. "I thought you'd be able to use this."

He put on the table a black-and-white rendering of a large sneaker tread.

"You remember that shoe print we pulled off of the tar at the shooter's position of Art Davidson's killing?"

"Of course," I said.

He placed a second rendering beside the first. "This is one we were able to take from a patch of wet soil at the Mercer scene."

The imprints were identical.

A hush filled the room. I looked at Agent Ruddy first, then Agent Hull.

"Course, they're just a standard pair of Reebok cross trainers," Charlie explained.

From a pocket in his white lab coat, he removed a slide. On it were tiny grains of powder. "We picked this up at the chief's crime scene."

I leaned over and stared at traces of the same white chalk.

"One killer," I said. "One shooter."

Chapter 55

I CALLED THE GIRLS TOGETHER for a quick lunch. I couldn't wait to see them.

We met at Yerba Buena Gardens, and sat in the courtyard outside the new IMAX, watching the kids play in the fountains, munching on take-out salads and wraps. I went through everything, from the moment I left them at Susie's, to the suspicion someone was following me, to taking down my father outside my apartment.

"My God," uttered Claire. "The prodigal father."

For a moment, it was as if a dome of silence had shut us off from the rest of the world. Everybody fixed on me with incredulous faces.

"When was the last time you'd seen him?" Jill asked.

"He was at my graduation from the academy. I didn't invite him, but he knew somehow."

"He followed you?" Jill gasped. "From our meeting? Like some kind of creepy perp? *Yick,*" she said, cringing.

"Typical Marty Boxer." I exhaled. "That's my dad."

Claire put her hand on my arm. "So, what did he want?"

"I'm still not sure. It's like he wanted to make amends. He said my sister Cat told him I was sick. He followed the bride and groom case. He said he wanted to tell me how proud he was of me."

"That was months ago." Jill snorted, taking a bite of a chicken-and-avocado wrap. "He sure took his time."

"That's what I said." I nodded.

Cindy shook her head. "He just decided *after twenty years* to show up at your door?"

"I think it's a good thing, Lindsay," injected Claire. "You know me — positive."

"A *good thing* that after twenty years he marches back in with a guilty conscience."

"No, a good thing because he needs you, Lindsay. He's alone, right?"

"He told me he got married again for two years, but he's divorced. Imagine, Claire, finding out years after the fact that your father got married again."

"That's not the point, Lindsay," Claire replied. "He's reaching out. You shouldn't be too proud to accept it."

"How *do* you feel?" inquired Jill.

I wiped my mouth, took a sip of iced tea and then a long breath. "The truth? I don't even know. He's like some ghost from the past who brings back a lot of bad memories. Everything he's touched has only hurt people."

"He's your father, honey," Claire said. "You've carried this hurt around since I've known you. You should let him in, Lindsay. You could have something you never had before."

"He could also kick her in the shins again," said Jill.

"Gee." Cindy looked over at Jill. "The prospect of motherhood hasn't exactly made you all soft and gooey, has it?"

"One date with the reverend," Jill chuffed

back, "and suddenly you're the conscience of the group? I'm impressed."

We looked at Cindy, all of us suppressing smiles.

"That's true." Claire nodded. "You don't think you're going to get off the hook, do you?"

Cindy began to blush. Never since I'd known her had I seen Cindy Thomas blush.

"You guys do make quite the couple." I sighed.

"I like him," Cindy blurted. "We talked for hours. At a bar. Then he took me home. The end."

"Sure." Jill grinned. "He's cute, he's got a steady job, and if you're ever tragically killed, you don't have to worry about who will preside over your service."

"I hadn't thought of that one." Cindy finally smiled. "Look, it was one date. I'm doing a piece on him and the neighborhood. I'm sure he won't ask me out again."

"But will you ask him out again?" said Jill.

"We're friends. No, we're friendly. It was a great couple of hours. I guarantee, all of you would have enjoyed yourselves. It's *research*," Cindy said, and she folded her arms.

We all smiled. But Cindy was right — none of us would have turned down a couple of hours with Aaron Winslow. I still got chills when I remembered his talk at Tasha Catchings's funeral.

As we crumpled our trash, I turned to Jill. "So, how're you feeling? You okay?"

She smiled. "Pretty good, actually." Then she linked her hands around her barely swollen belly and puffed out her cheeks as if to say, *Fat* . . . "I've just got this last case to finish up on. Then, who knows, I might even take some time off."

"I'll believe that when I see it." Cindy chortled. Claire and I mooned our eyes in support.

"Well, you just might be surprised," Jill said.

"So what're you gonna do?" Claire turned to me as we got up to leave.

"Keep trying to link the victims. They'll connect."

She kept her eyes on me. "I meant about your dad."

"I don't know. It's a bad time, Claire. Now Marty comes barging in. If he wants a dispensation, he can wait in line."

Claire stood up. She shot me one of her wise smirks.

"You obviously have a suggestion," I said.

"Naturally. Why not do what you normally do in situations of doubt and stress?"

"And that is . . . ?"

"Cook the man a meal."

Chapter 56

THAT AFTERNOON, Cindy hunched in front of her computer at the *Chronicle,* sipping a Stewart's Orange n' Cream, as she scrolled down another futile query.

Somewhere, in the deepest bin of her memory, there was *something* she had filed away, a nagging recollection she couldn't place. *Chimera* . . . the word used in another context, some other form that would help the case.

She'd gone through CAL, the *Chronicle*'s on-line archives, and come back with zilch. She had browsed through the usual search engines: Yahoo, Jeeves, Google. Her antennae were buzzing on high mode. She felt, as did Lindsay, that this fantastical monster led somewhere other than hate groups. It led to one very twisted and clever individual.

C'mon. She exhaled, jabbing the enter key

in frustration. *I know you're in here some-where.*

The day was nearly gone, and she'd come up with nothing. Not even a lead for tomorrow morning's edition. Her editor would be pissed. *We have readers,* he would grumble. *Readers want continuity.* She'd have to promise him something. *But what?* The investigation was stalled.

When she found it, she was in Google, wearily eyeing down the eighth page of responses. It hit her like a slap.

Chimera . . . Hellhole, an exposé of prison life in Pelican Bay, by Antoine James. Posthumous publication of prison hard-ships, cruelties, life of crime.

Pelican Bay . . . Pelican Bay was where they threw the worst of the worst trouble-makers in the California prison system. Violent offenders who couldn't be controlled anywhere else.

She remembered now that she had read about Pelican Bay in the *Chronicle,* maybe two years before. That was where she'd heard of Chimera. It was how it fit. *That* was what had been needling her.

She spun her chair over to the CAL terminal

on a nearby shelf. She pushed her glasses up on her forehead and typed in the query. *Antoine James.*

Five seconds later, a response came up. One article, August 10, 1998. Two years before. Written by Deb Meyer, a Sunday section feature writer. Headlined: "POSTHUMOUS JOURNAL DETAILS NIGHTMARE WORLD OF VIOLENCE BEHIND BARS."

She clicked on the display bar, and in another few seconds a facsimile of the article flashed on the screen. It was a Lifestyle article in a Sunday Metro section. Antoine James, while serving a ten-to-fifteen sentence at Pelican Bay for armed robbery, had been stabbed and killed in a prison squabble. He had kept a journal detailing the unsettling story of life on the inside, alleging a routine of forced snitching, racial attacks, beatings by guards, and perpetual gang violence.

She printed the article, closed out of CAL, and spun her chair back across to her desk. She leaned back in her chair and rested her feet on a stack of books. She scanned the page.

"From the moment they process you through the doors, life in Pelican Bay is a constant war of guard intimidation and gang violence," James had written in a black composition book. "The gangs provide your status, your identity, your protection, too. Everyone pledges out, and whatever group you belong to controls who you are and what's expected of you."

Cindy's eyes raced further down. The prison was a viper's nest of gangs and retaliation. The blacks had the Bloods and the Daggers, as well as the Muslims. The Latinos had the Nortenos in their red headbands and the Serranos in their blue, and the Mexican Mafia, Los Eme. Among the whites, there were the Guineas and the Bikers, and some white-trash shitbags called the Stinky Toilet People. And the supremacist Aryans.

"Some of the groups were ultra-secret," James wrote. "Once you were in, nobody touched you.

"One of these white groups was particularly nasty. All 'max' guys, serving violent felony time. They'd cut a brother open just to bet on what he had to eat."

Adrenaline shot through Cindy as she stopped on the next sentence.

James had a name for the group — *Chimera*.

235

Chapter 57

I WAS JUST FINISHING UP for the day —
nothing further on the four victims and the
white chalk still a mystery, when I got a call
from Cindy.

"The Hall still under martial law?" she
quipped, referring to the mayor's moratorium
on the press.

"Trust me, it's no picnic on the inside
either."

"Why don't you meet me? I've got something."

"Sure. Where?"

"Look out your window. I'm right outside."

I peered out and saw Cindy, leaning on a
car parked outside the Hall. It was almost
seven. I cleared my desk, called a quick good-
night to Lorraine and Chin, and ducked out
the rear entrance. I ran across the street and

went up to Cindy. She was in a short skirt and embroidered jean jacket, with a faded khaki knapsack slung over her shoulder.

"Choir practice?" I winked.

"You should talk. Next time I see you in SWAT gear, I'll assume you have a date with your dad."

"Speaking of Marty, I called him. I asked him over tomorrow night. So, Deep Throat, what's so important that we're meeting out here?"

"Good news, bad news," Cindy said. She pulled off her knapsack and came up with an 8 × 11 envelope. "I think I found it, Lindsay."

She handed me the envelope, and I opened it: a *Chronicle* article dated two years ago about a prison diary, *Hellhole,* by someone named Antoine James. A few passages were highlighted in yellow. I began to read.

"Aryan . . . worse than Aryan. All max guys. White, bad, and hating. We didn't know who they hated worse, us, the 'swarms' they had to share their meals with, or the cops and guards who had put them there.

"These bastards had a name for them-selves. They called themselves Chimera. . . ."

My eyes fixed on the word.

237

"They're animals, Lindsay. The worst troublemakers in the penal system. They're even committed to carrying out each other's hits on the outside.

"That's the good news," she said. "The bad news is, it's Pelican Bay."

Chapter 58

IN THE ANATOMY of the California state prison system, Pelican Bay was *the place where the sun don't shine*.

The following day, I took Jacobi and "req'd" a police helicopter for the hour's flight up the coast to Crescent City, near the Oregon border. I had been to Pelican Bay twice before, to meet with a snitch on a murder case and attend a parole hearing for someone I had put away. Each time, as I flew over the dense redwood forest surrounding the facility, it left a hole in the pit of my stomach.

If you were a law-enforcement agent — especially a woman — this was the kind of place you didn't want to go. There's a sign, as they process you through the front gate, warning that if you're taken hostage you're on your own. *No negotiations.*

I had arranged to meet with the assistant warden, Roland Estes, in the main administrative building. He kept us waiting for a few minutes. When he showed up, Estes was tall and serious, with a hard face and tight blue eyes. He had that clenched-fist unconfidingness that comes from years of living under the highest discipline.

"I apologize for being late," he said, taking a seat behind his large oak desk. "We had a disturbance down in O block. One of our resident Nortenos stabbed a rival in the neck."

"How'd he get the knife?" Jacobi asked.

"No knives." Estes smiled thinly. "He used the filed-down edge of a gardening hoe."

I wouldn't have had Estes's job for a heartbeat, but I also didn't like the reputation this place had for beatings, intimidation, and the motto "Snitch, Parole, or Die."

"So, you said this was related to Chief Mercer's murder, Lieutenant?" The warden leaned forward.

I nodded, removing a case file from my bag. "To a possible string of murders. I'm interested in what you may know about a prison gang here."

Estes shrugged. "Most of these inmates have been in gangs from the time they were ten. You'll find that every territory or gang domain that exists in Oakland or East L.A. exists here."

"This particular gang is called Chimera," I said.

Estes registered no immediate surprise. "No starting with the small stuff, huh, Lieutenant? So what is it you want to know?"

"I want to know if these murders lead to these men in Chimera. I want to know if they're as bad as they're made out to be. And I want to know the names of any reputed members who are now on the outside."

"The answer to all of that is yes." Estes nodded flatly. "It's a sort of a trial by fire. Prisoners who can take the worst we can dish out. The ones who have been in the SHU's, isolation, for a substantial time. It earns them rank — and certain privileges."

"Privileges?"

"Freedom. In the way we define it here. From being debriefed. From snitching."

"I'd like a list of any paroled members of this gang."

The warden smiled. "Not many get paroled. Some get transferred to other facilities. I suspect there are Chimera offshoots at every max facility in the state. And it's not like we have a file of who's in and who's not. It's more like who gets to sit next to the Big Motherfucker at mess."

"But you know, don't you? You know who's in."

"*We* know." The warden nodded. He stood up as if our interview had come to an end. "It'll take some time. Some of this I need to consult on. But I'll see what I can do."

"While I'm here, I might as well meet with *him*."

"Who, Lieutenant?"

"The Big Motherfucker. The head of Chimera."

Estes looked at me. "Sorry, Lieutenant, no one gets to do that. No one gets into the Pool."

I looked Estes in the eyes. "You want me to come back with a state order to get it done? Listen, our chief of police is dead. Every politician in this state wants this guy caught. I've got backing all the way. You already know that. Bring the bastard up."

The warden's taut face relaxed. "Be my guest, Lieutenant. But he doesn't leave. You go to him."

Estes picked up his phone and dialed a number. After a pause, he muttered sharply, "Get Weiscz ready. He has a visitor. It's a woman."

Chapter 59

WE WENT THROUGH a long underground walkway, accompanied by Estes and a club-toting head guard named O'Koren.

When we came to a stairway marked SHU-C, the warden led us up, waving at a security screen, then through a heavy compression door that opened into the ultra-modern prison ward.

Along the way, he filled me in. "Like most of our inmates, Weiscz came in from another facility, Folsom. He was the leader of the Aryan Brotherhood there, until he strangled a black guard. He's been iso-ed here for eighteen months now. Until we start sending people to the death house in this state, there's nothing more we can do to him."

Jacobi leaned over and whispered, "You sure of what you're doing here, Lindsay?"

I *wasn't* sure. My heart was starting to gallop, and my palms had busted out in a nervous sweat. "That's why I brought you along."

"Yeah," Jacobi muttered.

Pelican Bay's isolation unit was unlike anything I had ever seen. Everything was painted a dull, sterile white. Burly khaki-uniformed guards, of both sexes but uniformly white, manned glassed-in command posts.

Monitors and security cameras were everywhere. *Everywhere.* The unit was configured like a pod with ten cells, the compression-sealed doors tightly shut.

Warden Estes stopped in front of a metal door with a large window. "Welcome to ground zero of the human race," he said.

A muscular, balding senior guard holding a face visor and some sort of Uzi-like taser gun came up. "Weiscz had to be extracted, Warden. I think he'll need a few moments to loosen up."

I looked up at Estes. *"Extracted?"*

Estes sniffed. "You would think after being holed up a couple of months, he'd be happy to get out. Just so you know what's coming next, Weiscz was uncooperative. We had to send a team in to pretty him up for you."

He nodded toward the window. "There's your man. . . ."

I stepped in front of the solid pressure-sealed door. Strapped to a metal chair, his feet bound in irons, his hands cuffed from behind, hunched a hulking, muscular shape. His hair was long and oily and straggly, and he wore a thin, unkempt goatee. He was dressed in an orange short-sleeved jumpsuit, open at the chest, revealing ornate tattoos covering his pumped-up arms and chest.

The warden said, "There'll be a guard in there with you and you'll be monitored at all times. *Stay away from him.* Don't get closer than five feet. If he as much as juts his chin in your direction, he'll be immobilized."

"The guy's bound and chained," I said.

"This sonofabitch eats chains," Estes said. "Believe it."

"Anything I can promise him?"

"Yeah." Estes smirked. "A Happy Meal. You ready . . . ?"

I winked at Jacobi, who widened his eyes in caution. My heart nearly stopped, like a skeet target exploded out of the sky.

"Bon voyage," Estes muttered. Then he signaled the control booth. I heard a *ka-shoosh* as the heavy compression door unlocked.

Chapter 60

I STEPPED INTO THE STARK WHITE CELL. It was completely empty except for a metal table and four chairs, all bolted to the floor, and two security cameras high up on the walls. In a corner stood a silent, tight-lipped guard holding a stun gun.

Weiscz barely acknowledged me. His legs were fastened and his hands tightly cuffed behind the chair. His eyes had a steely, inhuman quality to them.

"I'm Lieutenant Lindsay Boxer," I said, stopping about five feet from him.

Weiscz said nothing, only tilted his eyes toward me. Narrow, almost phosphorescent slits.

"I need to talk to you about some murders that have taken place. I can't promise you much. I'm hoping you'll hear me out. Maybe help."

"Blow me," he spat with a hoarse voice.

The guard took a step toward him, and Weiscz stiffened as if he'd taken a jolt from the taser. I put up my hand to hold him back.

"You may know something about them," I continued, a chill shooting down my spine. "I just want to know if they make sense to you. These killings . . ."

Weiscz looked at me curiously, probably trying to size up if there was something he could get from this. "Who's dead?"

"Four people. Two cops. One was my chief of police. A widow and an eleven-year-old girl. All black."

An amused smile settled over Weiscz's face. "In case you haven't noticed, lady, my alibi's airtight."

"I'm hoping you may know something about them, then."

"Why me?"

From my jacket pocket, I took out the same two chimera photos I had shown Estes and held them in front of his face. "The killer's been leaving these behind. I believe you know what it means."

Weiscz grinned broadly. "I don't know what

you came in here for, but you don't fucking know how that warms my heart."

"The killer's a Chimera, Weiscz. You cooperate, you could gain back some privileges. They can always move you out of this hole."

"Both of us know I'll never get out of this hole."

"There's always something, Weiscz. Everybody wants something."

"There is something," he finally said. "Come closer."

My body stiffened. "I can't. You know that."

"You got a mirror, don't you?"

I nodded. I had a makeup mirror in my purse.

"Shine it on me."

I looked at the guard. His head twitched a firm no.

For the first time, Wciscz looked in my eyes. "Shine it on me. I haven't seen myself in over a year. Even the shower fixtures are dulled here so you can't see a reflection. These bastards just want you to forget who the fuck you were. I want to see."

The guard stepped forward. "You know that's impossible, Weiscz."

"Fuck you, Labont." He glared viciously up at the cameras. "Fuck you, too, Estes." Then he turned back to me. "They didn't send you in here with much to bargain with, did they?"

"They said I could take you out for a Happy Meal," I said with a slight smile.

"Just you and me, huh?"

I glanced at the guard. "And *him.*"

Weiscz's goatee split into a smile. "These bastards, they know how to ruin everything."

I stood there nervously. I didn't laugh. I didn't want to show the slightest empathy for him.

But I sat myself at the table across from Weiscz. I fumbled in my bag, took out a compact. I expected any minute a loud voice was going to blare over the intercom, or the stone-faced guard was going to rush over and knock it away. To my amazement, no one interfered. I cracked the compact open, looked at Weiscz, then I turned it toward him.

I don't know what he looked like before, but he was a horrific sight now. He stared at himself, wide-eyed, the truth of his harsh confinement setting in. He fixed on the mirror as if it were the last thing he would see on earth.

Then he looked at me and grinned. "Not much to go on, for that blow-me thing, is there?"

I don't know why, but I gave him a begrudging smile.

Then he twisted his neck around to the cameras. "Fuck you, Estes," he roared. "See? I'm still there. You try to squeeze me out, but I'm still there. The reckoning is going on without me. Chimera, baby . . . Glory to the unstained hand who stills the rabble and swarm."

"Who would do this?" I pressed. "Tell me, Weiscz." He knew. I knew he knew. Someone he had shared a cell with. Someone he had traded histories with in a prison yard.

"Help me, Weiscz. Someone you know is killing these people. You've got nothing to gain anymore."

His eyes lit up with a sudden fury. "You think I give a shit about your dead niggers? Your dead cops? Soon the state will be gathering them up anyway. Putting them in pens. A twelve-year-old nigger whore, some monkeys dressed up as cops. I only wish it was my finger on the trigger. We both know, whatever I say to you, I'll never get as much as a second meal out of these bastards. The minute you leave, Labont's gonna stun me anyway. There's a better chance you'll suck my dick."

I shook my head, stood up, and motioned for the door.

"Maybe one of your own assholes has come to his senses," he yelled with a smirk. "Maybe that's what it was, an inside job."

A tremor of rage burned through me. Weiscz was an animal. There wasn't an ounce of humanity in him. All I wanted to do was slam the door in his face. "I did give something to you, even if it was for a moment," I said.

"And don't be so sure you didn't get something in return. You'll never catch him. He's Chimera. . . ." Weiscz jerked his head down to his chest, pointing at a tattoo high on his shoulder. All I could make out was the tail of a snake. "We can endure as much as you can dish, copper lady. Look at me. . . . They stuff me in this hellhole, they make me eat my own shit, but I can still win." Suddenly, he was loud and angry again, twisting at his restraints. "Victory comes in the end. God's grace is the white race. Long live Chimera. . . ."

I moved away from him, and Weiscz

twisted defiantly. "So what about that Happy Meal, bitch?"

As I got to the door, I heard a zap followed by a garbled grunt, and turned as the guard pumped a thousand watts into Weiscz's twitching chest.

Chapter 61

WE CAME BACK TO TOWN with a few names, courtesy of Estes. Recent parolees thought to be members of Chimera. Back at the Hall, Jacobi parceled out the list to Cappy and Chin.

"I'm gonna start calling a few PO's," he said to me. "You want to join?"

I shook my head. "I have to leave early, Warren."

"Whatsamatter, don't tell me you got a date?"

"*Yeah.*" I nodded. No doubt my face sort of lit into an incredulous smile. "I've got a date."

The downstairs buzzer rang about seven.

When I opened the door, my father was peeking out from behind a catcher's mask, his hands outstretched in a defensive pose. *"Friends . . . ?"* he asked, an apologetic smile sneaking through.

254

"Dinner . . ." I smiled begrudgingly. "That's the best I can do."

"That's a start," he said, stepping in. He had cleaned himself up. He was wearing a brown sport jacket, pressed pants, an open-collared white shirt. He handed me a bottle of red wine wrapped in paper.

"You didn't have to," I said, unfurling the wine, then gasping in surprise as I read the label. It was a first-growth Bordeaux, Chateau Latour, the year *1965.*

I looked at him; 1965 was the year I was born.

"I bought it a year after you were born. It was about the only thing I took with me when I left. I always figured we'd drink it on your graduation or something, maybe your wedding."

"You kept it all these years." I shook my head.

He shrugged. "Like I said, I bought it for you. Anyway, Lindsay, there's nothing I'd rather do than drink it here tonight."

Something warm rose inside me. "You're making it hard to continue to completely hate you."

"Don't hate me, Lindsay." He tossed me the

catcher's mask. "This doesn't fit. I don't ever want to have to use it again."

I took him into the living room, poured him a beer, and sat down. I had on a wine-colored Eileen Fisher sweater, my hair pulled up in a ponytail. His eyes seemed to twinkle at me.

"You look gorgeous, Buttercup," my father said.

When I scowled, he smiled. "I can't help it, you just do."

For a while we talked, Martha lying beside him as if he were an old friend. We talked about trivial things, things we knew. Who was left from his old cronies on the force. Cat, and her new daughter he hadn't seen. Whether Jerry Rice would call it quits. We skirted the subject of Mercer and the case.

And as if I were meeting someone for the first time, I found him different from what I imagined. Not garrulous and boastful and full of stories as I remembered, but humble and reserved. Almost contrite. And he still had his sense of humor.

"I've got something to show *you*," I said. I went into the hall closet and came back with the satin Giants baseball jacket he'd given me over twenty-five years before. It was embroidered with a number 24 and had the name Mays on the front chest.

My father's eyes flashed in surprise. "I'd forgotten about that. I got it from the equipment manager in nineteen sixty-eight." He held it in front of him and looked at it a long time, like an old relic that had made the past suddenly vivid. "You have any idea what that thing must be worth today?"

"I always called it my inheritance," I told him.

Chapter 62

I DID SALMON on the grill in a ginger-miso sauce, fried rice with peppers, leeks, and peas. I remembered that my father liked Chinese. We cracked the '65 Latour. It was a dream wine, silky and gemlike. We sat in the alcove overlooking the bay. My father said it was the best bottle of wine he'd ever tasted.

The conversation gradually drifted toward more personal things. He asked what kind of man I had been married to, and I admitted, unfortunately, someone like himself. He asked if I resented him, and I had to tell him the truth. "Yeah. A lot, Dad."

Gradually, we even talked about the case. I told him how tough it was to solve, how I held it against myself that I couldn't crack it. How I was sure it was a serial, but four murders into the case, I still had nothing.

We talked for three more hours, until after eleven, the wine bottle empty, Martha asleep at his feet. Every once in a while I had to remind myself that I was talking to my own father. That I was sitting across from him for the first time in my adult life. And slowly, I began to see. He was just a man who had made mistakes, and who had been punished for them. He was no longer someone I could blindly resent, or hate. He hadn't murdered anybody. He wasn't Chimera. By the standards I dealt with, his sins were forgivable.

Gradually, I could no longer hold back the question I'd been wanting to ask for so many years. "I have to know the answer to this. Why did you leave?"

He took a swallow of wine and leaned back against the couch. His blue eyes looked so sad. "There's nothing I could say that would make sense of it to you. Not now . . . You're a grown woman. You're on the force. You know how things get. Your mother and I . . . Let's just say we were never a good match, even for the old school. I had squandered most of what we had on the games. I had a lot of debts, borrowed money on the street. That's

259

not exactly kosher for a cop. I did a lot of things I wasn't very proud of . . . as a man and as a cop."

I noticed his hands were trembling. "You know how sometimes, someone commits a crime simply because the situation gets so bad that one by one, the options just close off and they're unable to do anything else? That's how it was for me. The debts, what was going on on the job . . . I didn't see any other choice. I just left. I know it's a little late to say this, but I've regretted it every day of my life."

"And when Mom got sick . . . ?"

"I was sorry when she got sick. But by then I had a new life, and no one made it seem like I was welcome to come back. I thought it would hurt her more than help."

"I know Mom always told me you were a pathological liar."

"That's the truth, Lindsay," my father said. I liked the way he admitted it. I liked my father, actually.

I had to get up, shift gears. I started taking the dishes into the kitchen. My chest was heaving. I felt like I might be going to cry. My father was back, and I was starting to realize how much I had missed him. In a crazy way, I still wanted to be his girl.

My father helped with the dishes. I rinsed them off, and he loaded them in the dishwasher. We barely said a word. My whole body was vibrating.

When the dishes were done, we just sort of turned and met each other's eyes. "So where're you staying?" I asked.

"With an ex-cop buddy of mine, Ron Fazio. He used to be a district sergeant out in Sunset. He's got me on his couch."

I washed out a pasta pot. "I have a couch," I said.

Chapter 63

ALL THE FOLLOWING DAY we pounded on the list of names Warden Estes and his people had given us. Two we crossed off immediately. A computer check indicated they had become re-associated with the California penal system, currently residing in other institutions.

Something Weiscz had said the day before had stuck in my head.

"I gave you something," I had said, as the convict raved about the white race.

"And I gave you something back," he had replied. The words hung in my mind. They had first hit me at two in the morning, and I rolled back to sleep. They had accompanied me on my morning drive. And they were still with me now.

I gave you something back. . . .

I slipped my feet out of my pumps and

stared out my window at the freeway ramp starting to back up with traffic. I tried to retrace my encounter with Weiscz.

He was an animal who never had a chance of seeing the light of day. Still, I felt there had almost been a moment with him, a bond. All he wanted in that hellhole was to see what he looked like. *I gave you something back.*

So what did he give me?

"You think I give a shit about your dead niggers?" he had seethed. *"Long live Chimera,"* he had hollered as they put him under. . . .

Then, slowly, my mind settled on it.

"Maybe one of your own assholes has come to his senses. Maybe that's what it was, an inside job."

I didn't know if I had gone off the deep end or what. Was I reaching for something that wasn't there? Was Weiscz actually telling me something he could never be held accountable for?

An inside job . . .

I dialed Estes at Pelican Bay. "Any of your inmates up there ever been an ex-cop?" I asked.

"A cop . . . ?" The warden paused.

"Yeah." I explained why I wanted to know.

"Excuse my French," Estes shot back, "but Weiscz was fucking with you. He was trying to get inside your head. The bastard hates cops."

"You didn't answer my question, Warden."

"*A cop . . . ?*" Estes grunted a derisive snort. "We had a bad narcotics inspector out of L.A., Bellacora. Shot three of his informants. But he was transferred out. To my knowledge, he's still in Fresno." I remembered reading about the Bellacora case. It was as dirty and low as law enforcement got.

"We had a customs inspector, Benes, who on the side was running a dope ring at San Diego Airport."

"Anyone else?"

"No, not in my six years."

"What about before that, Estes?"

He grunted impatiently. "How far back do you want me to go, Lieutenant?"

"How long has Weiscz been there?"

"Twelve years."

"Then that's how far."

It was clear the warden thought I was crazy. He hung up saying he would have to get back to me.

I put down the phone. This was wild — trusting Weiscz for anything. He hated cops. I was a cop. He probably hated women, too.

Suddenly, Karen, my secretary, burst in. She looked stunned. "Jill Bernhardt's assistant just called in. Ms. Bernhardt's collapsed."

"Collapsed . . . ?"

Karen nodded blankly. "She's bleeding. Upstairs. She needs you up there, *now*."

Chapter 64

I RACED DOWN THE HALL to the elevator and then to Jill's office.

As I charged in, she was on the couch, reclined.

An EMS team, which had fortunately been at the morgue, was already there. There were towels, *bloody* towels, stuffed under her dark blue skirt. Her face was averted, but she looked as gray and listless and afraid as I had ever seen her. In an instant, it was clear what had happened.

"Oh, Jill," I said, kneeling beside her. "Oh, sweetie. I'm here."

She smiled when she saw me, slightly wary and afraid. Her normally sharp blue eyes reflected the color of dismal skies. "I lost it, Lindsay," she said. "I should've quit work. I should've listened to them. *To you.* I thought

I wanted the baby more than anything, but maybe I didn't. I lost it."

"Oh, Jill." I grasped her hand. "It wasn't you. Don't say that. This was medical. There was a chance of this. You knew that going in. There was always this risk."

"It was *me*, Lindsay." Her eyes suddenly welled with tears. "I think I didn't want it badly enough."

A female EMS tech asked me to step away, and they hooked Jill up to an IV line and a monitor. My heart went out to her. She was usually so strong and independent. But I had seen a transformation in her; she had looked forward to this baby so much. How did she deserve this?

"Where's Steve, Jill?" I leaned down to her.

She sucked in a breath. "Denver. April reached him. He's on his way back."

Suddenly, Claire burst into the room. "I came as soon as I heard," she said. She glanced worriedly at me, then asked the med tech, "What do you have?"

She was told that Jill's vitals were good, but she'd lost a lot of blood. When Claire mentioned the baby, the technician shook her head.

"Oh, honey," Claire clasped Jill's hand, kneeling down. "How're you feeling?"

Tears were running down Jill's face. "Oh, Claire, I lost it. I lost my baby."

Claire stroked a curl of damp hair off Jill's forehead. "You're going to be all right. Don't worry. We're going to take good care of you."

"We have to move her now," the EMS tech said. "Her doctor's been called. She's waiting for us at Cal Pacific."

"We're going with you," I said. "We're gonna be with you all the way."

Jill forced a smile, then stiffened. "They're going to make me deliver, aren't they?"

"I don't think so," Claire replied.

"I know they are." Jill shook her head. She had more resolve than anyone I knew, but the scary truth forming in her eyes was something I'll remember the rest of my life.

The door opened, and another EMS tech wheeled in a gurney. "It's time to go," said the woman who'd been working on her.

I bent down close to Jill. "We're going to be with you," I said.

"Don't leave me," she said, and held my hand.

"You can't get rid of us that easily."

"Homicide Chicks, right?" Jill murmured with a tight smile.

They eased her onto the gurney. Claire and I helped. A bloody towel fell limply onto the floor of her spotless office.

"It's going to be a boy," Jill whispered, letting out a pained breath. "I wanted a boy. I guess I can admit it now."

I folded her hands gently on her lap.

"I just didn't want it badly enough," Jill said, and then she finally started to sob and couldn't stop.

Chapter 65

WE RODE IN THE BACK of the EMS truck with Jill to the hospital, ran alongside the gurney as they wheeled her up to obstetrics, and waited as her doctors tried to save the child.

As they moved her into the OR, she gripped my hand. "They always seem to win," she murmured. "No matter how many of these bastards you put away, they always find a way to win."

Cindy had rushed down, and the three of us hung there waiting to see Jill. About two hours later, her husband, Steve, hurried in. We exchanged some awkward hugs, and part of me wanted to tell him, *Don't you fucking realize this baby was for you?* When the doctor came out, we let them be alone.

Jill was right. She had lost the baby. They called it a placental abruption, made worse from the stress of the job. The only good news was that the fetus had been removed surgically. Jill hadn't had to deliver it.

Afterward, Claire, Cindy, and I filed out of the hospital onto California Street. No one wanted to go home. There was this Japanese place nearby that Cindy knew. We went there and sat around drinking beer and sake.

It was hard to accept that Jill, who worked tirelessly at the office, who rock-climbed at Moab and biked the rough terrain in Sedona, had twice been denied a child.

"The poor girl's just too damn hard on herself." Claire sighed, warming her hands with her sake cup. "We all told her she had to ratchet it down."

"Jill doesn't have that gear," said Cindy.

I picked up a California roll and turned it over and over in the sauce. "She did it to please Steve. You could see it on her face. She keeps that impossible schedule. She doesn't give anything up. And he's running around the country wining investment bankers."

"She loves him," protested Cindy. "They're a team."

"They're not a team, Cindy. Claire and Edmund are a team. The two of them, they're in a race."

"It's true," Claire agreed. "That girl always has to be number one. The girl can't fail."

"So which one of us is any different?" Cindy asked. She looked around. Waited.

There was a moment of protracted silence. Our gazes met with contrite smiles.

"But it's deeper than that," I said. "Jill's different. She's tough as nails, but in her heart she feels alone. Any of us could be where she is now. We're not invincible. Except you, Claire. You have this mechanism that just keeps it together, you and Edmund and your kids, like that fucking battery rabbit, on and on and on."

Claire smiled. "Someone has to provide the balance around here. You saw your dad last night, didn't you?"

I nodded. "It went pretty well. I guess. We talked, we got some things out."

"No fisticuffs?" Cindy asked.

"No fisticuffs." I smiled. "When I opened the door, he had on a catcher's mask. I'm serious."

Claire and Cindy laughed out loud.

"He brought me this bottle of wine. Fancy French first-growth. Nineteen sixty-five. He bought it the year I was born. Kept it all these years. How do you figure that? He never even knew if he'd ever see me again."

"He knew he'd see you again," Claire said with a smile. She sipped her sake. "You're his beautiful daughter. He loves you."

"So how'd you leave it, Lindsay?" Cindy asked.

"I guess you could say we agreed to a second date. Actually, I told him he could stay with me for a while."

Cindy and Claire both blinked.

"We told you to loosen up and see him, Lindsay." Cindy snorted. "Not ask him to share the rent."

"What can I tell you? He was camped out on someone's couch. It seemed like the right thing to do."

"It is, honey." Claire smiled. "Here's to you."

"Uh-uh." I shook my head. "Here's to Jill."

"Yeah, here's to Jill," Cindy said, lifting her beer.

We all clinked. Then it was quiet for a moment or two.

"I don't mean to change the subject," Cindy said, "but you want to share where you are on the case?"

I nodded. "We're looking into the Chimera names Warden Estes gave us. But today I came up with a new theory."

"New theory?" Cindy wrinkled her brow.

I nodded. "Look, this guy's a trained shooter. He's made no mistakes. He's been one step ahead of us on every move. He knows how we work."

Cindy and Claire were listening. Not a word. I told them what Weiscz had said to me. *An inside job* . . .

"What if Chimera isn't a crazy, racist killer from one of these radical groups?" I leaned forward. "What if he's a cop?"

Chapter 66

IN A DARK BAR, Chimera sipped his Guinness. The best for the best, he thought.

Next to him, a white-haired man with a blotchy red, dry-as-parchment face was downing Tom Collinses, glancing up at the TV. The news was on. An insipid reporter was giving the latest on the Chimera case, getting it all wrong, insulting the public, insulting *him*.

He kept his eyes peeled across the street through the bar's large window. He had followed the next victim here. This one he would relish. All those cops, chasing down the wrong leads. This kill would really set them on their heels.

"It's not over," he muttered under his breath. *And don't ever get the idea that I'm predictable. I'm not.*

The drunk old-timer next to him gave him

a nudge. "I think the bastard's one of *them,*" he said.

"One of *them?*" Chimera asked. "Watch your elbows. And what the hell are you talking about?"

"Black as the ace of spades," the old man said. "They're combing through those hate groups. Ha, what a laugh. This is some sick jungle bunny minus one jar on the shelf. Probably plays in the NFL. Hey, Ray," he called to the bartender. "Probably plays in the NFL . . ."

"What makes you say that?" Chimera asked, his eyes flicking across the street. He was curious about what his public was thinking. Maybe he ought to do more man-on-the-street interviews like this one.

"You think any motherfucker with a set of brains would leave clues like that?" the old man whispered conspiratorially.

"I think you're jumping a little fast, old-timer." Chimera finally grinned. "I think this killer's pretty smart."

"How smart can you be to be a fucking murderer?"

"Smart enough not to get caught," Chimera said.

The man scowled at the screen. "Yeah, well,

when it comes out, you watch. They're looking under the wrong rug. There's gonna be
one big surprise. Maybe it's O. J. Hey, Ray,
someone should check if O. J.'s in town. . . ."

He had taken just about as much as he
could of the drunk. But the guy was right
about one thing. The San Francisco cops were
lost in space. Man, they didn't have a clue.
Lieutenant Lindsay Boxer was nowhere on
this. Not even close to him.

"I'll bet you something." Chimera grinned
at the old man. He put his face close to him,
his eyes wide. "If they catch him, I'll bet you
he has green eyes."

Suddenly, across the street, he spotted his
target on the street. *Well, maybe this will
help Lieutenant Boxer focus. A hit real close
to home. A little sidebar that he just couldn't
resist.* He tossed a few dollars on the bar.

"Hey, what's the rush?" The old man turned
to him. "Let me buy you another brew. Hey,
what the hell, *you got green eyes, buddy.*"

Chimera spun out of his seat. "Gotta go.
There's my date."

Chapter 67

ON THE LONG DRIVE HOME, Claire Washburn kept coming back to what had happened to poor Jill. The whole ride down 101 to her home in Burlingame, she couldn't put the terrible thought away.

She exited the highway at Burlingame and wound her way up into the hills. Her head pounded with weariness. It had been such a long day. These terrible murders, pulling the city apart. Then Jill losing her baby.

The digital clock on the dashboard said twenty past ten. Edmund was playing tonight. He wouldn't be back until sometime after eleven. She wished he would be home. Tonight of all nights.

Claire swung onto Skytop and, a few yards later, into the driveway of her modern Georgian home. The house was dark; that's how it was these days now that Reggie was away at college. Willie, her high school sophomore, was no doubt in his room playing video games.

All she wanted to do was to peel off her work clothes and slip quietly into her pajamas. Put an end to this horrible day . . .

Inside, Claire called out for Willie and, hearing no response, flashed through the mail on the kitchen table and brought it into the study. She leafed absently through a Ballard Designs catalog.

The phone rang. Claire tossed down the catalog and picked up the phone. "Hello . . ."

There was a hollow pause, as if someone were waiting.

Maybe one of Willie's friends.

"Hello . . . ?" Claire called again. "Once, twice . . . last time . . ." Still no answer. "Goodbye."

She placed the phone back on the receiver.

A shiver of nervousness went through her. Even after all these years, when she was alone in the house, an unexpected noise, the lights on in the basement, sent a tremor through her.

The phone rang again. This time, she picked it up quickly. *"Hello . . ."*

Another annoying pause. This was starting to get her pissed. "Who is this?" she demanded.

"Take a guess," a male voice said.

Claire's breath came to a stop. She glanced at her caller ID. "Listen, 901-4476," she said, "I don't know what your game is or how you got our number. If you've got something to say, say it fast."

"You know about Chimera?" the voice replied. "You're speaking to him. Aren't you honored?"

Claire froze. She arched upright in her chair. Her mind shot into gear: *Chimera was a police department name.* Had it ever been in print? Who knew she was involved in the investigation?

She pressed a separate line, about to punch in 911. "You better tell me who this really is," she said.

"I told you. The little black choir girl was number one," the voice replied. "The old bitch, the fat, unsuspecting cop, the boss . . . You know what they all had in common, don't you? Think about it, Claire Washburn. Do *you* have anything in common with the first four victims?"

Claire's body had begun to shake. Her mind drew a picture of the elaborate shots that had killed two of the victims.

Her eyes shifted outside the study window, to the darkness around her house.

The voice came back, *"Lean a little to the left, huh, Doc?"*

Chapter 68

CLAIRE SPUN just as the first bullet splintered through the glass.

A second shot shattered the study window, and Claire felt burning pain sear her neck. She was down on the floor as a third and fourth shot exploded into the room.

A startled cry came from her throat. There was blood on the floor, blood from her own neck, seeping onto her dress, her hands. Her heart beat madly. *How bad was it? Had it severed the carotid artery?*

Then she looked to the doorway, and her blood froze. *Willie* . . .

"Mom!" he exclaimed. His eyes were bulging with fear. He was only wearing a T-shirt and briefs. *He was a target.*

"Willie, get down," she screamed at him. "Someone's shooting at the house."

The boy dove to the floor, and Claire

scrambled over to him. "It's okay. Just stay down. Let me think," she whispered. "Don't you raise your head an inch."

The pain in her neck was excruciating, like the skin had been sheared off. She could breathe, though. If the bullet had pierced her carotid, she'd be choking. The gash was surface, had to be.

"Mom, what's going on?" Willie whispered. His body was trembling like a leaf. She'd never seen him this way.

"I don't know. . . . Just *stay down*, Willie."

Suddenly, four more shots blazed from outside. She held her son tight. Whoever it was was shooting blindly, trying to hit anything. *Did the killer know she was still alive?* A jolt of panic set in. *What if he came in the house? Did the killer know about her son? He knew her name!*

"Willie," she gasped, cupping his head between her hands. "Get down in the basement. *Lock the door.* Call nine one one. Crawl! Now! On your stomach!"

"I'm not going to leave you," he cried.

"Go," her voice replied sharply. *"Go now. Do as I say. Stay down! I love you, Willie."*

Claire pushed Willie forward. "Call nine one

one. Tell them who you are and what's happening. Then call Dad in the car. He should be on his way home."

Willie shot her a last, pleading look, but he understood. He crawled, face and body pressed to the floor. *Good boy. Your mother didn't raise any dumb ones.*

Another blast of gunfire came from outside. Sucking in a breath, Claire pleaded, "Please, God, don't let that bastard come into our house. Don't let that happen, I beg you."

Chapter 69

CHIMERA SQUEEZED OFF four more rounds through the shattered window, smoothly swiveling the PSG-1 rifle in his hands.

He knew he'd hit her. Not with the first shot; she had spun around at the last second. But with the next one, as she was trying to hit the deck. He just didn't know if he had done the job. He wanted to send a message to Lieutenant Lindsay Boxer, and just wounding her friend wasn't good enough. Claire Washburn had to die.

He sat in the cover of the dark street, the barrel of the rifle protruding from the car window. He needed to make sure she was dead, but, damn it, he didn't want to go into the house. She had a son, and he might be in there. One of them might have called 911.

Suddenly, outside lights flashed from a house down the street. At another, someone stepped out onto the lawn.

"Goddamnit," he seethed. "Son of a bitch." Part of him wanted to charge the shattered window and spray the room with a barrage. Washburn had to die. He didn't want to leave without finishing her.

From behind him came noise. A car turned wildly onto the street, its horn blaring, bright lights flickering on and off. The car sped toward him like some meteor barreling right into his sight.

"What the hell is this now?"

Maybe she had called the cops. Maybe as soon as they heard the shots, the neighbors had. He couldn't risk it. She wasn't the one he would put himself on the line for. He wasn't going to get caught.

The honking, flashing car spun sharply into the driveway of the house. It screeched to a halt. The neighbors began to emerge from their homes.

He slammed the wheel with his hand and pulled in his gun. He put his car in gear and floored it.

It was the first time he had messed up. Ever. Jesus, he never made mistakes.

You're lucky, Doc. But you were target practice anyway.

It was the next one that mattered.

Chapter 70

I HAD TAKEN OFF MY MAKEUP and curled up to watch the late news when Edmund's call came.

Claire's husband was frantic, stammering. The impossibility of what he was struggling to describe slammed into me with the force of a train. "She'll be all right, Lindsay. She's at Peninsula Hospital now."

I yanked a fleece pullover over my head, tugged on some jeans, and, throwing a top hat on the roof of the car, raced down to Burlingame. I made the forty-minute drive in under twenty minutes.

I found Claire still in one of the treatment rooms, sitting upright, dressed in the same rust-colored suit I had left her in only three hours before. A doctor was applying a bandage to her neck. Edmund and Willie were by her side.

"Jesus, Claire . . ." was all I could manage, my eyes hot and moist. I melted into Edmund, resting my head on his shoulder, and gave him my warmest, most grateful hug. Then I threw my arms all over Claire.

"Go easy on the TLC, honey." She winced, jerking her neck. Then she managed a smile. "I always told you one day these fat cells would come in handy. It takes a helluva shot to reach anything vital in me."

I was still squeezing her. "Do you have any idea how lucky you are?"

"*Yeah.*" She exhaled. I could see it in her eyes. "Believe me, I know."

The bullet had only grazed her. The ER doctor had cleaned the wound, bandaged it, and was releasing her without even keeping her overnight. Another inch, and we wouldn't have been talking now.

Claire reached out for Edmund's and Willie's hands and smiled. "My men did okay, didn't they? Both of them. Edmund's car scared the sniper away."

Edmund grimaced. "I should've chased that bastard myself. If I'd caught him . . ."

"Down, tiger." Claire smiled. "Let Lindsay be the heat. You stay a drummer. I always told you," she said, squeezing his hand, "Rachmaninoff might be in his head, but when it comes to his heart, the man's all Doggy Dogg."

Almost at once, the reality of what had almost happened seemed to overwhelm him. Edmund's bravado melted away. He sat down, just leaned against Claire for a while, and as he tried to speak, put a hand over his eyes. Claire held his hand without speaking.

A little more than an hour later, after going through the story with the Burlingame Police, we walked the grounds outside her house.

"It was *him,* wasn't it, Claire? It was Chimera." She nodded her head, *yes.*

"He's a real cold sonofabitch, Lindsay. I heard him say, 'Lean a little to the left, Doc.' Then he started firing."

Local cops and the San Mateo County sheriff's office were still scrambling all over the house and yard. I had already called Clapper to come down and lend a hand.

Claire said, "Why *me,* Lindsay?"

"I don't know, Claire. You're black. You work in law enforcement. I don't understand it myself. Why would he change his pattern?"

"We're talking calm and deliberate, Lindsay. It was like he was toying with me. He made it sound . . . *personal.*"

I thought I saw something I had never seen in her before. *Fear.* Who could blame her? "Maybe you should take some time off, Claire," I told her. "Stay out of sight."

"You think I'm gonna let him push me under a rock? That's not a possibility, Lindsay. No way I let him win."

I gave her a gentle hug. "You're okay?"

"I'm okay. He had his chance. Now I want mine."

Chapter 71

I FINALLY DRAGGED MYSELF back to my apartment at sometime after two in the morning.

The events of the long, horrible day — Jill losing her child, Claire's terrifying ordeal — flipped by like some old-time nightmare film sequence. The man I was tracking had almost killed my best friend. *Why Claire? What could it mean?* Part of me felt responsible, dirtied by the crime.

My body ached. I wanted to sleep; I needed to wash away the day. Suddenly, the door to the guest bedroom opened, and my father shuffled out. In the madness of the day, I had almost forgotten he was here.

He was wearing a long white T-shirt and boxers with a seashell pattern. Somehow, with the deprivation of sleep, I found this funny.

"You're wearing boxers, Boxer," I said. "You're a witty old bastard." Then I told him what had happened. As a former cop, he would understand. Surprisingly, my father was a good listener. Just what I needed right about then.

He came around to my side of the couch. "You want coffee? I'll go make it, Lindsay."

"Brandy would do the trick better. But there's some Moonlight Sonata tea on the counter there if you're up to it." It was nice to have someone here, and he seemed eager to calm me.

I sank back in the couch, shut my eyes, and tried to figure out what I was going to do next. *Davidson, Mercer, and now Claire Washburn . . .* Why would Chimera come after Claire? What did it mean?

My father came back with a cup of tea and a snifter of Courvoisier two inches full. "I figure you're a big girl. So why not *both.*"

I took a sip of tea, then drank about half the brandy in a gulp. "Oh, I needed that. Almost as much as I need a break on this case. He's leaving clues, but I still don't get it."

"Take it easy on yourself, Lindsay," my father said in the gentlest voice.

"What do you do," I asked, "when everyone in the world is watching and you have no idea what to do next? When you realize that whatever you're fighting isn't giving in, that you're fighting a monster?"

"That's about where we usually called in Homicide," my father said with a smile.

"Don't try to make me laugh," I begged. But my father had me smiling in spite of everything. Even more surprising to me, I was starting to think of him as my father.

His tone suddenly changed. "I can tell you what I did when it really got tough. I took off. You won't do that, Lindsay. I can tell. You're so much better than me."

He was looking squarely at me, no longer smiling.

What happened next, I would never have believed. My father's arms just sort of parted, and almost without resistance, I found myself burrowing into his shoulder. He wrapped his arms around me, a little tentatively at first, then, just like any father and any daughter, he squeezed me with tender care. I didn't resist. I could smell the same cologne he wore when I was a child. It felt both strange and, at the same time, like the most natural thing in the world.

Having my father hold me unexpectedly, it felt like layers of pain were suddenly stripped away.

"You're going to catch him, Lindsay," I heard him whisper, squeezing me and rocking. "You will, Buttercup. . . ."

It was just what I needed to hear.

"Oh, Daddy," I said. Nothing more, though.

Chapter 72

"LIEUTENANT BOXER." Brenda buzzed me early Monday. "Warden Estes from Pelican Bay. Line two." I picked up the phone, not expecting much.

"You asked if we had ever had a policeman imprisoned here," Estes said.

I perked up immediately. "And?"

"Mind you, I don't give a shit about some lunatic ravings from Weiscz. But I did go back through the old files. There *was* a case here that might have some relevance. *Twelve* years ago. I was the warden at Soledad when this scum arrived here."

I took the phone off speaker, pressing the receiver to my ear.

"They had him here for five years. Two of them in iso. Then they shipped him back to

Quentin. A special case. You may even remember the name."

I picked up a pen and started racking my brain. A cop at Pelican? Quentin?

"Frank Coombs," Estes said

I did recognize the name. It was like a headline flashing back from my youth. *Coombs.* A street cop, he had killed a kid in the projects some twenty years before. Got run up on charges. Sent away. To any San Francisco cop, his name was like a warning bell for the use of excessive force.

"Coombs turned into more of a bastard in prison than he was on the outside," Estes went on. "He choked a cell mate blue down in Quentin, which is why they shipped him here. After a stay in the SHU's, they were able to cure him of some of his antisocial tendencies."

Coombs... I wrote down the name. I couldn't remember anything about the case except that he had choked and killed this black kid.

"What makes you think this Coombs might fit?" I asked.

"As I said..." Estes cleared his throat. "I don't much care about Weiscz's ravings. What made me call was that I asked some of our staff. When he was here, Coombs was a charter member of that little group of yours."

"My group?"

"That's right, Lieutenant. *Chimera.*"

Chapter 73

YOU KNOW THE SAYING — when one door slams in your face, another one opens. Half an hour later, I rapped on my window for Jacobi. "What do you know about Frank Coombs?" I asked when he came into my office.

Warren shrugged. "Dirtbag street cop. Got some teenager in a stranglehold during a drug bust years ago. The kid died. Major departmental scandal when I was in uniform. Didn't he get a dime up in Quentin?"

"Uh-uh, *twenty*." I slid Coombs's personnel file toward him. "Now tell me something I can't find in *here*."

Warren opened the file. "As I remember, the guy was a tough cop, decorated, a solid arrest record, but at the same time, I figure this file's got enough OCC reprimands for excessive force to rival Rodney King."

I nodded. "Keep going . . ."

"You read the file, Lindsay. He busted up a basketball game in one of the projects. Thought he recognized one of the players as some kid he put away for drugs but was spit back out. The kid said something to him, then he took off. Coombs went after him."

"We're talking about a black kid," I injected. "They gave him fifteen to twenty, second-degree manslaughter."

Jacobi blinked. "Where're we going with this, Lindsay?"

"*Weiscz,* Warren. At Pelican Bay. I thought he was just ranting, but something he said stuck. Weiscz said he'd given me something. He said it sounded like an inside job."

"You dredged up this old file because Weiscz said it was an inside job?" Jacobi screwed his brow.

"Coombs was *Chimera.* He spent two years in the SHU's. Take a look. . . . The guy had SWAT training. *He was qualified for marksman status.* He was an avowed racist. And he's *out.* Coombs was released from San Quentin a few months ago."

Jacobi sat there stone-faced. "You're still short a motive, Lieutenant. I mean, granted, the guy was a major asshole. But he was a cop. What would he have against other cops?"

"He pleaded self-defense, that the kid was resisting. No one backed him, Warren. Not his partner, not the other officers on the scene, not the brass.

"You think I'm reaching?" I grabbed the file, skimmed through, and stopped where I had circled something in red marker. "You said Coombs killed this kid in the projects?"

Jacobi nodded.

I pushed the page at him.

"*Bay View,* Warren. *La Salle Heights.* That's where he choked that kid. Those projects were torn down and rebuilt in nineteen ninety. They were renamed . . ."

". . . Whitney Young," Jacobi said.

Near where Tasha Catchings had been killed.

Chapter 74

MY NEXT MOVE was to dial up Madeline Akers, assistant warden at San Quentin prison. Maddie was a friend. She told me what she knew about Coombs. "Bad cop, bad guy, real bad inmate. A cold sonofabitch." Maddie said she would ask around about him. Maybe Frank Coombs had told somebody what he planned to do once he got outside.

"Madeline, this absolutely can't leak out," I insisted.

"Mercer was a friend, Lindsay. I'll do anything I can. Give me a couple of days."

"Make it one, Maddie. This is vital. He's going to kill again."

For a long time I sat at my desk trying to piece together just what I had. I couldn't place Coombs at a crime scene. I had no weapon. I didn't even know where he was. But for the first time since Tasha Catchings was killed, I had the feeling I was onto something good.

My instinct was to ask Cindy to troll through the *Chronicle*'s morgue for old stories. These events had happened more than twenty years before. Only a few people in the department were still around from those days.

Then I remembered I had someone who'd been there staying under my own roof.

I found my father watching the evening news when I walked through the door. "Hey," he called. "You're home at a decent hour. Solve your case?"

I changed my clothes, grabbed a beer from the fridge, then I pulled up a chair across from him.

"I need to talk to you about something." I looked in his eyes. "You remember a guy named Frank Coombs?"

My father nodded. "There's a name I haven't heard in a long time. Sure, I remember him. Cop who choked the kid over in the projects. They brought him up on murder charges. Sent him away."

"You were on the force, right?"

"Yes, and I knew him. Worst excuse for a cop I ever ran into. Some people were impressed with him. He made arrests, got things done. In his own way. It was different then. We didn't have review committees looking over our shoulder. Not everything we did got into the press."

"This kid he choked, Dad, he was fourteen."

"Why do you want to know about Coombs? He's in jail."

"Not any longer. He's out." I pulled my chair closer. "I read that Coombs claimed he killed the kid in self-defense."

"What cop wouldn't? He said the kid tried to cut him with a sharp object he took to be a knife."

"You remember who he was partnered up with back then, Dad?"

"Jesus." My father shrugged. "Stan Dragula, as I recall. Yeah, he testified at the trial. But I think he died a few years back. No one wanted to work with Coombs. You were scared to walk through the neighborhoods with him."

"Was Stan Dragula white or black?" I asked.

"Stan was white," my father answered. "I think Italian, or maybe Jewish."

That wasn't the answer I had been expecting. No one had backed Coombs up. But why was he killing *blacks?*

"Dad, if it *is* Coombs doing these things . . . if he is out for some kind of revenge, why against blacks?"

"Coombs was an animal, but he was also a cop. Things were different then. That famous blue wall of silence . . . Every cop is taught at the academy, Keep your yap shut. It'll be there for you. Well, it didn't hold up for Frank Coombs; it came tumbling down on him. Everyone was glad to give him up. We're talking, what, twenty years ago? The affirmative action thing on the force was strong. Blacks and Latinos were just starting to get placed in key positions. There was this black lobby group, the OFJ . . ."

"Officers for Justice," I said. "They're still around."

My father nodded. "Tensions were strong. The OFJ threatened to strike. Eventually, there was pressure from the city, too. Whatever it was, Coombs felt he was handed over, hung out to dry."

It started coming clear to me. Coombs felt he had been railroaded by the black lobby of the department. He had chewed on his hatred in prison. Now, twenty years later, he was back on the streets of San Francisco.

"Maybe, another time, this kind of thing might've been swept under the rug," I said. "But not then. The OFJ nailed him."

Suddenly, a sickening realization wormed into my brain. "Earl Mercer was involved, wasn't he?"

My father nodded his head. "Mercer was Coombs's lieutenant."

Part III

THE BLUE WALL OF SILENCE

Chapter 75

THE NEXT MORNING, the case against Frank Coombs, which only a day ago had seemed flimsy, was bursting at the seams. I was pumped.

First thing, Jacobi rapped at my door. "One for your side, Lieutenant. Coombs is looking better and better."

"How so? You make any progress with Coombs's PO?"

"You might say. He's gone, Lindsay. According to the PO, Coombs split from this transient hotel down on Eddy. No forwarding address, hasn't checked in, hasn't contacted his ex-wife."

I was disappointed that Coombs was missing, but it was also a good sign. I told Jacobi to keep looking.

A few minutes later, Madeline Akers called from San Quentin.

"I think I've got what you want," she announced. I couldn't believe she was responding so soon.

"Over the past year, Coombs was paired with four different cell mates. Two of them have been paroled, but I spoke with the other two myself. One of them told me to stuff it, but the other, this guy Toracetti . . . I almost didn't even have to tell him what I was looking for. He said the minute he heard on the news about Davidson and Mercer, he knew it was Coombs. Coombs told him he was going to blow the whole thing wide open again."

I thanked Maddie profusely. *Tasha, Mercer, Davidson* . . . It was starting to fit together.

But how did Estelle Chipman fit in?

A force took hold of me. I went outside and dug through the case files. It had been weeks since I'd looked at them.

I found it buried at the bottom. The personnel file I'd called up from Records: *Edward C. Chipman.*

In his thirty unremarkable years on the force, only one thing stood out.

He had been his district's representative to the OFJ . . . *the Officers for Justice.*

It was time to put this on the record. I buzzed Chief Tracchio. His secretary, Helen, who had been Mercer's, said he was in a closed-door meeting. I told her I was coming up.

I grabbed the Coombs file and headed up the stairs to five. I had to share this. I barreled into the chief's office.

Then I stopped, speechless.

To my shock, seated around the conference table were Tracchio, Special Agents Ruddy and Hull of the FBI, the press flack Carr, and Chief of Detectives Ryan.

I hadn't been invited to the latest task force meeting.

Chapter 76

"THIS IS BULLSHIT," I said. "It's total crap. What is this — some kind of a men's club?"

Tracchio, Ruddy and Hull from the FBI, Carr, Ryan. Five boys seated around the table — minus me, the woman.

The acting chief stood up. His face was red. "Lindsay, we were about to call you up."

I knew what this meant. What was going on. Tracchio was going to shift control on the case. *My case.* He and Ryan were going to hand it over to the FBI.

"We're at a critical moment in this case," Tracchio said.

"You're damn right," I cut him off. I swept my gaze over the group. *"I know who it is."*

Suddenly, all eyes turned my way. The boys were silent. It was as if the lights had been cranked up, and my skin prickled as if it had been cauterized.

I leveled my eyes back on Tracchio. "You want me to lay it out for you? Or do you want me to leave?"

Seemingly dumbfounded, he pulled out a chair for me.

I didn't sit. I stood. Then I took them through everything, and I enjoyed it. How I had been skeptical at first, but then it began to fit. Chimera, Pelican Bay . . . Coombs's grudge against the police force. At the sound of Coombs's name, the departmental people's eyes grew wide. I linked the victims, Coombs's qualification as a marksman, how only a marksman could have made those shots.

When I finished, there was silence again. They just stared. I wanted to pump my arm in victory.

Agent Ruddy cleared his throat. "So far, I haven't heard a thing that links Coombs directly to any of the crime scenes."

"Give me another day or two and you will," I said. "Coombs is the killer."

Hull, Ruddy's broad-shouldered partner, shrugged optimistically toward the chief. "You want us to follow this up?"

I couldn't believe it. This was *my* case. *My*

breakthrough. *Homicide's.* Our people had been murdered.

Tracchio seemed to mull it over. He pursed his thick lips as if he were sucking a last drop through a straw. Then he shook his head at the FBI man.

"That won't be necessary, Special Agent. This has always been a *city* case. We'll see it through with city personnel."

Chapter 77

ONLY ONE THING was standing in the way now. We had to find Frank Coombs.

Coombs's prison file mentioned a wife, Ingrid, who had divorced him while he was in prison and remarried. It was a long shot. The PO said he hadn't been in touch. But long shots were coming in right now.

"C'mon, Warren." I nudged Jacobi. "You're coming with me. It'll be like old times."

"Aww, ain't that sweet."

Ingrid Thiasson lived on a pleasant middle-class street off of Laguna.

We parked across the street, went up, and rang the bell. No one answered. We didn't know if Coombs's wife worked, and there was no car in the driveway.

Just as we were about to head back, an old-model Volvo station wagon pulled into the driveway.

Ingrid Thiasson looked about fifty, with stringy brown hair; she wore a plain, shapeless blue dress under a heavy gray sweater. She climbed out of the car and opened the rear hatch to unload groceries.

An old cop's wife, she ID'd us the minute we walked up. "What do you people want with me?" she asked.

"A few minutes. We're trying to locate your ex-husband."

"You got nerve coming around here." She scowled, hoisting two bags in her arms.

"We're just checking all the possibilities," Jacobi said.

She snapped back, "Like I told his parole officer, I haven't heard a word from him since he got out."

"He hasn't been to see you?"

"Once, when he got out. He came by to pick up some personal stuff he thought I had held for him. I told him I threw it all out."

"What kind of stuff?" I asked.

"Useless letters, newspaper articles on the trial. Probably the old guns he kept around. Frank was always into guns. Stuff only a man with nothing to show for his life would find value in."

Jacobi nodded. "So what'd he do then?"

"What'd he do?" Ingrid Thiasson snorted. "He left without a word about what life had been like for us for the past twenty years. Without a word about me or his son. You believe that?"

"And you have no idea where we could contact him?"

"None. That man was poison. I found someone who's treated me with respect. Who's been a father to my boy. I don't want to see Frank Coombs again."

I asked, "You have any idea if he might be in touch with your son?"

"No way. I always kept them apart. My son doesn't have any links to his father. And don't go buzzing around him. He's in college at Stanford."

I stepped forward. "Anyone who might know where he is, Ms. Thiasson, it would be a help to us. This is a murder case."

I saw the slightest sign of hesitation. "I've lived a good life for twenty years. We're a family now. I don't want anyone knowing this came from me."

I nodded. I felt the blood rushing to my head.

"Frank kept up with Tom Keating. Even when he was locked away. Anyone knows where he is, it'd be him."

Tom Keating. I knew the name.

He was a retired cop.

Chapter 78

LESS THAN AN HOUR LATER, Jacobi and I
pulled up in front of condo 3A at the Blakesly
Residential Community, down the coast in
Half Moon Bay.

Keating's name had stuck in my mind from
when I was a kid. He'd been a regular at the
Alibi after the nine-to-four shift, where many
afternoons I'd been hoisted up on a bar stool
by my father. In my mind, Keating had a ruddy
complexion and a shock of prematurely
white hair. *God,* I thought, *that was almost
thirty years ago.*

We knocked on the door of Keating's mod-
est slatted-wood condo. A trim, pleasant-
looking woman with gray hair answered.

"Mrs. Keating? I'm Lieutenant Lindsay
Boxer of the San Francisco Homicide detail.
This is Inspector Jacobi. Is your husband at
home?"

"Homicide . . . ?" she said, surprised.

"Just an old case," I said with a smile.

A voice called from inside, "Helen, I can't find the damned clicker anywhere."

"Just a minute, Tom. He's in the back," she said as she motioned us into the house.

We walked through the sparsely decorated house and into a sunroom overlooking a small patio. There were several framed police photos on the wall. Keating was as I remembered him, just thirty years older. Gaunt, white hair thinning, but with that same ruddy complexion.

He sat watching an afternoon news show with the stock market tape streaming by. I realized he was sitting in a wheelchair.

Helen Keating introduced us, then, finding the clicker, put the TV volume down. Keating seemed pleased to have visitors from the force.

"I don't get to many functions since my legs went. Arthritis, they tell me. Brought on by a bullet to lumbar four. Can't play golf anymore." He chuckled. "But I can still watch the old pension grow."

I saw him studying my face. "You're Marty Boxer's little girl, aren't you?"

I smiled. "The Alibi . . . A couple of five-oh-ones, right, Tom?" A 5-0-1 was the call for backup, and how they used to call a favorite drink, an Irish whiskey with a beer chaser.

"I heard you were quite the big shot these days." Keating nodded with a toothy smile. "So, what brings you two honchos down to talk to an old street cop?"

"Frank Coombs," I said.

Keating's features suddenly turned hard. "What about Frank?"

"We're trying to find him, Tom. I was told you might know where he is."

"Why don't you call his parole officer? That wouldn't be me."

"He's split, Tom. Four weeks now. Quit his job."

"So they got Homicide following up on parole offenders now?"

I held Keating's eyes. "What do you say, Tom?"

"What makes you think I'd have any idea?" He glanced toward his legs. "Old times are old times."

"I heard you guys kept in touch. It's important."

"Well, you're wasting your time here, Lieutenant," he said, suddenly turning formal.

I knew he was lying. "When was the last time you spoke with Coombs?"

"Maybe just after he got out. Could be once or twice since then. He needed some help to get on his feet. I may have lent him a hand."

"And where was he staying," Jacobi cut in, "while you were lending him this hand?"

Keating shook his head. "Some hotel down on Eddy or O'Farrell. Wasn't the St. Francis," he said.

"And you haven't spoken with him since?" My eyes flicked toward Helen Keating.

"What do you want with the man, anyway?" Keating snapped. "He's paid his time. Why don't you just leave him alone?"

"It would be easier this way, Tom," I said. "If you'd just talk to us."

Keating pursed his dry lips, trying to size up where his loyalties fell.

"You put in thirty years, didn't you?" Jacobi said.

"Twenty-four." He patted his leg. "Got it cut short at the end."

"Twenty-four good years. It'd be a shame to

dishonor it in any way by not cooperating now. . . ."

He shot back, "You want to know who was a goddamn expert in *lack of cooperation?* Frank Coombs. Man was only doing his job and all those bastards, supposedly his friends, looked the other way. Maybe that's the way you do things now, with your community action meetings and your sensitivity training. But then we had to get the bad guys off the streets. With the means that we had."

"Tom." His wife raised her voice. "Frank Coombs killed a boy. These people, they're your friends. They want to speak with him. I don't know how far you have to take this duty-and-loyalty thing. Your duty's here."

Keating glared at her harshly. "Yeah, sure, my duty's here." He picked up the TV clicker and turned back to me. "Stay here all day if you like; I don't have the slightest idea where Frank Coombs is."

He turned up the volume on his TV.

Chapter 79

"FUCK HIM," Jacobi said as we left the house. "Old-school asshole."

"We're halfway down the peninsula already," I said to him. "You want to drive down to Stanford? See Frankie's kid?"

"What the hell." He shrugged. "I can use the education."

We hooked back onto 280 and made it to Palo Alto in half an hour.

As we pulled onto the campus drive — the tall palms lining the road, the stately ocher buildings with their red roofs, the Hoover Tower majestically rising over the Main Quad — I felt the spell of being part of campus life. Every one of these kids was special and talented. I even felt some pride that Coombs's son, despite his rough beginnings, had made it here.

We checked in at the administrative office

on the Main Quad. A dean's assistant told us Rusty Coombs was probably at football practice down at the field house. Said Rusty was a good student, and a great tight end. We drove there, where a student manager in a red Stanford cap took us upstairs and asked us to wait outside the weight room.

Moments later, a solidly built, orange-haired kid in a sweaty Cardinals T-shirt wandered out. Rusty Coombs had an affable face spotted with a few freckles. He had none of the dark, brooding belligerence I had seen in photos of his father.

"I guess I know why you guys are here," he said, coming up to us. "My mom called, told me."

The heavy sound of weight irons and lifting machines clanged in the background. I smiled affably. "We're looking for your father, Rusty. We were wondering if you have any idea where he might be?"

"He's not my father," the boy said, and shook his head. "My father's name is Theodore Bell. He's the one who brought me up with Mom. Teddy taught me how to catch a football. He's the one who told me I could make it to Stanford."

"When was the last time you heard from Frank Coombs?"

"What's he done, anyway? My mother said you guys are from Homicide. We know what's in the news. Everyone knows what's going on up there. Whatever he did before, he paid his time, didn't he? You can't believe just because he made some mistakes twenty years ago he's responsible for these terrible crimes?"

"We wouldn't have driven all the way down unless it was important," Jacobi said.

The football player shifted back and forth on the balls of his feet. He seemed to be a likable kid, cooperative. He rubbed his hands together. "He came here once. When he first got out. I had written him a couple of times in jail. I met with him in town. I didn't want anybody to see him."

"What did he say to you?" I asked.

"I think all he wanted was to clear his own conscience. And know what my mother thought of him. Never once did he say, 'Hey, great job, Rusty. Look at you. You did *good*.' Or, 'Hey, I follow your games. . . .' He was more interested in knowing if my mom had thrown out some of his old things."

"What sort of things?" I asked. What would be so important that he would drive all the way here and confront his son?

"Police things," Rusty Coombs said and shook his head. "Maybe his guns."

I smiled sympathetically. I knew what it was like to look at your father with something less than admiration. "He give you any idea where he might go?"

Rusty Coombs shook his head. He looked like he might tear up. "I'm not Frank Coombs, Inspectors. I may have his name, I may even have to live with what he did, but I'm not *him*. Please leave our family alone. Please."

Chapter 80

WELL, THAT SUCKED. Stirring up bad memories for Rusty Coombs made me feel terrible. Even Jacobi agreed.

We made it back to the office about four. We'd driven all the way down to Palo Alto just to run into another dead end. What fun.

There was a phone message waiting for me. I called Cindy back immediately. "There's a rumor floating around that you've narrowed on a suspect," she said. "Truth or dare?"

"We have a name, Cindy, but I can't tell you anything. We just want to bring him in for questioning."

"So there's no warrant?"

"Cindy . . . not just yet."

"I'm not talking about a story, Lindsay. He went after our friend. Remember? If I can help . . ."

"I got a hundred cops working on it, Cindy.

Some of us have even handled an investigation or two before. Please, trust me."

"But if you haven't brought him in, then you haven't *found* him, right?"

"Or maybe we haven't made the case yet. And Cindy, that's not for print."

"This is *me* talking, Linds. Claire, too. And Jill. We're in this case, Lindsay. All of us."

She was right. Unlike any other homicide case I had worked, this one seemed to be growing more and more personal. *Why was that?* I didn't have Coombs and I could use the help. As long as he stayed free, anything could happen.

"I do need your help. Go through your old files, Cindy. You just didn't go back far enough."

She paused, then sucked in a breath. "You were right, weren't you? The guy's a cop."

"You can't go with that, sweetie. And if you did, you'd be wrong. But it's damned close."

I felt her analyzing, and also biting her tongue. "We're still going to meet, aren't we?"

I smiled. "Yeah, we're going to meet. We're a team. More than ever."

I was about to pack it in for the night when a call buzzed through to my line. I was sitting around thinking that Tom Keating had been lying. That he'd spoken to Coombs. But until we put out a warrant, Keating could hold back all he wanted.

To my utter surprise, it was his wife on the line. I almost dropped the phone.

"My husband's a stubborn man, Lieutenant," she began, clearly nervous. "But he wore the uniform with pride. I've never asked him to account for anything. And I won't start now. But I can't sit back. Frank Coombs killed that boy. And if he's done something else, I refuse to wake up every morning for the rest of my life knowing I abetted a murderer."

"It would be better for everybody, Mrs. Keating, if your husband told us what he knows."

"I don't know what he knows," she said, "and I believe him when he says he hasn't spoken to Coombs in some time. But he wasn't telling the whole truth, Lieutenant."

"Then why don't you start."

She hesitated. "Coombs *did* come by here. Once. Maybe two months ago."

"Do you know where he is?" My blood started to rush.

"No," she answered. "But I did take a message from him. For Tom. I still have the number."

I fumbled for a pen.

She read me the number. *434-9117*. "I'm pretty sure it was some kind of boarding house or hotel."

"Thank you, Helen."

I was about to hang up when she said, "There's one more thing. . . . When my husband said he lent Coombs a hand, he wasn't telling the whole story. Tom did give him some money. He also let him rummage through some old things in our storage locker."

"What sort of things?" I asked.

"His old *department* things. Maybe an old uniform, and a badge."

That's what Coombs had been looking for in his ex-wife's house. His old police uniforms. My mind clicked. *Maybe that's how he got so close to Chipman and Mercer. . . .*

"That's all?" I asked.

"No," Helen Keating said. "Tom kept guns down there. Coombs took those, too."

Chapter 81

WITHIN MINUTES I traced the number Helen Keating had given me to a boarding house on Larkin and McAllister. The Hotel William Simon. My pulse was jumping.

I called Jacobi, catching him as he was about to sit down to dinner. "Meet me at Larkin and McAllister. The Hotel William Simon."

"You want me to meet you at a hotel? Cool. I'm on my way."

"I think we found Coombs."

We couldn't arrest Frank Coombs. We didn't have a single piece of evidence that could tie him directly to a crime. I might be able to get a search warrant and bust into his room, though. Right now, the most important thing was to make certain he was still there.

Twenty minutes later, I had driven down to the seedy area between the Civic Center and

Union Square. The William Simon was a shabby one-elevator dive under a large bill-board with a slinky model wearing Calvin Klein underwear. As Jill would say, *yick*.

I didn't want to go up to the desk, flashing my badge and his photo, until we were ready to make a move. Finally, I said *what the hell,* and placed a call to the number Helen Keating had given me. After three rings, a male voice answered, *"William Simon . . ."*

"Frank Coombs . . . ?" I inquired.

"Coombs . . ." I listened as the desk clerk leafed through a list of names. "Nope."

Shit. I asked him to double-check. He came back negative.

Just then, the passenger door of my Explorer opened. My nerves were twanging like a bass guitar.

Jacobi climbed in. He was wearing a striped golf shirt and some sort of short, hideous Members Only jacket. His belly bulged. He grinned like a john. "Hey, lady, what does an Andrew Jackson get me?"

"Dinner, maybe, if you're treating."

"We got an ID?" he asked.

I shook my head. I told him what I had found out.

"Maybe he's moved on," Jacobi offered. "How 'bout I go in and flash the badge? With Coombs's photo?"

I shook my head. "How 'bout we sit here and wait."

We waited for over two hours. Stakeouts are incredibly dull. They would drive the average person nuts. We kept our eyes peeled on the William Simon, going over everything from Helen Keating, to what Jacobi's wife was serving for dinner, to the 49ers, to who was sleeping with who at the Hall. Jacobi even sprung for a couple of sandwiches from a Subway.

At ten o'clock, Jacobi grumbled, "This could go on forever. Why don't you let me go inside, Lindsay?"

He was probably right. We didn't even know if Helen Keating's number was current. She had taken it weeks ago.

I was about to give in when a man turned the corner on Larkin headed toward the hotel. I gripped Jacobi's arm. "Look over there."

It was Coombs. I recognized the bastard instantly. He was wearing a camouflage jacket, hands stuffed in his pockets, a floppy hat pulled over his eyes.

"Son of a fucking bitch," Jacobi muttered.

Watching the bastard slink up to the hotel, it took everything I had not to jump out of the car and slam him up against a wall. I wished I could slap him in cuffs. But we had Chimera now. We knew where he was.

"I want someone stuck to him, twenty-four hours," I told Jacobi. "If he makes the tail, I want him picked up. We'll figure out the charges later."

Jacobi nodded.

"I hope you brought a toothbrush." I winked. "You've got first watch."

Chapter 82

AS THEY WALKED hand in hand toward her Castro apartment, Cindy admitted to herself that she was scared shitless.

This was the fifth time she and Aaron Winslow had been out together. They had seen Cyrus Chestnut and Freddie Hubbard at the Blue Door; been to *Traviata* at the opera; taken the ferry across the bay to a tiny Jamaican café that Aaron knew. Tonight, they had seen this dreamy film, *Chocolat*.

No matter where this went tonight, she enjoyed being with him. He was deeper than most men she'd dated, and he was definitely more sensitive. Not only did he read unexpected books like Dave Eggers's *A Heartbreaking Work of Staggering Genius* and Amy Tan's *The Bonesetter's Daughter,* he lived the life that he preached. He worked twelve-to-sixteen-hour days and was loved in his neighborhood, but he still managed to keep his ego in check. She'd heard it over and over again interviewing people for her story. Aaron Winslow was one of the good guys.

All the while, though, Cindy had felt this moment looming in the distance. Hurtling closer and closer. Ticking. This was the natural step, she told herself. As Lindsay would say, their foxhole was about to explode.

"You seem a little quiet tonight," Aaron said. "You okay, Cindy?"

"I'm great," she fibbed. She thought he was just about the sweetest man she had ever gone out with, but, *Jesus, Cindy, he's a pastor. Why didn't you think of this then? Is this a good idea? Think it through. Don't hurt him. Don't get hurt yourself.*

They stopped walking in front of the entrance to Cindy's building and stood in the lighted arch. He sung a line from an old R&B tune, "I've Passed This Way Before." He even had a good singing voice.

There was no use postponing it any longer. "Look, Aaron, someone has to say this. You want to come up? I'd like it if you did, *hate* it if you didn't."

He exhaled and smiled. "I don't exactly know where to take this, Cindy. I'm a little out of my range. I, uh, I've never dated a blonde before. I wasn't expecting any of this."

"I can relate to that." She smiled. "But it's only two floors up. We can talk about it there."

His lip was quivering slightly, and when he touched her arm it sent a shiver down her spine. God, she did like him. And she trusted him.

"I feel like I'm about to cross this line," he said. "And it's not a line I can cross casually. So I have to know. Are we there together? In the same place?"

Cindy elevated on her toes and pressed her lips lightly against his mouth. Aaron seemed surprised and at first he stiffened, but slowly he placed his arms around her and gave himself over to the kiss.

It was just as she had hoped, that first real kiss. Tender and breathtaking. Through his jacket, she could feel the rhythm of his heart pounding. She liked it that he was afraid, too. It made her feel even closer to him.

When they parted, she looked in his eyes

and said, "We're *there.* We're in the same place."

She took out her key and led him up the two floors to her place. Her heart was pounding.

"It's great," he said. "I'm not just saying that." A two-story wall of bookshelves and an informal open kitchen. "It's you. . . . Cindy, it seems silly that I haven't been up here before."

"It wasn't for lack of trying." Cindy grinned. God, she was so *nervous.*

He took hold of her again, this time giving her a longer kiss. He certainly knew how to kiss. Every cell in her body felt alive. The small hairs on her arms, the warmth in her thighs; she pressed herself against him. She wanted, needed, to be close to him now. His body was slender, but he was definitely strong.

Cindy started to smile. "So what were you waiting for?"

"I don't know. Maybe some kind of sign."

She pressed herself into the grooves of his body, felt him come alive. "*There's* a sign," she said, close to his face.

"I guess my secret's out now. Yes, I *do* like you, Cindy."

Suddenly, the phone rang, almost blasting in their ears.

"Oh, God," she groaned. "Go away, leave us alone."

"I hope that's not another sign." He laughed.

Each ring seemed more annoying than the last. Mercifully, the answering machine finally kicked on.

"Cindy, it's Lindsay," the voice shot. "I've got something important. *Please.* Pick. Up."

"Go ahead," Aaron said.

"Now that you're finally up here, don't use the time I'm on the phone to change your mind."

She reached behind the couch, fumbled for the receiver, put it to her ear. "I wouldn't do this for anyone but you," she said.

"Funny, that's just what I was about to say. Listen to this." Lindsay shared her news, and Cindy felt a rush of triumph surge through her. This was what she had wanted. It had been her angle that put Lindsay onto him. Yes!

"Mañana," she said, "and thanks for the phone call." She placed the receiver down, squeezed back with Aaron, and looked into his eyes.

"You wanted a sign. I think I've got the best one in the world." A glimmer lit her face.

"They found him, Aaron."

Chapter 83

WE KEPT WATCH all night at the William Simon. Unofficially. So far, Coombs hadn't come out again. I knew where he was. Now all I had to do was make the case.

That was the morning Jill came back to work. I headed to her office to bring her up to date. Coming off the elevator on the eighth floor, I ran into Claire, who must've had the same idea.

"Great minds and all that," she said.

"I've got big news," I told her, beaming with anticipation. "C'mon . . ."

We knocked on her door and found Jill at her desk, looking a little peaked. Stacks of documents and legal files gave the impression she hadn't missed a single day. At the sight of us, her blue eyes sprang alive, but as she stood, her arms outstretched for a hug, Jilly seemed to be moving at half her usual speed.

"Don't," I said. I went over and gave her a hug. "You've got to take it easy."

"I'm fine," she answered quickly. "Abdomen's a little stiff, heart's a little broken. But I'm *here.* And this is the best thing for me."

"You *sure* this is the smartest thing?" Claire asked her.

"It is for me," Jill shot back. "I promise, Doc, I'm *fine.* So please, don't start trying to convince me otherwise. You want to help me start to heal, just bring me up to date on what's going on."

We looked at her a little skeptically. But then I had to share the news. "I think we found him."

"Who?" Jill asked.

I beamed. *"Chimera."*

Claire gave me a stare. She closed her eyes for a moment, as if in prayer, then opened them with a sigh.

Jill looked impressed. "Jesus, you sonofabitches *have* been busy while I've been away."

They asked all the right questions, and I laid it all out for them. When I told them the name, Jill muttered, *"Coombs* . . . I remember the case from law school. . . ." A spark lit in

343

her sharp eyes. "Frank Coombs. He killed a teenage boy."

"You're *sure* it's *him?*" Claire asked. She was still wearing a bandage on her neck.

"I hope so," I said. Then, without any doubt, "Yes, I'm sure it's him."

"You arrest him yet?" Claire asked. "Can I visit him in his cell? Hmm? I've got this bull bat I've been meaning to try out."

"Not yet. He's holed up at some dive in the Tenderloin. We've got him under twenty-four-hour watch."

I turned to Jill. "What do you say, Counselor? I want to bring him in."

She came over, a little gingerly, and leaned on the corner of her desk. "Okay, tell me exactly what you have."

I went through each link: the loose connections to three of the victims, Coombs's history as a marksman, his documented grudge against blacks, how the OFJ had sealed his fate. But with each strand of evidence, I saw her conviction dim.

"Jill, listen." I held up my hand. "He took a department-issued thirty-eight from a retired cop, and Mercer was killed with a thirty-eight. Three of the targets tie directly to his own history. I've got a guy in San Quentin who says he boasted he was out for revenge. . . ."

"Thirty-eights are a dime a dozen, Lindsay. Do you have a match on the gun?"

"No, but Jill, Tasha Catchings's murder took place in the same neighborhood where Coombs went down twenty years before."

She cut me off. "What about a witness who can place him at the scene? One witness, Lindsay?"

I shook my head.

"A print, then, or a piece of clothing. Something that ties him to one of the murders?"

With an exasperated breath, I reacted. "No."

"Circumstantial evidence can convict, Jill," Claire cut in. "Coombs is a monster. We can't just let him stay out on the streets."

Jill looked sharply at both of us. Jeez, she was almost the Jill of old. "You don't think I want him as much as you? You don't think I look at you, Claire, and think just how close we came . . . ? But there's no weapon, barely a motive. You haven't even placed him within sight of a murder scene. If you bust in and don't find anything, you've lost him for good."

"Coombs is Chimera, Jill," I said. "I know I don't have it buttoned up yet, but I've got a motive and links that tie him to three victims. As well as outside testimony that corroborates his intentions."

"Jailhouse testimony," said Jill. "Juries laugh at it these days."

She got up, came over, and put a hand on both Claire's and mine. "Look, I know how badly you want to close this. I'm your friend, but I'm still the law. Bring me anything, someone who saw him at a scene, a print he left on a door. Give me *anything,* Lindsay, and I'll be bashing down his door to get at him same as you. Turn him upside down, rattle him until his spare change falls out."

I stood there, teeming with frustration and anger but knowing that Jill was right. I shook my head and made my way toward the door.

"What are you going to do?" asked Claire.

"*Rattle* the fucker. Turn his life upside down."

Chapter 84

FIFTEEN MINUTES LATER, Jacobi and I picked up Cappy outside the William Simon and headed into the rundown lobby of the hotel. A sleepy-eyed Sikh was leafing through a newspaper in his native tongue behind the front desk. Jacobi thrust Coombs's photo and his badge in front of the man's startled eyes.

"What room?"

It took about three seconds for the turbaned clerk to squint at the photo, flip through a bound black register, and in a tight accent say, "Tree-oh-seven. He is registered with the name *Burns.*" He pointed. "Ele-vator to the right."

Moments later, we stood in the dingy, paint-chipped hallway on the third floor outside Coombs's room, flicking our automatics off safety.

"Remember, we're only talking," I cautioned. "Keep your eyes open for anything we can use."

Jacobi and Cappy nodded, then each took a position on either side of the door. Cappy knocked.

No one answered.

He knocked again. "Mr. Frank Burns?"

Finally, a heavy, grumbling voice. "Go the fuck away. Get lost, huh. I'm paid up through Friday."

Jacobi shouted, "San Francisco Police, Mr. Burns. We got you your morning coffee."

There was a long pause. I heard some commotion, the sound of a chair being dragged and a drawer closed. Finally, the sound of footsteps coming closer and a voice barking, "What the fuck do you want?"

"Just to ask a few questions. You mind opening the door?"

It took about a minute of waiting with our fingers tensed on the triggers for the door to finally unlatch.

It swung open, revealing an angry Coombs.
Chimera.

His face was round and heavy, with eyes that sagged into deep-set craters. Short, graying hair, a large, flat nose, mottled skin. He had on a white short-sleeved undershirt pulled over rumpled gray trousers. And his eyes *burned* with hatred and disdain.

"*Here . . .*," exclaimed Jacobi, swatting him in the chest with a rolled-up *Chronicle*. "Your morning paper. Mind if we come in?"

"Yeah, I mind." Coombs scowled.

Cappy smiled. "Anyone ever tell you you're a dead ringer for this cat who used to be on the force? What the hell was the cat's name? Oh yeah, Coombs. *Frank Coombs.* You ever hear that from anybody before?"

Coombs blinked impassively, then his mouth curled into a half smile. "Wouldn't you know, I get boarded on planes for him all the time."

If he recognized Jacobi or Cappy from years ago on the force, he didn't register it, but he squinted a look of familiarity as his gaze fell on me. "Don't tell me, after all this time, you bozos are the department's welcome-home committee?"

"How 'bout you let us in?" Jacobi asked.

"You come with a warrant?" Coombs leered.

"I told you nicely, we're just delivering your morning paper."

"Then make a fucking scene. C'mon," Coombs said between gritted teeth. His eyes were something else; they burned a hole right into the back of your skull.

Cappy pressed the door firmly in Coombs's face, then he and Jacobi pushed their way into the room. "As long as we're here, we might as well run a couple of questions by you."

Coombs rubbed his unshaven chin, glaring vicious darts at us. He finally pulled out a wooden chair from a small table and took a seat with his arms wrapped around its back. "Fuckers," he muttered. "Useless shitbirds."

The tiny room was littered with newspapers, Budweiser bottles lined up on the sill, cigarette butts in Coke cans. I had the sense that if I could only poke around, *something was there.*

"This is Lieutenant Boxer of the Homicide Detail," Jacobi said. "We're Inspectors Jacobi and McNeil."

"Congratulations." Coombs grinned. "I feel safer already. What do you Three Stooges want?"

"Like I said," Jacobi replied, "you should

read the papers. Keep abreast of what's going on. You follow what's in the news much?"

"You got something to say, say it," Coombs said.

"Why don't you start by telling us where you were four nights ago," I started in. "Friday? Around eleven o'clock."

"Why don't you kiss my ass." Coombs sneered. "You want to play games, let's play. I was either at the ballet or the opening of that new art exhibition. I can't recall. My schedule's too full these days."

"Simplify it for us," Cappy snapped.

"Sure. Yeah. Actually, I was with friends."

"These friends," Jacobi cut in. "They have names, phone numbers? I'm sure they'd be happy to vouch for you."

"*Why?*" Coombs's mouth puckered into a slight grin. "You got someone who says I was somewhere else?"

"I guess what I was thinking" — I met his eyes — "was when was the last time you made it out to Bay View? Your old stomping grounds? Maybe I should say your choking grounds."

Coombs glared. I could tell he wanted to wrap his hands around my neck.

"So he *does* read the papers," Cappy chortled.

The ex-con continued to glare. "What the fuck, Inspector, you think I'm some rookie whose knees start to shake when you wag your dick at him? Sure, I read the papers. You assholes can't solve your case so you come up here and shake my bush for old times. You've got zip on me, otherwise you wouldn't be lap dancing in my face and we'd be having this talk down at the Hall. You think I killed all those dingo bastards, then lock me up. Otherwise, *oh, look at the time. . . .* My Town Car's waiting. Are we done?"

I wanted to take *him* by the throat and smack his smug face against the wall. But Coombs was right. We *couldn't* take him in. Not with what we had. "There are a few questions you're going to have to answer, Mr. Coombs. You'll have to answer why three people are dead who had a connection to your murder charge twenty years ago. You'll have to answer what you were doing on the nights they were killed."

The veins on Coombs's forehead started to bulge. Then he calmed, and curled his lips into a smile. "You must be up here, Lieutenant, 'cause you've got some eyewitness that can place me at one of the murder scenes."

I stared at his face without answering.

"Or my prints all over some weapon? Or fibers from this rug, right, or my clothing? You just came up here to let me turn myself in with dignity?"

I stood there inches from Chimera, watching his arrogant grin. "You think, just because you affirmative action flunkies come up here and look tough at me, I'm gonna shove up my ass and say, 'Hey, stick it here. . . .' It gives me a real kick seeing those assholes drop one by one. You took my life away. You want to make me sweat, Lieutenant, then *pretend* you're real cops. Find something that will stick."

I stood there staring into those cold, haughty eyes. I wanted to take him down so bad. I was tempted. "Consider yourself a murder suspect, Mr. Coombs. You know the routine. Don't leave town. We'll be back to see you soon."

I nodded at Cappy and Jacobi. We moved toward the door.

"One more thing." I turned back with a grin of my own. "Just so you know . . . From Claire Washburn . . . *Lean a little to the left, huh, asshole?*"

Chapter 85

I WAS TOTALLY WIRED after work. There was just no way I could go home and unwind.

I headed down Brannan toward Potrero, my mind replaying the gut-stabbing interview with Coombs. He was taunting us, laughing in our faces, knowing we couldn't bring him in.

I knew who Chimera was . . . but I couldn't touch him.

I stopped at a light, not wanting to go home but not knowing where else to go. Cindy had a date; Jill and Claire were home with their husbands; I probably could have had a date if I made myself the least bit available.

I thought about calling Claire, but my cell phone was down — I needed to recharge the damn battery. I wanted to *do something* — the urgency was ripping through me.

If I could only get into Coombs's hotel room . . . I felt torn between heading home and possibly making the biggest mistake of my career. My rational voice said, *Lindsay, go home, get him tomorrow. . . . He's going to mess up soon.*

The pounding in my heart said, *Uh-uh, baby . . . stay on him.*

Rattle the fucker.

I swung my Explorer onto Seventh and headed for the Tenderloin district. It was almost nine o'clock.

My car seemed to drive itself to the William Simon. My chest felt tight and pressurized. Pete Worth and Ted Morelli had night watch, and as I pulled up, I spotted them in a blue Acura. They had orders, if Coombs left, to follow and radio in. Earlier that day, Coombs had sauntered out, strolled conspicuously around the block, and finally settled in a coffee shop to read the paper. *He knew he was being watched.*

I climbed out of my Explorer and went over to Worth and Morelli. "Any sign?"

Morelli leaned out the driver's-side window. "Nada, Lieutenant. He's probably up there watching the Kings game. The scum-bag. He knows we're stuck down here. Why don't you go home? We've got him covered for the night."

Much as I hated to admit it, he was proba-bly right. There was nothing much I could do here.

I started the engine again and flashed a wave to the boys as I passed by. But at the cor-ner, on Eddy, some controlling impulse restrained me from leaving. It was as if some-thing were saying, *What you want is here.*

He knows he's being watched. . . . And? . . . He wants to show up the SFPD.

I drove down Polk, back toward the William Simon. I passed pawnshops, an all-night liquor store, a storefront Chinese take-out. A parked patrol car sat at the end of the block.

I drove past the rear of the hotel. Several garbage cans outside. Not much else. The street was deserted. I turned off my lights and sat there. I don't know what I was expecting to happen, but I was driving myself crazy.

I finally climbed out of the Explorer and went inside the back door of the hotel. *Rattle the fucker.* I was thinking about going back upstairs to talk to Coombs again. Yeah, maybe we could watch the Kings game together.

There was a narrow, dingy bar just off the lobby. I took a peek inside, saw a couple of real skulls, but not Frank Coombs. Goddamn it, a murderer was here in this hotel, a cop murderer, and we couldn't do a thing about it.

A movement near the back stairs caught my eye. I ducked back inside the shadowy bar. A real oldie was playing on the juke, Sam and Dave's "Soul Man." I watched a person coming down the stairs, casting glances around like *The Fugitive.*

What the hell was this?

I recognized the camouflage jacket, the floppy hat pulled over his face. I stared hard to be sure.

It was Frank Coombs.

Chimera was on the move.

Chapter 86

COOMBS DUCKED into the kitchen of a greasy spoon attached to the hotel. I waited a few seconds, then I followed him.

Now I was the one keeping my head down, casting furtive looks. I saw Coombs, but he'd *changed*. He'd put on a white kitchen jacket and a greasy chef's hat. I remembered my cell phone — and then that it was dead. I wasn't on duty; I hadn't really needed it.

Coombs walked right out the back door of the hotel. Before I had a chance to signal the patrol car, *discreetly*, he ducked into an alleyway.

I looked down the alley and saw that it angled toward the street where I was parked. I ran for my car.

Thank God I could still see him. Coombs hurried across the street, not twenty feet in front of my car. I hoped I'd have a chance to signal the patrol car, but I didn't.

Coombs ducked into an empty lot, heading toward Van Ness. I was angry at our people — they had let him out. They had blown it.

I waited until he disappeared into the lot, then I spun the Explorer around and headed toward the intersection. At the light, I made a right, throwing on the car lights. The busy street was crowded. A Kinko's, a Circuit City, people passing by.

I watched where I thought the empty lot might come out.

I sat there, scanning up and down the block. *Could he have beaten me out here? Could he have slipped into the crowd? Shit!*

Suddenly, up ahead, I spotted the camou-flage jacket slinking out of an alley between the Kinko's and a Favor shoe store.

He'd dumped the cook's jacket and hat.

I was pretty sure he hadn't seen *me.* He looked around in both directions, then, hands in pockets, started south toward Market. I wanted to run him down with my car.

At the next intersection, I spun the Explorer around and headed back on the other side of the street, about twenty yards behind Coombs.

He was pretty good at this. He moved well. Obviously, he was in shape. Finally, he seemed satisfied he'd made a clean escape. He *nearly* had.

At Market Street, Coombs jogged into the middle of the street at a BART station. He hopped an electric bus heading south.

I followed as the bus continued south on Mission. Each time it stopped I slowed on the brakes, craning to see if Coombs had jumped off. He never did. He was taking it out of the city center.

Out near Bernal Heights, at the Glen Park station, the bus hung at the stop for a few seconds. Just as it was starting up again, Coombs hopped off.

It was too late for me to stop. I had no choice but to pass right by. I hunched low, every nerve in my body on edge. I'd been on lots of stakeouts, tailed dozens of cars, but never with so much at risk.

Coombs hung on the platform, scanning in both directions. I had no choice but to continue on. In the rearview mirror, I watched him. He seemed to be following my car as it faded out of sight.

Damn. . . . All I could do was drive. I was incredibly angry, so pissed. When I was sure I was out of sight, I accelerated, climbing a residential hill, cutting a three-point U-turn out of a driveway, and prayed Coombs would still be there.

I sped across the street and spun around to the Glen Park station from the other side.

The sonofabitch was gone! I frantically scanned every direction, but there was no sign of him. I pounded the wheel in anger. "Fucker!" I yelled.

Then, about thirty yards ahead, I spotted a mustard-colored Pontiac Bonneville pulling out of a side street, then stopping at the side of the road. The only reason I fixed on it was that it was the only thing moving.

Suddenly, there was Coombs. He ducked out of a storefront and jumped into the Bonneville's passenger's-side door.

Back at ya, I said to myself.

Then the Bonneville sped away.

So did I.

Chapter 87

I FOLLOWED, ten car lengths or so behind. The Bonneville spun onto the entrance ramp for 280 and headed south. I hung at a distance, my pulse racing. I was pretty much running on adrenaline now. I had no choice except to follow Coombs as best I could.

After a few miles, the Bonneville signaled and veered onto the exit for South San Francisco. It wound through the working-class part of town, then up a steep street that I knew to be South Hill. The streets grew dark, and I shut off my lights.

The Bonneville turned down a dark, isolated street. Middle-class row houses badly in need of repair. At the end of the street, it pulled into the driveway of a white clapboard house perched on a hill overlooking the valley. The location was pretty enough, but the house was a shambles.

Coombs and his partner got out of their car, talking. They went into the house. I turned into a dark driveway three houses down. I'd never had such a chilling feeling of being alone. It was just that I couldn't let Coombs go, couldn't let him run on us.

I pulled the Glock out of my glove compartment and checked the clip. Full load. *Jesus Christ, Lindsay. No vest, no backup, no cell phone that works.*

I crept along the shadowy sidewalk toward the white house, the automatic at my side. I was good with the gun, but *this* good?

Several beat-up cars and pickups were parked in a random pattern at the top of the driveway. The downstairs lights were on. I could hear voices. *Well, I'd come this far.*

I made my way up the narrow driveway toward the garage. It was a two-car standalone, separated from the main house by a blacktop walkway. The voices grew louder. I tried to listen, but they were too far away. I took a breath and moved closer. Hugging the house, I looked inside a window. If Coombs looked as if he was going to stay for a while, then I could get backup here.

Six outlaw types, beer bottles, smokes, huddled around a table. Coombs was one of them. On the arm of one man I spotted a tattoo that made it all so clear.

The head of a lion, the head of a goat, the tail of a reptile.

This was a meeting of Chimera.

I inched closer, trying to hear. Suddenly came the rumble of another car climbing South Hill. I froze. I clung to the house, hugging the space between the main house and the garage. I heard the car door slam, then voices and footsteps coming my way.

Chapter 88

I SAW TWO MEN coming, one with a blond beard and long ponytail, the other in a sleeveless denim vest with massive tattooed arms. I had absolutely nowhere to go.

They fixed on me. "Who the hell are you?"

Two possibilities: back away with my gun aimed at them, or make a stand and take Coombs in right now. The latter seemed the better idea to me.

"Police," I shouted, freezing the two new arrivals. My automatic was extended with both hands. "San Francisco Homicide. Get your hands up."

The two men had measured, unpanicked reactions. They glanced at each other calculatingly, then back at me. I was sure they were armed, and so were the others inside. A terrifying thought flashed through me: *I could die here.*

Noise erupted from all over. Two other men arrived from the street. I spun around, jerking my gun at them.

Suddenly, the lights inside the house went out. The driveway got dark, too. *Where was Coombs? What was he doing now?*

I jerked into a shooting crouch. This wasn't about Coombs anymore.

I heard a noise behind me. Someone coming fast. I spun in that direction — and then I was blindsided by somebody else. I was grabbed, taken down. I hit the ground hard under a couple of hundred pounds.

Then I was looking at a face I didn't want to see. A face I hated.

"Look what the tide rolled in." Frank Coombs grinned. He wagged a .38 at my eyes. "Marty Boxer's little girl."

Chapter 89

COOMBS CROUCHED down close and leered at me with that haughty, smirking grin I'd come to hate already. Chimera was right here. "Seems *you're* the one who's leaning to the left a little now," he said.

I had just enough clearheadedness to realize what incredible trouble I was in. Everything that could have possibly gone wrong had.

"This is a murder investigation," I said to the men around me. "Frank Coombs is wanted in connection with four killings, including two cops. You don't want a piece of that."

Coombs continued to grin. "You're wasting your breath if you think that bullshit carries any weight here. I heard you talked to Weiscz. Neat guy, huh? Friend of mine."

I forced myself into a sitting position. How the hell did he know I'd been to Pelican Bay? "People know I'm here."

Suddenly, Coombs's fist flashed out. He caught me flush on the jaw. I felt a warm ooze fill my mouth, my own blood. My mind flickered for some way to escape.

Coombs continued to smile down at me. "I'm gonna do what you bastards did to me. Take something precious from you. Take something you can never have back. You don't understand anything yet."

"I understand enough. You killed four innocent people."

Coombs laughed again. His coarse hand stroked my cheek. The venom in his stare, the coldness of his touch nearly made me retch.

I heard the gunshot, loud and close by, only it was Coombs who howled and grabbed his shoulder.

The others scattered. There was chaos in the darkness, and I was as confused as anyone. Another bullet whined through the air.

A skinny thug with tattoos yelped and grabbed his thigh. Two more shots thudded into the garage wall.

"What the fuck is going on?" Coombs yelled. "Who's shooting?"

More shots rang out. They were coming from the shadows at the end of the driveway.

I got up and ran in a crouch away from the house. No one stopped me.

"Here," I heard someone shout up ahead. I churned my legs toward the sound. The shooter was crouched behind the mustard-colored Bonneville.

"Let's go," he hollered.

Then all at once I saw, but I couldn't believe my eyes.

I reached out and fell into the arms of my father.

Chapter 90

WE SPED AWAY from the house, getting most of the way to San Francisco before we could even speak. Finally, my father pulled his car into the busy parking lot of a 7-Eleven. I faced him, still breathing, my heart pounding.

"Are you okay?" he asked in the softest voice I could imagine.

I nodded, not quite sure, taking an inventory of where it hurt. *My jaw . . . the back of my head . . . my pride.*

Slowly, the questions that needed to be answered crept through the daze.

"What were you doing there?" I asked.

"I've been worried about you. Especially after somebody came after your friend Claire."

The next thought hit me hard. "You've been following me?"

He dabbed the corner of my mouth with his thumb to wipe away a trickle of blood. "I was a cop for twenty years. I followed you after you left work tonight. Okay?"

My head rung in disbelief, but somehow it didn't matter. Then, as I stared at my father, something else flashed in my mind. Something that wasn't adding up. I remembered Coombs leering over me. "He knew who I was."

"Of course he knew. You met him face-to-face. You're in charge of his case."

"I don't mean from the case," I said. "He knew about *you*."

My father's eyes looked confused. "What do you mean?"

"That I was your daughter. He knew. He called me Marty Boxer's little girl."

A light was blinking from a beer sign in the 7-Eleven window. It illuminated my father's face.

"I already told you," he said, "Coombs and I were familiar. Everybody knew me back then."

"That wasn't what he meant." I shook my

head. "He called me Marty Boxer's little girl. It was about *you.*"

I had a flash of my face-to-face with Coombs that morning at the hotel. I'd had the same fleeting sensation then. That he knew me. That there was something *between him and me.*

I pulled away, my voice straining. "Why were you following me? I need to hear every-thing."

"To protect you. I swear. To do the right thing for once."

"I'm a cop, Dad, not your little Buttercup. You're holding something back. You're involved in this somehow. You want to do the right thing for once, this is the time to start."

My father leaned his head back, eyes fixed straight ahead. He sucked in a sharp breath. "Coombs called me when he got out of jail. He managed to trace me down south."

"Coombs called *you?*" I said, wide-eyed, completely in shock. "Why would he call you?"

"He asked how I'd enjoyed the last twenty years of my life, while he was away. If I'd made something of myself. He said it was time to pay me back."

"Pay you back? Pay you back for what?" As soon as I asked the question, the answer shot through me. I stared hard into my father's lying eyes.

"You were there that night, weren't you? You were in this twenty years ago."

Chapter 91

MY FATHER AVERTED HIS EYES. I'd seen the shamed and guilty look before — too many times — when I was just a little girl.

He started to explain. *Here we go again, huh, Daddy?*

"Six of us got to the crime scene, Lindsay. I was only there by chance. I was subbing for this guy, Ed Dooley. We were last on the scene. I didn't see shit. We got there after everything had been played out. But he's been badgering us, all of us, ever since.

"I never knew he was Chimera, Lindsay," my father said. "That you have to believe. I never heard of this cop *Chipman* until you told me the other day. I thought he was just threatening me."

"Threatening you, Dad?" I blinked in disbelief. My heart was breaking a little.

"Threatening you with what? Please make me understand. I *really* want to understand."

"He said he was going to make me feel the way *he* did all these years. Watching himself lose everything. He said he was going after *you.*"

"That's why you came back," I said with a sigh, "wasn't it? All that stuff about wanting to set things right. Make amends with me. That wasn't it at all."

"No." He shook his head. "I'd already pissed away so much. I couldn't let him take the rest, the part that was good. That's why I'm here, Lindsay. I swear it. I'm not lying this time."

My head was ringing. I had a murder suspect loose. Shots had been fired. I didn't know what to make of this. What to do about my father? How much did he really know? How to deal with Coombs now? *With Chimera?*

"You're telling me the truth? For once? This is my case, my big, important case. I have to know the truth. Please don't lie to me, Dad."

"I swear," he said, his eyes hooded with shame. "What're you going to do?"

I glared at him. "About what? About Coombs, or *us* . . . ?"

"About this whole mess. What happened tonight."

"I don't know." I swallowed. "But I do know one thing. . . . If I can, I'm bringing Coombs in."

Chapter 92

BY TEN THE NEXT MORNING, I had a search warrant in my hands. It granted access to Coombs's room at the William Simon. Half a dozen of us rushed over there in two cars.

Coombs was out in the open. There were things we could nail him for: like attempted murder of a police officer and resisting arrest. I had put out an APB on him and sent a team to go over the meet house where everyone had scattered the night before.

I asked Jill to meet Jacobi and me at the William Simon. I was hoping against hope that we'd find something in Coombs's room that would tie him to one of the murders. If we did, I wanted a warrant in motion immediately.

The same Indian desk clerk let us in the room. It was unkempt, a row of crushed beer bottles and soda cans lining the windowsill.

The only furniture was a metal-frame bed with a thin mattress, and a chest of drawers with his toiletries on top, a desk, a table, and two chairs.

"What'd ya expect" — Jacobi smirked — ". . . a Holiday Inn?"

Several newspapers were littered about, *Chronicle*s and *Examiner*s. Nothing out of the ordinary. On a ledge to the side of the bed, my eyes fell on a small marksmanship trophy — a prone sharpshooter aiming a rifle with the inscription *Regional 50 Meter Straight Target Champion* and Frank Coombs's name.

It made my stomach turn.

I went over to the desk. Stuck under the phone were crumpled receipts and a few numbers I didn't recognize. I found a map of San Francisco and the surrounding areas. I yanked out the drawers of the desk. An old Yellow Pages, some take-out menus to local restaurants, an out-of-date city guide.

Nothing . . .

Jill looked at me. She shook her head, grimaced.

I kept searching the room. Something had to be here. *Coombs was Chimera.* . . .

I kicked a desk drawer in, sending a lamp toppling to the floor. In the same frustrated fit, I grabbed hold of the mattress and angrily ripped it off the bed.

"It's here, Jill. Something has to be."

To my surprise, a manila envelope that had been between the mattress and the box spring fell to the floor. I picked it up and spilled the contents onto Coombs's bed.

It wasn't a gun or something taken from the victims . . . but it was a virtual history of the Chimera case. Newspaper and magazine articles, some of them going back twenty-two years to the trial, one from *Time* magazine, detailing the case. One, headlined "POLICE LOBBY DEMANDS COOMBS ARREST," had a picture of an Officers for Justice rally at City Hall Square. Scanning through it, my eye was drawn by a slashing red circle Coombs had made, highlighting a quote ascribed to a group spokesman, Patrol Sergeant Edward Chipman.

"*Bing-o.*" Jacobi whistled.

Continuing on, we came upon articles on the trial and copies of letters from Coombs to the POA demanding a new trial. A faded copy of the original Police Commission's report on the incident in Bay View. There were lots of angry comments penned in the margins by Coombs. *"Liar,"* boldly underlined, and "Fucking coward." A bold red bracket highlighted the testimony of Field Lieutenant Earl Mercer.

Then a series of current articles, tracing the most recent murders: Tasha Catchings, Davidson, Mercer . . . a blurb in the *Oakland Times* about Estelle Chipman with a scrawled-in comment, "A man without honor dishonors everything."

I looked at Jill. It wasn't perfect; it wasn't something we could tie directly to a murder case. But it was enough to remove all doubt that we had found our man. "It's all here," I said. "At least we can make this stick for Chipman and Mercer."

She thought awhile, then finally bunched her lips together and gave me a satisfied nod.

As I rebundled the file, perfunctorily leafing through the last few items, something hit my eye. My jaw stiffened.

It was a newspaper clipping from the first press conference after the Tasha Catchings murder. The photo showed Chief Mercer standing behind several microphones.

Jill noticed my changed expression. She took the clipping out of my hand. *"Oh God, Lindsay . . ."*

In the photo's background, behind Mercer, were several people connected to the investigation. The mayor, Chief of Detectives Ryan, Gabe Carr.

Coombs had drawn a bold red circle around one face.

My face.

Chapter 93

BY THE END OF THE DAY, Frank Coombs's description was in the hands of every cop in the city. This was personal. We all wanted to bring him down.

Coombs had no belongings, no real money, no network that we knew of. By all reckoning, we should have him soon.

I asked the girls to get together in Jill's office after everyone else had left. When I arrived, they were cheerful and smiling, probably thinking about congratulating me. The newspapers had Coombs's picture on the front page. He *looked* like a killer.

I sank down on the leather couch next to Claire.

"Something's wrong," she said. "I don't think we want to hear this."

I nodded. "I need to talk about something."

As they listened, I described my experience of the night before. The *real* version. How tailing Coombs had been risky and impulsive, though I hadn't had any real choice. How I had gotten trapped. How, when I was sure there was no hope, my father had rescued me.

"Jesus, Lindsay." Jill's jaw hung incredulously. "Will you *please* try to be more careful . . . ?"

"I know," I said.

Claire shook her head. "You said to me the other day, *I don't know what I would do without you,* and you go off taking a risk like that. Don't you think it works the same for us? You're like a sister. Please stop trying to be a hero."

"A cowboy," Jill said.

"Cowgirl," Cindy chimed.

"A couple of seconds either way" — I smiled — "and you guys would be out on a membership drive about now."

They sat staring at me, somber and serious. Then a ripple of laughter snaked its way around the room. The thought of losing my girls, or them losing me, made what I had done seem all the more insane. *Now* it was funny.

"Thank God for Marty," Jill exclaimed.

"Yeah, good old Marty." I sighed. "My dad."

Sensing my ambivalence, Jill leaned forward. "He didn't hit anyone, did he?"

I took a breath. "Coombs. Maybe someone else."

"Was there blood at the scene?" asked Claire.

"We've been over the house. It was rented to this small-time punk who's disappeared. There was evidence of blood in the driveway."

They stared back in silence. Then Jill said, "So how'd you leave it, Lindsay? With the department?"

I shook my head. "I *didn't*. I kept my father out of it."

"Jesus, Lindsay," Jill shot back, "your dad may have shot someone. He stuck his nose into a police situation and fired his gun."

I looked at her. "Jill, he saved my life. I can't just turn him in."

"But you're taking a huge risk. For what? His gun is properly licensed. He was your father, and he was following you. He saved you. There's no crime in that."

"Truth is" — I swallowed — "I'm not sure he was following me."

Jill shot me a hard look. She wheeled her chair closer. "You want to run that by me again?"

"I'm not sure he was following *me*," I said.

"Then why the hell was he there?" Cindy shook her head.

All their eyes fell on me.

Piece by piece, I laid out the exchange with my father in the car after the shooting. How after I confronted him, my father had admitted to being a material witness twenty years ago in Bay View. "He was there with Coombs."

"Oh, shit," Jill said with blank eyes. "Oh Jesus, Lindsay."

"That's why he came back," I said. "All those uplifting conversations about reconnecting with his little girl. His little Buttercup. Coombs was threatening him. He came back to face him down."

"That may be," said Claire, reaching out for my hand, "but he was threatening him with you. He came back to protect you, too."

Jill leaned forward, her eyes narrowed. "Lindsay, this may not be about protecting your dad from getting involved. He may have known Coombs was killing people and not come forward."

I met her eyes. "These past weeks, having him back in my life, it was like, all of a sudden I could put aside the things he had done, the hurt he caused, and he was just a person, who made some mistakes but who was funny and needing, and who seemed happy to be with me. When I was little, I dreamed of something like this happening, my dad coming back."

"Don't give up on him yet," Claire said.

Cindy asked, "So if you don't think your father came back for *you*, Lindsay, what *is* he protecting?"

"I don't know." I looked around the room, my eyes stopping at every face. "That's the big question."

Jill got up, went over to the credenza behind her desk, and hoisted up a large cardboard box file. On the front was marked, "Case File 237654A. *State of California vs. Francis C. Coombs.*"

"I don't know either," she said, patting it. "But I'll bet the answer's somewhere in here."

Chapter 94

AS SOON AS SHE GOT TO WORK the next morning, Jill opened the case file and waded in. She told her secretary to hold all calls and canceled what only yesterday had seemed an urgent meeting on another murder case she'd been working on.

With a mug of coffee on her desk and her DKNY suit jacket slung over her chair, Jill lifted out the first heavy folder. The massive trial record — pages and pages of testimony, motions, and judicial rulings. In the end, it would be better that she didn't find anything. That Marty Boxer ended up being a father who had come back to protect his kid. But the prosecutor in her wasn't convinced.

She groaned and started reading the file.

The trial had taken nine days. It took the rest of the morning for her to go through it. She sifted through the pretrial hearings, jury selection, the opening statements. Coombs's previous record was brought out. Numerous citations for mishandling situations on the street where blacks were involved. Coombs was known for off-color jokes and pejorative remarks. Then came a painstaking re-creation of the night in question. Coombs and his partner, Stan Dragula, on patrol in Bay View. They encounter a schoolyard basketball game. Coombs spots Gerald Sikes. Sikes is basically a good kid, the prosecution conveys. Stays in school, is in the band; one blemish when he had been rounded up two months before in a sweep of the projects looking for pushers.

Jill read on.

As Coombs busts up the game, he starts taunting Sikes. The scene gets ugly. Two more patrol cars arrive. Sikes shouts something at Coombs, then he takes off. Coombs follows. Jill studied several hand-drawn diagrams illustrating the scene. After the crowd is subdued, two other cops give chase. Patrol Officer Tom Fallone is the first to arrive. *Gerald Sikes is already dead.*

The trial and notes ran over three hundred pages . . . thirty-seven witnesses. A real mess. It made Jill wish she'd been the prosecuting attorney. But nowhere was there anything implicating Marty Boxer.

If he was there that night, he was never called.

By noon, Jill had made her way through the depositions of witnesses. The murder of Sikes had taken place in a service alley between Buildings A and B in the projects. Residents claimed to have heard the scuffle and the boy's cries for help. Just reading the depositions turned Jill's stomach. Coombs was Chimera; he had to be.

She was tired and discouraged. She'd spent half a day plowing through the file. She had almost gotten to the end when she found something odd.

A man who claimed he'd witnessed the murder from a fourth-story window. *Kenneth Charles.*

Charles was a teenager himself. He had a juvie record. Reckless mischief, possession. He had every reason, the police said, to create trouble.

And no one else backed up what Charles said he saw.

As she read through the deposition, a throbbing built in Jill's head. Finally, it was sharp, stabbing. She buzzed her secretary. "April, I need you to get me a police personnel file. An old one. From twenty years ago."

"Give me the name. I'm on it."

"Marty Boxer," Jill replied.

Chapter 95

A CHILLY BAY BREEZE sliced through the night as Jill huddled on the wharf outside the BART terminal station.

It was after six. Men in blue uniforms, still wearing their short-billed caps, came out of the yard, their shift over. Jill searched the exiting group for a face. He may have been a juvie with a police record twenty years before, but he had straightened his life out. He'd been decorated in the service, married, and for the past twelve years worked as a motorman with BART. It had taken April only a few hours to track him down.

A short, stocky black man in a black leather cap and a 49ers windbreaker waved good-bye to a few coworkers and made his way over to her. He eyed her warily. "Office manager said you were waiting for me? Why's that?"

"Kenneth Charles?" Jill asked.

The man nodded.

Jill introduced herself and handed him her card. Charles's eyes widened. "I don't mind saying, it's been a long time since anyone at the Hall of so-called Justice took an interest in me."

"Not you, Mr. Charles," Jill answered, trying to set him at ease. "This is about something you might have witnessed a long time ago. You mind if we talk?"

Charles shrugged. "You mind walking? My car's over here." He motioned her through a chain-link gate to a parking lot on the wharf.

"We've been digging through some old cases," Jill explained. "I came across a deposition you had given. The case against Frank Coombs."

At the sound of the name, Charles came to a stop.

"I read your deposition," Jill went on. "What you said you saw. I'd like to hear about it."

Kenneth Charles shook his head in dismay. "No one believed anything I said back then. They wouldn't let me come to trial. Called me a punk. Why you interested now?"

"You were a kid with a rap sheet who'd been in the system twice," Jill answered honestly.

"All that's true," Kenneth Charles said, "but I saw what I saw. Anyway, there's a lot of water under the bridge since then. I'm twelve years toward my pension. If I read right, a man served twenty years for what he did that night."

Jill met his eyes. "I guess I want to make sure the right man did spend twenty years for that night. Look, this case hasn't been re-opened. I'm not making any arrests. But I'd like the truth. Please, Mr. Charles."

Charles took her through it. How he was watching TV and smoking weed, how he'd heard scuffling outside his window, shouting, then a few muffled cries. How when he looked out, there was this kid, being choked.

Then, as Jill listened, everything changed. She took in a sharp breath.

"There were *two* men in uniform. *Two* cops holding Gerald Sikes down," Charles told her.

"Why didn't you do something?" Jill asked.

"You have to see it like it was back then. Then, you wore blue, you were God. I was just this punk, right?"

Jill looked deeply into his eyes. "You remember this second cop?"

"I thought you said you weren't making any arrests."

"I'm not. This is something personal. If I showed you a picture, you think you could pick him out?"

They resumed walking and arrived at a shiny new Toyota. Jill opened her briefcase, took out the picture. She held it out for him. "Is this the policeman you saw, Mr. Charles?"

He stared at the photo for a long moment. Then he said, "That's the man I saw."

Chapter 96

I SPENT THAT WHOLE DAY at the Hall, on the phone with the field or at a grid map of the city, overseeing the manhunt for Frank Coombs.

We placed a watch on several of his known acquaintances and places where we thought he might run, including Tom Keating's. I did a trace on the yellow Bonneville that had picked Coombs up and ran the phone numbers found on his desk. No help there. By four, the guy who had rented the house in South San Francisco had turned himself in — insisting it was the first time he had met Coombs.

Coombs had no money, no belongings. No known manner of transport. Every cop in the city had his likeness. *So where the hell was he?*

Where was Chimera? And what would he do next?

I was still at my desk at seven-thirty when Jill walked in. She was only a few days out of the hospital. She had on a brown wrap raincoat, with a Coach briefcase slung over her shoulder. "What're you still doing here?" I shook my head. "Go home and rest."

"You got a minute?" she asked.

"Sure, pull up a chair. Afraid I don't have a beer to offer."

"Don't worry." She smiled, opening her bag and removing two Sam Adamses. "I brought my own." She tilted one toward me.

"What the hell." I sighed. We had no trace on Coombs, and it was clear in Jill's face that something was bothering her. I figured it was Steve, already humping some new deal, leaving her alone again.

But as soon as she unzipped her case, I saw the blue personnel folder. And then a name, *Boxer, Martin C.*

"I must've told you," Jill said, cracking her beer and sitting herself down across from me, "that my father was a defense lawyer back in Highland Park."

"Only a hundred times." I flashed her a smile.

"Actually, he was the best lawyer I ever saw.

397

Totally prepared, unswayed by race or what a client could pay. My dad, the totally upright man. Once, I watched him work a case at night at home for six months to overturn the conviction of an itinerant lettuce farmer who was falsely convicted on a rape charge. A lot of people back then were pushing my dad to run for Congress. I loved my dad. Still do."

I sat there silently, watching her eyes grow moist. She took a swig of beer. "Took me until I was a senior in college to realize the bastard had cheated on my mother for twenty years. The big upstanding man, my hero."

I broke into a faint smile. "Marty's been lying to me all along, hasn't he?"

Jill nodded, pushing my father's dog-eared personnel file along with a deposition across my desk. The deposition had been folded open to a page highlighted in yellow. "You might as well read it, Lindsay."

I braced myself and, as dispassionately as I could, read through Kenneth Charles's testimony. Then I read it over again. All the while, a sinking feeling of disappointment. And then fear. My first reaction was not to believe it; anger filled me. But at the same time, I knew it had to be true. My father had lied and covered up his whole life. He had conned and bullshitted and disappointed anyone who ever loved him.

My eyes welled up. I felt so betrayed. A tear burned its way down my cheek.

"I'm so sorry, Lindsay. Believe me, I hated to show you this." Jill reached out a hand and I took it, squeezed hard.

For the first time since becoming a cop, I had no idea what to do. I felt a chasm widening; it couldn't be filled with anything that resembled duty, or responsibility, or right.

I shrugged, draining the last of my beer. I smiled at Jill. "So whatever happened to your father? Is he still with your mom?"

"*Fuck*, no," she said. "She was so tough sometimes, so cool. I just loved her. She threw him out when I was in law school. He's been living in a two-bedroom condo in Las Colinas ever since."

I started to laugh, a painful laugh that mixed with the disappointment and the tears. When I stopped, I was left with this crushed feeling in my heart and all these questions that wouldn't go away. How much had my father known? What had he kept silent about? And finally, what was his connection to Chimera?

"Thanks," I said. I squeezed Jill's hand again. "I owe you, sweetie. . . ."

"What are you going to do, Lindsay?"

I folded my jacket over my arm. "What I should've done a long time ago. I'm going to find out the truth."

Chapter 97

MY FATHER WAS IN THE MIDDLE of a game of solitaire when I got home.

I shook my head, slightly averting my eyes. I trudged into the kitchen, pulling a Black & Tan out of the fridge. I came over and sank into the chair across from him.

My father looked up, maybe feeling the heat of my eyes. "Hey, Lindsay."

"I was thinking, Dad . . . about when you left. . . ."

He continued flipping through the deck of cards. "Why do you want to go through that now?"

I kept my gaze on him. "You took me down to the wharf for some ices. Remember? I do. We watched the ferries coming in from Sausalito. You said something like, 'I'm gonna get on one of those in the next few days, Buttercup, and I won't be back for a while.' You said it was something between you and Mom. And for a while I waited. But for years I always wondered, *Why did you have to leave?*"

My father's lips moved as if he were trying to frame a response, then he stopped.

"You were dirty, weren't you? It was never about you and Mom. Or the gambling, or the booze. *You helped Coombs murder that boy.* That's what it was all along. Why you left? Why you came back? None of it had anything to do with *us*. It was all about you."

My father blinked, trying to spit out a reply. "No . . ."

"Did Mom even know? If she did, she always gave us the party line, that it was your gambling, and the alcohol."

He put down the deck of cards. His hands were trembling. "You may not believe it, Lindsay, but I always loved your mother."

I shook my head, and I wanted to get up and hit my father. "You couldn't have. No one could hurt someone they love that much."

"Yes, they can." He wet his lips. "I've hurt *you*."

We sat there, frozen in silence, for a few

moments. The washed-over anger of so many years was hurtling back at me.

"How did you find out?" he asked.

"What does it matter? I was going to find out eventually."

He looked stunned, like a fighter hit with a solid uppercut. "That trust, Lindsay . . . it's been the best thing to happen to me in twenty years."

"Then why did you have to use me, Dad? You used me to get to Coombs. You and Coombs killed that boy."

"I didn't kill him," my father said, and shook his head back and forth, back and forth. "I just didn't do anything to stop it."

A breath came out of him that seemed as if it had been held inside for twenty years. He told me how he had run after Coombs and found him in the alley. Coombs's hands were wrapped around Gerald Sikes's throat. "I told you things were different then. Coombs wanted to teach him a little respect for the uniform. But he kept squeezing. 'He's got something,' he told me. I shouted at him, *'Let go!'* When I realized it had gone too far, I went for him. Coombs laughed at me. 'This is my territory, Marty-boy. If you're scared, get the fuck out of here.' I didn't know the kid was going to die. . . . When Fallone came on the scene, Coombs let the kid drop and said, 'Little bastard was trying to pull a knife on me.' Tom was a vet; he sized it up fast. Told me to get lost. Coombs laughed and said, '*Go . . .*' No one ever disclosed my name."

My eyes stung with tears. My heart felt as if it had a rip in it. "Oh, how could you? At least Coombs stood up. But *you* . . . you ran."

"I know I ran," he said. "But I didn't run the other night. I was there for you."

I closed my eyes, then opened them again. "It's truth time. You weren't there for *me*. You were following *him*. That's why you're back here. Not to protect *me* . . . to protect yourself. You came back to kill Frank Coombs."

My father's face turned ashen. He ran his hand through his thick white hair. "Maybe at first." He swallowed. "But not *now* . . . It changed, Lindsay."

I shook my head. Tears were running down my cheeks, and I angrily wiped them away.

"I know you think that everything that comes out of my mouth is a lie. But it's not.

The other night, helping you escape, was the proudest moment of my life. You're my daughter. I love you. I always have."

My eyes were still wet, and words came out I wished I could grab back. "I want you to go. I want you to pack up and go back to wherever you were for the past twenty years. I'm a cop, Dad, not your little Buttercup. Four people have been killed so far. You're involved somehow. And I have no idea how much you know or what you're hiding."

My father's face went slack. I could see in the evaporating glow of his eyes how much this hurt.

"I want you out," I said again. "Right now."

I sat there, my arms folded around Martha, while he went into the guest room. A few moments later, he came out with his things packed. He looked small suddenly, and alone.

Martha's ears stood up. She sensed that something was wrong. She moseyed over to him, and he gently patted her head.

"Lindsay, I know how much reason I've given you to hate me, but don't do this now. You've got to watch out for Coombs. He's going to come after you. Please, let me help. . . ."

My heart was breaking. I knew that the minute he walked out the door, I would never see him again.

"I don't need your help," I said. Then I whispered, "Good-bye, Daddy."

Chapter 98

FRANK COOMBS leaned stiffly against a pay phone on the corner of Ninth and Bryant. His eyes were riveted on the Hall of Justice. It had all been leading here.

The pain in his shoulder cut through his body, as if someone were probing at the edges of the wound with a scalpel. For two days he had kept undercover, slipping down to San Bruno, hiding out. But his picture was on the front page of every paper. He had no money. He couldn't even go back and get his things.

It was almost two o'clock. The afternoon sun pierced his dark glasses. There was a crowd on the front steps of the Hall. Lawyers huddling in discussions.

Coombs took in a calming breath. *Hell, what do I have to be afraid of?* He continued to stare toward the Hall of Justice. *They should be afraid.*

The service revolver was holstered to his waist, thanks to old faithful, Tom Keating. The clip was filled with hollow points. He extended his shooting arm. Okay. He could do this.

Coombs turned toward the pay phone. He placed a quarter in the slot and dialed. *No more second chances. No more waiting. This was his time. Finally, after twenty-two years in hell.*

On the second ring, a voice answered, "Homicide Detail."

"Put me through to Lieutenant Boxer."

Chapter 99

WE HAD A LINE on one of Coombs's prison cronies who had fled to Redwood City. I was waiting for a call back.

All morning, I had pushed the murder case forward — while in the back of my mind I replayed the devastating scene with my father. Was I right to judge him for things that had happened twenty years before? More important, *what was my father's involvement with Chimera?*

I was finishing a sandwich at my desk when Karen stuck her head in. "Call on line one, Lieutenant."

"Redwood City?" I asked as I reached for the phone.

Karen shook her head. "This person said you would know him. Said he was an old friend of your father's."

My body stiffened. "Put it on four," I said. Four was the common line shared by the office. "Start a trace, Karen. *Now* . . ."

I jumped out of my chair, urgently signaling to Jacobi in the outer room. I held up four fingers, pointing to the phone.

In seconds, the office exploded into a state of alert. Everybody knew this had to be Chimera.

We needed ninety seconds to get a solid read on the trace. Sixty to narrow it down to a sector of town. *If* he was even calling from town. Lorraine, Morelli, and Chin all ran in, their faces tight with anticipation.

I picked up the phone. In the squad room, Jacobi picked up as well. "Boxer," I said.

"Sorry we missed out on all the real fun the other night, Lieutenant." Coombs laughed. "I wanted to do you. In my own special way."

"Why are you calling?" I asked. "What do you want, Coombs?"

"I have important things to tell you. Might help you make sense of the last twenty years."

"I'm fine with them, Coombs. You were put away for murder."

He chuckled grimly. "Not *my* twenty years . . . *yours.*"

410

My heart jumped. I was talking to a man who had raised a pistol to my head. I had to engage him. Anger him . . . Anything to keep him on the goddamn line.

I looked at my watch; thirty-five seconds had gone by. "Where are you, Coombs?"

"Always the departmental small talk, huh, Lieutenant? I'm starting to lose some respect for you. You're supposed to be a smart chick. Make your Marty-boy proud. So tell me, how come all these people are dead and you still don't have it figured right?"

I could feel him sneering at me. God, I hated this man. "What is it, Coombs? What haven't I figured out?"

"I heard your daddy ran out on you about the time I went to jail," he said.

I knew what he was building up to tell me. Still, I had to keep him on the line. In the outer room, Jacobi was listening, but he was also watching me.

Coombs snickered. "You probably thought that the old man was jacking off some bar-maid. Or that he left some bad markers out on the street." Coombs put on a voice of mock sympathy. "God, it must've been tough when he took off and your mom died."

"I'm going to enjoy nailing you, Coombs. I'll be there when they start the drip at San Quentin."

"Too bad you won't have the chance, sweetheart. But I wanted to tell you something important. *Listen.* Your old man *did* leave markers. *To me . . . I own them. . . .* I took the fall. For him. For the whole police department. I own them all. I did the time. But guess what, little Lindsay? I wasn't alone."

Every fiber in my body tightened. My chest nearly exploded with rage. I glanced at Jacobi. He nodded to me as if to say, *A few more beats . . . Keep him on.*

"You want me, Coombs? I saw the photo in your room. I know what you want. I'll meet you anywhere. . . ."

"You want the killer so bad, it's almost touching. But sorry, I have to pass on your offer. I've got one more date."

"*Coombs,*" I said, glancing at the clock, "you want me, let's go at it. Can you beat a woman, Frank? I don't think you can."

"Sorry, Lieutenant. Thanks for the fun talk. But it seems like, everything that happens, you're just a tad too late. I still don't think broads belong in the department. Just an opinion."

I heard a click.

I ran out into the squad room. Cappy had a line going with Dispatch. I was desperately hoping Coombs hadn't used a cell phone. Cells were the hardest to trace. *One more date* . . . I didn't know what the hell Coombs was threatening. What was next? What?

"He's still in the city," Cappy shouted to me. He reached for a pen. "He's in a phone booth. They're trying to narrow it down."

The detective started to write, then he looked up. His face was screwed in disbelief. "He's in a booth . . . at the corner of Ninth and Bryant."

All of our eyes met, and then everybody in the room was moving.

Coombs was calling from a block away.

Chapter 100

I STRAPPED ON MY GLOCK and yelled a call for closest available unit. Then I charged out of the office. Cappy and Jacobi trailed on my heels.

Just a block away . . . What was Coombs going to do?

I didn't wait for the elevator. I bounded down the back stairs as fast as my legs would carry me. In the lobby, I pushed through staffers and civilians standing around and burst through the glass doors leading to Bryant Street.

There was the usual mass of people milling around on the front steps at lunchtime: lawyers, bondsmen, and detectives. I turned my gaze toward Ninth, craning my head to spot anyone who looked like Coombs.

Nothing.

Cappy and Jacobi caught up to me. "I'll go ahead," Cappy said.

Then it hit me. *One more date . . . Coombs was here, wasn't he?* He was at the Hall of Justice.

"Police," I shouted, signaling the unsuspecting crowd. "Everybody stand alert."

I scanned through the startled crowd for his face. My Glock was at the ready. Bystanders looked at me in wide-eyed surprise. Several crouched down or started to move away.

This is what I remember about what happened next:

A uniformed cop came up the stairs, walking toward me. I hardly noticed; I was scanning for Coombs's face.

The uniform came out of the crowd, the face obscured behind sunglasses and the visor of his hat. He was holding out his hand.

I focused right past him, scanning down the street, searching for Coombs. Then I heard someone shout my name. "Hey! *Boxer!*"

Everything exploded on the steps of the Hall. Jacobi, Cappy, yelling, *"Gun . . . "*

My eyes flashed toward the cop. In that

instant, the strangest thing came clear to me. *His blues* . . . He was wearing a patrolman's uniform that I hadn't seen in a while. I fixed on the face, and to my shock, it was Coombs. It was Chimera. I was the date he was planning to keep.

Someone spun me from behind as I raised my Glock. "Hey!" I yelled.

I saw Coombs's gun spurt orange. Twice. Nothing I could do to stop it.

Then everything got incredibly crazy and confused. Chaos. Terror.

I know that I got off a shot before my body went numb with pain.

I saw Coombs lurch forward, his glasses flying off, his gun pointed my way. He staggered, but he was still coming for me. His dark eyes glared with hate.

Then a scary shooting gallery erupted in front of the Hall. A cacophony of loud, echoing pops . . . *five, six, seven* in rapid succession, coming from all directions. People were screaming, running for cover.

Coombs's blue uniform erupted in bursts of bright red. Cappy and Jacobi were firing at him. His body hurtled backward, jerking with the hits. His face showed terrible pain. The air was laced with a burning cordite smell. The echo of each shot crashed in my ears.

Then it was eerily quiet. The silence was startling to me.

"Oh, Jesus," I remembered saying, finding myself down on the concrete steps. I didn't know for sure if I'd been shot.

Jacobi was leaning over me. "Lindsay, stay right there. Be still." His hands were on my shoulders, and his voice reverberated through my brain.

I nodded, inventorying my body for a wound. Shouts and wails echoed all around, people rushing everywhere.

I reached for Warren's arm and slowly pulled myself up. He tried to give me an order: "Lindsay, stay down. I'm telling you now."

Coombs was on his back, ruptures of crimson oozing out of his blue shirt.

I pushed by Jacobi. I had to see Coombs, had to look into his eyes. I hoped he was still alive, because when the monster took his last breath, I wanted him staring up at me.

A few uniforms had formed a protective ring around Coombs, ordering everyone to stay clear.

Coombs was still alive, labored sounds escaping from his heaving chest. An EMS team came running, two techs lugging equipment. One, a woman, began ripping at Coombs's bloody shirt. The other was taking his pressure and setting up an IV.

Our eyes met. Coombs's gaze was waxy, but then his mouth twitched into an ugly smile. He tried to say something to me.

The EMS woman was backing people off, shouting out his vitals.

"I have to hear what he's saying," I told the tech. "Give me a minute here."

"He can't talk," she said. "Give him room to breathe, Lieutenant. He's dying on us!"

"I have to hear," I said again, then I knelt down close. Coombs's uniform shirt had been cut open, a mosaic of ugly wounds exposed.

His mouth quivered. He was still trying to talk. *What did he want to tell me?*

I leaned closer, the blood on Coombs smearing my blouse. I didn't care. I put my ear close.

"One last . . . ," he whispered. Every breath was a fight for him now. Was this how it ended? With Coombs taking his secrets straight to hell?

418

One last . . . ? One last target, one last victim? I stared into his eyes, saw the hatred still there.

"One last *what,* Coombs?" I asked.

Blood bubbled out of his mouth. He took in a hard breath, husbanding the last of his strength, straining against the power of his own death.

"One last *surprise.*" He smiled.

Chapter 101

CHIMERA WAS DEAD. It was over, thank God.

I had no idea what Coombs had meant, but I wanted to spit his words back in his face. *One last surprise* . . . Whatever it was, Chimera was gone. He couldn't hurt us anymore.

I hoped it didn't mean he had left one last victim before he died.

"C'mon, Lieutenant," Jacobi muttered. He gently pulled me up.

Suddenly, my legs buckled. I felt as if I had no control over the lower part of my body. I saw the look of alarm on Warren's face. "You're hit," he uttered, wide-eyed.

I looked down at my side. Jacobi peeled back my jacket, and a wet red gash appeared on my right abdomen. All of a sudden my head began to spin. A current of nausea rose.

"We need help here," Jacobi shouted to the EMS tech. He and Cappy eased me back to the ground.

I found myself staring over at Coombs, as the female tech who had peeled away the dead man's shirt rushed over to me. *God, this was so unreal.* They took off my jacket, slapped a blood pressure monitor on my arm. It was as if it were happening to somebody else.

My gaze stayed fixed on the killer, the goddamn Chimera. Something a little strange, something not tracking. What was it?

I pulled myself out of Jacobi's grip. "I have to see something. . . ."

He held me back. "You have to stay right here, Lindsay. There's an ambulance on the way."

I pulled away from Jacobi. I got up and went over to the body. Coombs's police uniform had been peeled back off of his chest and arms. Raw wounds spotted his chest. But *something* was missing; something was all wrong. What was it?

"Oh, my God, Warren," I whispered. "Look."

"Look at what?" Jacobi frowned. "What the hell is wrong with you?"

"Warren . . . there's no tattoo."

My mind flashed back. Claire had discovered pigment from the killer's tattoo under Estelle Chipman's fingernails.

I put my hands underneath Coombs's shoulders and rolled him slightly. *There was nothing on his back. No tattoos anywhere.*

My mind was whirling. This was unthinkable — but Coombs couldn't be Chimera.

Then I passed out.

Chapter 102

I OPENED MY EYES in a hospital room, feeling the constraining pull of the IV line stuck in my arm.

Claire was standing over me.

"You are a lucky girl," she said. "I talked to the doctors. Bullet grazed your right abdomen but didn't lodge. What you've basically got is one of the nastiest *floor burns* you'll ever see."

"I heard floor burns go well with powder blue, don't they?" I said softly, my lips parting in a weak smile.

Claire nodded, tapping the taped bandage on her neck. "So I'm told. Anyway, congratulations. . . . You've earned yourself a cozy desk job for the next couple of weeks."

"I already have a desk job, Claire," I said. I blinked a confused look around the hospital room, then I pulled myself up into a sitting position. My side ached as if it were on fire.

"You did good, girl." Claire squeezed my arm. "Coombs is dead, and now safely ensconced in hell. There's a mob of people outside who want to talk with you. You're gonna have to get used to the accolades."

I closed my eyes, thinking of the misplaced attention about to come my way. Then, through the haze, it hit me. What I had discovered before I blacked out.

My fingers gripped Claire's arm. "Frank Coombs didn't have a tattoo."

She shook her head and blinked back. "So . . . ?"

It hurt to talk, so the words came out in a whisper. "The first murder, Claire. Estelle Chipman . . . She was killed by a man with a tattoo. You said it."

"I could've been wrong."

"You're never wrong." I flashed my eyes.

She eased back on her stool, her brow creased. "I'm doing the autopsy on Frankie-boy Monday morning. There could be a highly pigmented section of skin, or a discoloration somewhere."

I managed a smile. "Autopsy . . . ? My professional opinion is that he was shot."

"Thanks." Claire grinned. "But someone's got to take the bullets out of him and match them up. There'll be an inquiry."

"Yeah." I blew out a gust of air and dropped my head back on the pillow. The whole incident, seeing the cop coming up to me, realizing it was Coombs, the flash of his gun, all came back to me as broken fragments.

Claire stood up, brushed her suit skirt. "You ought to get some rest. Doctor said they might release you tomorrow. I'll check back in the A.M." She leaned down and gave me a kiss. Then she made her way to the door.

"Hey, Claire . . ."

She turned back. I wanted to say how much I loved her, how grateful I was to have such a friend. But I just smiled and said, "Keep your eyes peeled for that tattoo."

Chapter 103

I SPENT THE REMAINDER of the day trying to rest. Unfortunately, a steady stream of brass and press paraded through my room. It was credit by association, sound bite time. Everyone wanted to have their picture taken with the wounded hero cop.

The mayor stopped by, accompanied by his press liaison and Chief Tracchio. They held an impromptu press conference at the hospital, praising me, citing the great work done by the city's homicide detail, the same unit they had almost pulled off the case.

After the commotion finally died down, Cindy and Jill dropped in. Jill brought a single rose in a glass vase and placed it on my bedside table. "You won't be in here long enough to warrant more." She grinned.

Cindy handed me a wrapped videotape. I

opened it. *Zena, the Warrior Woman.* She winked. "I hear she does her own stunts, too."

I pulled myself up and lifted my stiff arms around them in a hug. "*Don't* squeeze back," I warned with a smile.

"They giving you any good pills?" Jill asked.

"Yeah. Percocets. You should try this sometime. Definitely worth the risk."

For a moment, we all just sat there without talking.

"You did it, Lindsay," Cindy said. "You may be fucking crazy, but no one can say you're not a helluva cop."

"Thanks."

"Don't think this getting-shot thing lets you out of my exclusive. I'll give you some time to recover. How's six?"

"Right." I chuckled. "Bring me back a chicken enchilada from Susie's."

"Doctor said we could only come in for a minute," said Jill. "We'll call you later." They both smiled and backed toward the door.

"You know where to find me, ladies."

Around five, Jacobi and Cappy stuck their heads in.

"We were wondering where you were,"

Jacobi muttered, deadpan. "You didn't show up for the afternoon meeting."

I grinned, climbed out of bed a little stiffly. "You guys are the heroes. All I did was dive out of the way to save my butt."

"Shit." Cappy shrugged. "We just wanted to say that despite the fact the mayor's recommending you for the Medal of Honor, we still love you."

I smiled, tugged at my green hospital gown, and slowly lowered myself into a chair. "You guys got a bead on what happened?"

"Chimera came at you is what happened," Jacobi said. "He shot, we took him out. End of story."

I tried to remember the sequence of events. "Who got off the shots?"

"I got four," Jacobi said. "Tom Perez, from Robbery, was next to me. He got off two."

I looked at Cappy.

"Two," he added. "But shots were coming from all around. IAB's taking statements."

"Thanks." I smiled gratefully. Then my expression changed. I looked hard at the two of them. "How do you figure this? The same guy who takes out Tasha Catchings and Davidson from a hundred yards like it's a layup only *grazes* me from point-blank range?"

Jacobi looked at me a little confused. "Is there something you're trying to tell us, Lindsay?"

I sighed. "All along, we were looking for a guy with a tattoo, right? The same man who killed Estelle Chipman. Linchpin of the case."

They nodded blankly.

"There was none on Coombs. Not a mark."

Jacobi shot a glance at Cappy, then back at me. "What're you trying to say? That Coombs isn't our man? That we tied him in to each of the murders, found those clippings in his room, that he tried to pop you not once but twice. But that it wasn't him?"

My mind wasn't working clearly. The events of the day, the medication. It was chickenshit compared to everything that pointed clearly at him. "I guess what I mean is, you ever know Claire Washburn to be wrong?"

"No." Jacobi shook his head. "But I don't know you to be wrong too often, either. Jeez, I can't believe I said that."

They told me to get a good night's sleep.

"My gut feeling," Jacobi said, turning back on his way out the door, "is that when the medication wears off and you have a chance to look at everything in the light of day, you'll see you made a pretty good bust."

I smiled at them. "We all did."

That night I couldn't sleep. I lay on my back, my side throbbing, but I was also feeling the blurry warmth of a couple of Percocets. I looked around the dark room, strange, unnatural, and the truth sank in about how lucky I was to be alive.

Jacobi was right; it *was* a good bust. Coombs was a murderer. All the facts played out. He had been trying to kill me at the end.

I shut my eyes and tried to drift off, but the tiniest voice tolled in my head. One voice, sneaking through all that was certain, all that seemed plausible.

I tried to force myself to sleep, but the voice got louder.

How could he have missed?

Chapter 104

I WAS RELEASED the following morning.

Jill came and got me, pulling her BMW up to the curb outside San Francisco General as they wheeled me out in a chair. The press was there. I waved to all my new pals, but I refused to talk to them. The next stop was home, a hug for Martha, a shower, a change of clothes.

By the time I walked into room 350 at the Hall with a slightly stiff gait Monday morning, it was as if it were business as usual: The entire detail gave me a round of applause.

"Game ball belongs to you, Lieutenant," Jacobi said, handing me the brush.

"C'mon" — I waved them off — "let's wait for the inquiry."

"The inquiry? What's that gonna prove?" he said. "Do the honors."

"L.T.," said Cappy, his eyes clear and proud, "we've been saving it. For you."

"Do it, L.T."

Maybe for the first time since Mercer promoted me, I felt like the head of Homicide, and that all the doubts of worth and rank I'd carried with me my whole career were markers on an old journey, miles behind.

I went over to the board where our active cases were listed and I brushed Tasha Catchings's name off the board. Art Davidson's, too.

I felt filled with a quiet but exultant joy. I felt relief and satisfaction.

You can't bring the dead back. You can't even make sense of why things happen. All you can do is the best you can to let the living believe their souls are at peace.

The detectives circled around me and watched.

I wiped Earl Mercer's name off the slate.

Chapter 105

I FIELDED PHONE CALLS for the next couple of hours. But mostly I just sat at my desk, giving some thought to my deposition. There was an inquiry pending on the Coombs shooting, standard practice whenever a police officer fired a gun.

The whole incident was still a blur to me. The doctors had told me it might be like that for a while. A kind of repressed shock.

I had a flash of that out-of-date uniform, and Coombs's eyes burning into me. His arm extended, the orange spurt of his gun. I was sure that someone had shouted my name, probably Cappy or Jacobi, then someone else said, *"Gun . . ."*

And my own Glock, flopping up in slow motion, knowing I was a beat too late, seeing the spurt of his gun. Then the gunfire — from all directions, *pop, pop, pop, pop, pop . . .*

Finally, I put it out of my mind and went back to work.

About an hour later, I was leafing through the file on one of our new outstanding cases when Claire appeared at my door.

"Hey!"

"Hey back at you, Lindsay."

I knew *Claire*. . . . I knew her look when she'd found what she expected and had put doubt to rest. And I knew the look when it was not so kosher.

This time, she was definitely wearing that not-kosher look.

"You didn't find any tattoo, did you?" I said.

She shook her head. Her expression couldn't have been more troubled if she had found something culpable about Edmund, or one of her sons.

I motioned her in and shut the door. "Okay, so what *did* you find?"

She shrugged somberly. "I guess I found out *why Coombs missed.*"

Chapter 106

CLAIRE SAT DOWN and started to explain. "I was doing a routine histology, in the substantia nigra —"

"In English, Claire," I cut in. "S'il vous plaît? Por favor?"

She smiled. "I scooped some cells, midbrain. Coombs was hit nine times. Eight from the front. One from the rear. That one smacked into his cervical spine. It's the only reason I would have been in there in the first place. I was looking for a specific cause of death."

"So what *did* you find?"

Her gaze bore right through me. "A marked absence of neurons . . . live nerve cells."

I sat upright. My heart was in my throat. "Meaning what, Claire?"

"Meaning . . . Coombs had Parkinson's, Lindsay. And not an unadvanced case."

Parkinson's . . . My first thought was, *That's why he missed.* That I had been so damn lucky . . .

Then, watching the look of blank-eyed nullity grow into alarm on Claire's face, I knew it wasn't so simple.

"Lindsay, someone with Coombs's stage of Parkinson's could *never* have pulled off those shots."

My mind went back to the scene at the La Salle Heights Church . . . Tasha Catchings, felled by that incredible shot . . . And Art Davidson, a single bullet hole in his head . . . The bullet had come through the window from an adjoining roof, at least a hundred yards away.

I fixed on Claire's eyes. "You're sure about this?"

She nodded slowly. "I'm not a neurologist . . ." But then with unwavering clarity, "Yes, I'm sure. I'm absolutely positive. His state of Parkinson's could never have allowed the necessary interaction between hand and brain for those shots. His case was too progressed."

With an almost nauseating chill, I flashed through all the things we knew about our killer. We had been certain that Chimera had a tattoo. But Coombs didn't have one. Then he barely grazed me on the steps of the Hall from point-blank range. And now this, *Parkinson's* . . . Whoever Chimera was, he was certifiable as a marksman. That much was irrefutable.

We looked at each other and I uttered the unutterable. "Jesus, Claire, Coombs isn't our man."

"Right," she said. "So, who is, Lieutenant?"

Chapter 107

FOR A LONG TIME, we just sat there, letting the stunning realization, and panic, sink in.

The newspapers, the TV, every sane person in the entire city was celebrating Chimera's death. Just that morning, I had wiped the murder cases off the board.

"Coombs was trying to tell me something," I said to Claire, recalling his dying moments. "'One last . . . ,' he whispered, and when I asked him, *one last what?* he seemed to smile. 'One last surprise.' He *knew* Chimera was still out there, Claire. He knew we would find out. The bastard was laughing at me as he drew his last breath. It has to be somebody else in his group. There's another madman."

Claire pressed her lips together. "Lindsay, if I could've come back with any other conclusion . . ."

I didn't know exactly what to do with this new information. The pattern had fit so seamlessly. Bay View . . . Chimera. The file in Coombs's room. And how he had come at me. I couldn't believe that somehow I had been wrong. And then the question again: *If not Coombs, who?*

The last thing I wanted to do was go upstairs and shatter the celebration of all the bureaucrats and brass. But at the same moment Claire and I were gaping at each other in disbelief, the real killer was out there, possibly scoping another hit. Jesus, *this just didn't make sense.*

"Come with me," I said, sucking in the sharp pain in my side. I ambled down the hall to Charlie Clapper's office.

"The returning hero." The rotund CSU man stood up and smiled. "A little bent over at the waist, but otherwise you look okay."

"Charlie," I said, "how long until we have a match on the gun?"

"Gun . . . ?" He screwed his brow.

"Coombs's gun. How long until we can match it up against the piece that killed Mercer?"

439

"It's a little late, gorgeous, if you're trying to narrow down your suspects. I'd start with the dude on Claire's slab."

"When, Charlie?" I shot back. "How long 'til you get a match?"

"Maybe Wednesday." He shrugged. "We've got to scan the inside of the gun, get a reading on the —"

"*Tomorrow,* Charlie," I said. "I *need* it by tomorrow."

"Lindsay," he said, looking a little confused, "what the hell is going on?"

I turned to Claire, a swallow of bile making an unpleasant retreat into my chest. "We have to bring this upstairs."

We grabbed an elevator up to the fifth floor. I was so dumbfounded and racked with emotions, I hardly felt the pain shooting through my side. We barged into Acting Chief Tracchio's office. He was scribbling at his desk.

"What are you doing *here?*" he exclaimed. "You should be home. Good God, Lieutenant, if anyone has a well-earned leave coming to them —"

I stopped him in midsentence. Then I told him what Claire had found. Suddenly, Tracchio looked as if he had swallowed a mouthful of bad oysters.

"I don't buy this, Lieutenant," he said. "You solved the case. It's over."

"You may not buy it," Claire said firmly, "but I've never been so sure of anything in my professional life. There is *no way* Coombs could've pulled off those shots."

"But this is all speculation," Tracchio objected. "The links to the Sikes killing . . . Coombs's Chimera background . . . his qualifications with weapons. These are all facts. *Your* facts, Lieutenant." He wagged his finger at me, stabbing me point by point with my own analysis. "No one else could possibly fit that profile. I can't argue with your conclusions, Dr. Washburn, but eliminating Coombs . . ."

"We can test his DNA against the sample of skin we found under Estelle Chipman's nails," Claire replied, "which is what I'm going to do. But I'll bet my reputation against yours, they *don't* match."

"In the meantime, we have to reopen the case," I said.

"Reopen the case?" Tracchio gasped. "I'm not going to give any such order."

"If Chimera's still out there," I pressed, "he could be planning another hit right now. I suspect that he is."

"Only yesterday," Tracchio blurted, "you were one hundred percent sure Coombs was Chimera."

"That was yesterday," I said. "We told you why it's changed. Right now I'm about one hundred percent sure Coombs *isn't* Chimera."

"What you've told me is medical speculation. I want solid proof. Get me the DNA check."

"That could take days," Claire said. "A week . . ."

"Then match the ballistics," Tracchio ordered. "Chief Mercer was killed with a thirty-eight. I'll guarantee you Clapper will show it was the same gun."

"I'm on it. But in the meantime —"

"There is no *meantime,* Lieutenant. As far as I'm concerned, you did one hell of a job. Put your own life on the line. What you should be on now is medical leave, not trying to start another investigation."

Claire and I looked at each other.

Then Tracchio picked up a few papers, the

way figures of authority learn to do to communicate that a meeting is over. *Fuck him.*

Back in the hallway, I looked at Claire. "I'm about to bring the whole city down on us. You better be damn sure."

"Course I'm sure," she replied. "What are you going to do?"

"I'm going to wait for ballistics, Claire. And pray that nothing happens in between. I'm also putting everybody back on the investigation."

Chapter 108

"CINDY THOMAS, is that you?"

Aaron Winslow almost couldn't believe what his eyes were telling him. When Cindy opened the door to her apartment, she was wearing a tailored black pantsuit, sling-back heels, a solitaire diamond necklace. Directly behind her, he could see her dining room — lit candles, china, silver flatware, and crystal.

Cindy stepped forward and gave Aaron a kiss. Then she pulled away. God, she did look stunning. She was absolutely radiant tonight.

"All right, I have a confession to make," she said. "The Armani suit belongs to my friend Jill, the lawyer. So do the Ferragamo shoes. If I spill anything on the Armani, or as much as scuff the shoes, she'll never talk to me again."

Cindy smiled and took Aaron's hand.

"Come in. Don't be too afraid. Even though

I am. Tonight we celebrate the end of a horrible siege and a terrible man."

Aaron had started to laugh. "You certainly look beautiful for the celebration."

Cindy continued to beam. "Yes, and I prepared almond-crusted chicken, a romaine salad, orzo pasta with peas and mint. Unfortunately, the chicken happens to be one of only three dinners I know how to make."

"Your honesty is refreshing," Aaron said. "Who belongs to the china and crystal?"

Cindy laughed out loud as she led him into the dining room. Jeez, she felt a little like Bridget Jones.

"Believe it or not, the china and crystal is all mine. My mother has been giving me pre-wedding gifts since I was eighteen. I thought Wedgwood and Waterford would be perfect for our special night. The grub is ready. Let's do it."

"May I help you serve the feast?" Aaron asked.

"That would be just perfect. Like everything else tonight."

Everything was, actually, and a few minutes later they were seated at the dining table with the delicious-looking food in front of them.

Cindy tapped her wineglass. "I want to make a toast," she said.

Just then, Aaron saw a reflection moving in the mirror over the sideboard behind Cindy. His heart fell. Not again; not here.

"Cindy, no!" he screamed. Suddenly he was out of his chair and he dove headfirst across the dining table. He only hoped he was in time.

He took Cindy and most of her china and crystal down. Everything hit the floor with a crash just as the first shot shattered the dining room window. Several more shots followed in quick succession. Trailer fire. Chimera was here. He was coming for them now.

Cindy had the presence of mind to grab the cord and pull the phone off the console in the hallway. She pressed the number four on her quick dial, then speaker, and she heard Lindsay's voice.

"He's here at my apartment. He's shooting at Aaron and me!" she screamed over the phone. "Chimera is here and he's still shooting!"

Chapter 109

THIS COULDN'T BE HAPPENING, but it was.

I called for all available units, then I rushed to Cindy's apartment. I got there as fast as humanly possible. Maybe a little faster. I saw Cindy and Aaron standing on the front porch. Half a dozen patrol cars were parked all around the house. But they were still targets, weren't they?

My hands were clutched tightly as I ran to her. I hugged Cindy, and she was still trembling badly. I'd never seen her look so vulnerable, so afraid and lost.

"Thank God a patrol car was here in minutes, Lindsay. It either scared him off or he was gone already."

"Are you all right?" I turned my attention to Aaron. He and Cindy both had stains all over their clothes. It looked as if they'd had a food fight. What the hell had happened here?

"Aaron saved me," Cindy said in a whisper. He just shook his head and held Cindy's hand. There was a tenderness between them that touched me a great deal.

"He's losing it," I muttered, more to myself than to either of them. Whoever Chimera was, he was in a rage. Obviously, he wanted to hurt me, or anyone I was close to. Or maybe he was offended by the idea of Aaron Winslow and Cindy. That could be part of it. He wasn't planning his hits as carefully now; he was reckless and rattled, but still very dangerous.

And he was out there somewhere. Maybe even watching us right now.

"C'mon, let's go back inside," I said.

"Why, Lindsay?" asked Cindy. "That's where he shot at us. Who the hell is this guy? What does he want?"

"I don't know, Cindy. Please go inside, sweetie."

Inspectors were already checking where the shots had come from. CSU was after the caliber of the weapon. But I knew. And I knew that it was him: *Chimera.*

I'm still here, he was telling us. Telling me.

Warren Jacobi's blue Ford pulled up, and I watched him get out and hurry over to me. "The two of them okay?"

"Yeah. They're inside now. Jesus, Warren. This has something to do with me. It has to."

I rested my head on his shoulder for a second. Tears welled in my eyes, and I felt them come. They ran down my cheeks, hot and stinging.

"I'm gonna kill this guy," I whispered.

Jacobi held me even tighter. Good old Warren.

We were back at zcro. I had no idea who it was. I didn't know where we would start to look for him.

A black Lincoln Town Car wound its way along the barricaded street and swooshed up to the curb. The door opened, and a grim-faced Chief Tracchio stepped out, surveying the shooting scene.

He caught my eye with a guilty swallow, the flashing lights of the crime scene reflected on his glasses.

I glared at him. *Proof enough?*

Chapter 110

THE NEXT MORNING, half of Homicide banged our heads together in the conference room, reexamining every piece of evidence, every assumption we had made. As the meeting was ending, I took Jacobi aside. "One other thing, Warren. I want you to look at something for me. Make certain that Tom Keating *really is in a wheelchair.*"

By one o'clock, I had to take a break. I needed thinking outside the box. We weren't seeing something.

I had to talk to the girls, so I called them together for a quick lunch at the Rialto, across the street from the Hall. Even Cindy said she was coming. She insisted on it.

When she arrived at the Rialto everybody hugged her, and tears came into our eyes. None of us could believe Chimera had gone after Cindy and Aaron — but he certainly had.

"This is crazy," I said as we huddled around a table, nibbling at salads and calzones. "Everything matched. Coombs's past, Chimera, the incident in Bay View. Everything pointed there. We *can't* be wrong."

"What you need to do first," Claire cautioned, "is take the pressure off yourself. It's horrible, what's happened. But we can't get too emotional."

"I know that." I exhaled. "It's probably what the killer wants. Jesus."

Jill shuffled in her seat. "Listen, Coombs has to be at the center of this. Too many things check out. He may not have pulled the trigger, but what if he got someone else to? What about those asshole buddies of his in South San Francisco?"

"Two are still missing," I said, "but my gut tells me no. Oh hell, I don't know anymore. Everybody in Homicide is stumped. Coombs was one madman. Who the hell is the other one?"

"You checked everything you found in his hotel room?" Cindy asked. She had been unusually quiet until then.

"Checked, double-checked," I replied.

For what seemed like the tenth time, my

mind went to the tiny, disheveled hotel room — the suitcase full of Coombs's prison things, the clippings stashed under his mattress, the numbers on the desk, his letters . . .

Except this time, something hit. . . .

Cindy was asking if we had ever considered the possibility that someone was trying to set Coombs up, but I didn't respond. My mind was elsewhere . . . rooted back in that dingy hotel room. The line of beer cans and cigarette butts on the sill above the bed. *Something else there.* I had never given it a second thought. I squinted into space, trying to visualize the sight. Then I saw what I was looking for — and what I might have missed.

"Lindsay?" Claire cocked her head. "Everything all right?"

"Earth to Lindsay . . . ," Jill taunted.

Cindy put her hand on my wrist. "Lindsay, what's going on?"

I grabbed my bag and stood up. "We've got to get back to the Hall. I think I just figured something out."

Chapter 111

EVIDENCE TAKEN INTO CUSTODY is kept under lock and key in a storage room in the basement of the Hall.

Fred Karl, the day duty officer, looked a little annoyed at the four of us. "This isn't a social room," he grumbled, pushing a clipboard in my direction and pressing a button that opened the chain-link gate. "You and Ms. Bernhardt can sign and go in. These other two, they'll have to wait out here."

"Arrest us, Fred," I said, waving everyone through.

The contents of Coombs's hotel room had been placed in large storage bins near the back. I led the girls to the spot and hung my jacket on a ledge as I pulled a couple of bins down from the shelf coded with Coombs's case number. I started rummaging through the contents.

"Would you mind telling me just what the hell we're looking for?" Jill asked, seeming annoyed. "What the hell didn't I see?"

"You saw it perfectly," I said as I pawed through Frank Coombs's effects. "So did I. But neither of us put it together at the time. Look at this."

As if it were a silver chalice, I picked up the polished brass trophy of a prone sharpshooter aiming a rifle. *50 Meter Straight Target Champion,* the inscription plate read. That was what I remembered from the first time I saw the trophy.

But the name above it changed everything.

Frank L. Coombs . . . *not Frank C.* Francis Laurence, not Francis Charles.

Rusty Coombs . . . The trophy had been awarded to Coombs's son.

All of a sudden, every assumption and insight changed for me. Maybe because of all the paperwork I had looked at recently, Coombs Sr.'s full name had sunk into my consciousness.

Frank C. was the father, *Frank L.* the son.

"I'm not my father," I remembered Rusty Coombs saying. I could see his face now, the convincing act he'd put on for Jacobi and me.

"It's the son," I whispered.

Jill sat back on the floor, stunned. "You're telling me, Lindsay, these horrifying murders were committed by Coombs's son? The boy at Stanford?"

Cindy blurted, "I thought he hated his father. I thought they hadn't been in touch."

"So did I," I said. "He fooled everyone, didn't he?"

We stood there, seeking one another's eyes in the dim basement room. Did the new theory work? Did it stand up to scrutiny? My mind flashed again — *the white van.* The getaway car from Tasha Catchings's murder . . . It had been stolen from Mountain View. Palo Alto and Mountain View were only a few minutes apart.

"The owner of the white van," I said, "taught anthropology at a community college down there. He said he took on students from other schools. Sometimes, some of the jocks . . ."

All of a sudden, things were fitting into place. "Maybe one of them was Rusty Coombs?"

Chapter 112

I HURRIED BACK UPSTAIRS. The first thing I did was place a call to Professor Stasic at Mountain View Junior College. I was only able to get his voice mail. I left an urgent message for him to call me.

I punched the name Francis L. Coombs into the CCI databank computer. The father's old conviction came up, but nothing on the son. No criminal record.

I felt that if the kid was cold enough to do these terrible crimes, he had to be in the system somewhere. I typed his name in the juvie databank. These records were sealed, unable to be used in a court, but we had access. After a few seconds, a file shot back. *A long one* . . . I blinked at the screen.

Rusty Coombs had had run-ins with the law at least seven times from the time he was thirteen.

In 1992, he'd been brought before a juvie court for shooting a neighbor's dog with a pellet gun.

A year later, he'd been indicted for criminal mischief for killing a goose in a corporate park.

At age fifteen, he and a friend had been charged with desecrating a public place for spray painting a synagogue with anti-Semitic slogans.

He had been charged, but not convicted, with throwing beer bottles through a neighbor's window. The complainant was black.

He was alleged to be part of a high school gang, the Kott Street Boys, known for race-based attacks on blacks, Latinos, and Asians.

One after another, I read on, stunned. Finally, I called Jacobi into my office. I laid the whole thing out for him. Rusty Coombs's violent past. His name on the marksmanship trophy. The stolen van in Mountain View, not that far from Palo Alto.

"Obviously, they've seriously relaxed the admission requirements at Stanford since I applied." Jacobi snorted.

"No jokes, Warren. Please. So what do you think? I'm losing it, right? Am I crazy?"

"Not so crazy we shouldn't pay the kid another visit," he said.

There were other things we could do to be sure. We could wait and see if Coombs Sr.'s DNA matched what was found under Estelle Chipman's nails. But that took time. The more I thought about it, the more Rusty Coombs made sense.

My brain was buzzing now. A tremor of recognition reverberated through me. "Oh my God, Warren . . . *the white chalk* . . ."

Jacobi leaned forward and narrowed his eyes. "What about it?"

"The white powder Clapper found at two of the scenes." I recalled an image of Rusty Coombs, his freckled face and wide lineman's shoulders in a sweaty Cardinals T-shirt. The epitome of a superior kid who'd turned his life around, right?

"Remember when we met him?"

"Sure, the gym at Stanford."

"He was lifting weights. What do weight lifters use, Warren, to hold on to the bar so it doesn't slip?" I stood up. My mind settled on the vivid image of Rusty Coombs rubbing his thick, white hands together.

"They use chalk," Jacobi muttered.

Chapter 113

JOGGING BACK from afternoon practice, Rusty Coombs took the four-mile loop from the field house around South Campus. He decided to make the last two hundred meters an all-out sprint.

A police car wailed past him. Then another speeding cruiser.

At first, the sight of the cruisers jolted him. But as he watched the cars trail away, he relaxed. His muscular legs churned on.

Everything was fine, just fine. He was safe here at Stanford. One of the privileged few, right?

He went back to what he'd been thinking about before the cops rudely interrupted. If he could get his body fat down to 7.8, and slice his time in the forty another tenth or two, he could maybe move up to the third round of the NFL draft. Third round meant guaranteed bonus. Stick to the plan, he told himself. *Fantasies had a way of becoming real, at least his did.*

Rusty chugged onto Santa Ynez, a block away from the frat house where he and several other football players lived. As he turned down the street, his body slammed to a halt.

What the fuck . . . They're here for me!

The street was ablaze with flashing lights. Police cars . . . three of them, and two maroon campus security vehicles in front of *his* house. A crowd milling in the street. Town cops weren't allowed on campus for anything trivial. No, this was bigger, *widescreen. . . .*

He knew in a sickening flash that everything was over. He wouldn't even have the chance to cut the lights out on the little bitch who had killed his father. His legs still moved, jogging in place.

What shot through his mind was, *How the fuck could they have known? Who figured it out? Not Lindsay Boxer!*

A geeky student in baggy red shorts with a red knapsack thrown over his shoulder came up the street toward him. Rusty continued to jog in place. "Hey, what the hell's going on?"

"Police are looking for someone," the guy said. "Must be something big, 'cause everyone's saying cops from San Francisco are on the way."

"No shit," Rusty muttered. "All the way from San Francisco, huh?"

Too bad, he thought. He was pissed. He was also sorry it had to end. But he'd always fantasized about how this might play out.

He reversed himself and started jogging back in the direction of the Main Quad. His stride picked up speed, swiftly and powerfully.

Rusty Coombs turned his head as another police car, siren wailing, shot by. No point hiding out any longer. The cops were here in numbers.

Fortunately, he had the perfect ending.

Chapter 114

JACOBI AND I SPED DOWN 101 toward Palo Alto at a steady ninety. Signs for Burlingame, San Mateo, and Menlo Park shot past. We were pumped to take this creep down within the hour.

I was hoping we could take Rusty Coombs by surprise. Maybe as he came out of a class. There were thousands of students on the Stanford campus. He was armed and very dangerous, so I wanted to avoid a confrontation if I could.

I had arranged to meet Lieutenant Joe Kimes of the Palo Alto Violent Crimes Detail at the dean of students' office in the Main Quad. As we closed in on Palo Alto, Kimes called back. He reported that Coombs couldn't be found. He had no scheduled classes that afternoon. He wasn't at his residence or the stadium, where the Stanford football team had finished practice about an hour ago.

"Does he know there's an APB out on him?" I asked. "What's happening down there, Joe?"

"It's hard to keep a low profile here," Kimes said. "He could've seen our cars."

I was starting to worry. I'd hoped we could get to Coombs before he knew we were coming. He liked attention — he wanted to be a star.

"What do you want us to do?" Kimes asked.

"I want you to put the local SWAT team on alert. Meanwhile, try to find the big creep, Joe. Don't let him out of our trap. And Joe, this guy is extremely dangerous. You have no idea."

Chapter 115

THE ELEVATOR ASCENDED RAPIDLY and when it opened, Chimera looked out on the observation deck of the Hoover Tower, more than two hundred and fifty feet over Stanford's Main Quad.

There was no one up there on the deck. No one to bother him, no one to kill right away. Just the flat blue sky, the concrete WPA-style dome, the giant carillon bells that tolled thunder across the campus.

Rusty Coombs flicked off the elevator power switch, freezing the doors open.

Then he slung the black nylon duffel bag he was carrying onto the floor and leaned against the concrete wall, his back to one of the eight barred windows. He opened the bag, removing his disassembled PSG-1, the sniper's scope, and two additional pistols, along with clips of ammunition.

This was something else — breathtaking, actually. The bomb, right? He could see mountains to the south and west, the outline of San Francisco to the north. It was a clear day. Everything was calm, perfect. The Stanford campus stretched out before him. Students crept like ants down below. The best and the brightest.

He began to hook together the rifle, clicking the barrel seamlessly into the stock, fitting on the customized shoulder rest, until the assembled piece rested in his arms like a prized musical instrument.

A sparrow perched on the carillon bells. He aimed and squeezed the trigger in a dry run. *Click.*

Then he screwed the sniper's sight onto the stock. He snapped in a twenty-round clip.

He crouched behind the cement wall. The wind rattled by, sounding like a gust snapping a canvas sail. The sky was a gorgeous turquoise blue. *I'm going to die, and you know what? I really don't care.*

Students were casually traversing crosswalks, lounging and reading on benches. Who knew . . . ? Who suspected any danger? He could have his pick. *He could immortalize any of them.*

Rusty Coombs swung the barrel of his rifle through the metal bars in one of the dome's six-foot-high windows. He squinted through the sight and searched out the first target. Students popped into view: a pretty Japanese girl with auburn hair and dark glasses nuzzling her Caucasian boyfriend on the green. A geek in a bright yellow sweatshirt riding a yellow bicycle. He shifted the sight. A black student with long corn braids walking toward the student bookstore. Coombs smiled. Sometimes it even amazed him how much hatred he had inside. He was smart enough to know that he didn't just despise them, he despised himself. Despised his buffed-up body, the imperfections only he knew about, but most of all he hated his thoughts, his obsessions, the way his goddamn mind worked. He'd felt so alone, for so goddamn long. Like right now.

In the distance, he caught sight of a blue Explorer with flashing lights. It pulled up in front of the administration building. The tight-assed bitch from San Francisco jumped out. His heart pounded.

She was here. He'd have his chance at her after all.

He fixed the sight on the pretty Oriental girl smooching her boyfriend on the lawn. Christ, he hated both of them. Disgraces to their races.

Then, as a second thought, he swung the rifle over to the jig girl with the cornstalks, a gold heart-shaped pendant bobbing on her neck, a glint in her brown eyes.

It's just my nature. He smirked, coiling his finger around the cold metal trigger.

Chimera was back in business.

Chapter 116

THE EXPLORER screeched to a stop outside the administration building. Jacobi and I got out and cut through the Spanish loggia overlooking the Main Quad.

We ran right into Kimes, barking orders into a handheld radio. He was with the grim-faced dean of students, Felix Stern. "We still haven't found Rusty Coombs," Kimes told me. "He was seen on the Quad twenty minutes ago. Now he's disappeared again."

"How are we doing with that SWAT team?" I asked him.

"They're on their way now. You think we'll need them?"

I shook my head. "I hope not. We won't need them if Coombs got spooked and split."

Just then, we heard shots. I knew that none of the police would fire first. Besides, it sounded like rifle fire.

"I think he's still here," Warren Jacobi deadpanned.

Screams of panicked students echoed down the loggia. Then they started to run toward us, fleeing the Quad.

Someone shouted, "He's in the Hoover Tower. The fucker, the fucking madman!"

Jacobi, Kimes, and I ran right into the stampeding students. Joe Kimes was on the radio. "Shots fired! All personnel and EMS to the Hoover Tower. Use extreme caution!"

We got to the green in the next few seconds. Students were hiding behind trees, pillars, large flower pots, anything that afforded some cover.

Two students were down. One of them was a black woman, a bloody circle widening on her chest. Goddamn him. Goddamn *Chimera.*

"Stay down! Stay where you are!" I yelled across the Quad. "Please keep your heads down!"

A shot rang out from the tower. Then a second and third. A male student dropped from behind a slatted bench.

"Please stay down!" I screamed again. "Stay the hell down!"

I fixed my eyes on the belfry of the tower, searching for a shape, a gun, anything to set Rusty Coombs's position.

Suddenly, two more shots echoed from the tower. Coombs was definitely up there. There was no way we could protect this many people. He had us where he wanted us. Chimera was still winning.

I grabbed Kimes. "How would I get up there?"

"No one's going up there," Joe Kimes snapped back, "without a SWAT escort." His eyes were wide and frozen. He shouted into the radio. "All SWAT and medical teams to the Main Quad! Sniper is shooting from the Hoover Tower. At least three down."

I looked him in the eye. "How do I get up there, Joe?" I demanded. "I'm going, so tell me the best way."

"There's an elevator on the ground floor," Dean Stern cut in.

I pulled my Glock out of my side holster and checked the smaller Beretta I had fastened to my ankle. Chimera was up in that dome, raining bullets down.

My eyes fixed on a building that would provide some cover. Jacobi reached for my arm. But he knew he wasn't going to stop me.

"You wouldn't give me a minute to grab us both a vest, would you, L.T.?"

"I'll see you up there, Warren." I winked. Then I broke for the tower in a tight crouch.

And somewhere in the back of my mind, I wondered — *why am I doing this?*

Chapter 117

JESUS, HE FELT GOOD.

Chimera pulled back the rifle and sat against the hard concrete wall. In a moment, hell on earth was going to bust loose in the Quad. SWAT teams, snipers, maybe even helicopters. He knew he had the advantage — he didn't care if he died.

He fixed on the big carillon bells. He'd always liked the stupid, damn bells. When they played, you could hear them all over campus. He wondered, when this was over, when he was no longer around, if he could have bells played at his funeral. Yeah, right.

Then he realized he was alone in the Hoover Tower and had just killed five people. What a fucking day this had been — what a life he'd had. He was going down in history, no doubt about that anymore.

He lifted himself up and peered over the side. Suddenly, everything was pretty quiet down there. The Quad had been cleared. Soon there'd be a high-tech SWAT team on the scene, then he'd just have to take out as many as he could get. They were going to have to earn their overtime pay.

But for now, up here, man, everything was beautiful. . . .

Then he spotted Lindsay Boxer! He squinted through the rifle sight to be sure. The "hero cop" who had killed his father. She had run from the cover of the administration building, zigzagging in a crouch toward the tower. He was glad she was here. Suddenly, everything changed. *He could still bring this bus in on time.* . . .

He followed the darting shape and gently closed his left eye. He let his breathing slow to an almost meditative rate.

He was thinking that his father had taken nine shots.

So should she.

He drew in a breath and fixed the crosshairs on her white blouse.

You're a dead woman.

Chapter 118

IT WAS QUIET NOW in the quadrangle. Rusty Coombs was either taking a breather or reloading.

Let's do it. Me and you, pal.

I headed for the building in front of me. I felt a kind of controlled hysteria. Not good. I knew I was a target, and that Coombs could shoot.

Suddenly, I heard a gun burst *behind* me. I glanced and saw Jacobi firing at the tower.

Before Coombs could train on me, I darted under the cover of thick poplar branches, then around the building to within a few yards of the base of the tower.

I looked around and saw Jacobi with Kimes. He shook his head at me. I knew it meant, *Please, Lindsay, stay put. I can't do backup once you're in the tower.* I winked at him almost apologetically.

I ran around the tower until I found an entrance on the north side. I headed up the stairs and found myself in a marbled WPA-style lobby.

Elevator straight ahead.

I pressed for the elevator over and over, my gun trained on the doors. They didn't open. In futility, I slammed my fist against the polished chrome doors. I screamed, *"Police."* The shout echoed down the halls. I needed someone, anybody. I had no idea how to get to the top of the tower from here.

An older man in a maintenance uniform emerged from down a corridor. He recoiled at the sight of my gun.

"Police," I yelled. "How do I get up there?"

"Man's blocked the elevator," he said. "Only way up is the auxiliary stairs."

"Show me. Please. It's a matter of life or death."

The caretaker led me through a door and up to the third floor, then down a corridor to a narrow set of stairs. "You got yourself thirteen flights. Fire door at the top. Opens from both sides."

"*Wait* in the lobby and tell anyone who comes that I'm up here," I said as I headed into the narrow stairwell. "That's a matter of life or death, too."

"Yes ma'am. Understood."

I started up. Thirteen flights. And I didn't know what to expect at the top. My heart was racing and my blouse clung to my back with cold sweat.

Lucky thirteen. With each story, my breaths grew tighter and sharper. My legs began to ache, top to bottom, and I run four times a week. I didn't know if I was crazy, going in there without backup. No, hell, I *knew* I was crazy.

Finally, I pushed past twelve and reached the top. *Jesus.* Only a solid metal fire door separated me from Chimera. My heart was exploding.

Through the door I heard more shooting. *K-pow, k-pow, k-pow.* He was at it again. I was scared that someone else might be killed. I was angry, pissed, I wanted him so bad. I checked my Glock and sucked in a breath. *Oh God, Lindsay ... whatever you do, do it fast.*

The fire door had one of those heavy emergency levers that had to be pushed down to release.

I pressed it down and burst onto the observation deck.

Chapter 119

I WAS STRUCK with a blast of blinding sunlight. Then the chilling sounds: *k-ping, k-ping, k-ping* . . . the ejecting shells from the rifle jangling to the floor.

Rushing onto the deck, I spotted Coombs. He was kneeling in front of an opening with his rifle extended through the bars.

Suddenly he pivoted toward me.

His gun exploded in my direction. A deafening burst, orange flashes all around. Loud metallic dings.

I dove away from the door, peeling off a burst of four shots. I didn't know if I'd hit him. I sucked in a breath, waiting for a stab of pain to see *if he'd hit me.* He hadn't.

"It's a lot harder when somebody's shooting back at you," I yelled.

I was crouched behind a tall metal grating. It housed a collection of seven massive bells. Each looked as if it could shatter my eardrums with a single ring. The rest of the observation deck was no more than an eight-foot-wide path. It circled the bells with viewing openings every six feet or so in the wall.

Coombs was on the other side — the bells acting as a cover for both of us.

His voice called out, an easy, arrogant twang, "Welcome to Camelot, Lieutenant. . . . All these big-shot brains down there . . . and now you coming all the way up here just to talk to *me*."

"I brought along friends. They won't be talking, Rusty. They'll be looking for any shot to take you down. Why die like this?"

"I don't know, seems like a good plan to me. You want to die up here with me, be my guest," Rusty Coombs called back.

I squinted through the grating, trying to get a fix on where Coombs was. Across the belfry, I heard him shove in a fresh clip.

"I'm glad it's you. I mean, it's fitting, don't you think? You nail my dad, now I get to do the same to you."

His voice seemed to shift, *as if he was circling*.

I started to circle as well, my Glock aimed toward the corner of the bell housing.

"I don't want you to die up here, Rusty."

"A little slow on the uptake, aren't you, Lieutenant? Just like always. I gave you everything I could think of. The chimera symbols, the van, the nine one one . . . What did I have to do, send you a fucking E-mail and say, *'Hey, fellas, I'm over here?'* Took you long enough to figure it out. Cost a few lives along the way."

Suddenly, a burst of gunfire rattled the iron grating, bullets clanging loudly off the bells.

I ducked down, holding my head between my hands.

"Your father's gone," I shouted. "This doesn't bring him back."

Where was he now? I peered through a gap in the grating. *Brain freeze.*

There was Rusty Coombs. He was smiling at me, his father's smug, hateful grin. I saw the rifle extended through the bell housing.

In that instant, I saw a sudden flash, felt a recoil of brute force. Then the powerful impact of the shot hurled me backward.

I landed hard on my back, scurried for cover as Coombs rushed around for a clear shot. My fingers groped for my Glock. Jesus, *my gun . . . wasn't there.*

Coombs had shot it out of my hand!

He walked forward until he stood over me. His rifle was pointed at my chest. "You have to admit, I sure can shoot, huh?"

Every lingering hope was gone. His eyes were green and held such a cold, impassive burn. I hated this bastard so much.

"Don't add any more deaths," I said, my mouth completely dry. "SWAT teams are coming. Kill me, five minutes later, it'll be you."

He shrugged. "At this point, it's gonna be a bitch to square myself with the coach. People like you" — he stared blankly — "you don't have the slightest idea what it's like to lose your father. You bastards took my father."

I watched his finger move to the trigger and realized I was going to die. I said a silent prayer and I thought, *I don't want to die.*

Then the deepest, ear-splitting sound interrupted. It had the force of a building crashing down. One resounding gong was followed by another, then another. I had to grab my ears to keep from going deaf.

It was the bells. They were going off, and it was the loudest noise I'd ever heard — by a lot. The entire tower shook with the thunderous sound.

Coombs's face twisted into a contortion of shock and pain. He staggered, reflexively crunching into a ball to protect himself.

When I saw him coil up, I reached inside my pant leg. I pulled out the Beretta strapped to my ankle.

Everything happened so quickly, like a film with the action running but the sound a high-pitched distortion.

Coombs, seeing me, swung his rifle into firing position.

I fired three times, spurts jerking back my hand. *The bells continued to gong . . . over and over.*

Three crimson bursts spattered across Coombs's broad chest. The force sent him tumbling backward.

Then the bells again. Each earsplitting clang felt like a sledgehammer slamming into my skull.

Coombs came to rest in a sitting position. He gazed down, saw his torn flesh. He blinked with a glazed, mystified look. He raised his rifle toward me. "You die, too, bitch!"

I squeezed the trigger of the Beretta. The bells gonged as a final blast thudded into his throat. He grunted loudly and his eyeballs rolled back into his head.

I realized that my hands were cupping my ears again. My head ached. I crawled to Coombs and kicked his rifle away. The bells continued to sound, a melody that was unidentifiable to me, maybe an answer to my prayer.

My eye fixed on something as I knelt beside Coombs. "There it is," I whispered.

A curled, reptilian tail in red and blue, leading into the body of a goat with the fierce and proud heads of a lion and a goat. *Chimera* . . . One of my shots had pierced the wicked beast's torso. It looked dead, too.

I heard shouts coming from behind, but I continued to kneel over Coombs. I felt I had to answer what he'd said at the end. *You don't have the slightest idea what it's like . . . to lose your father. . . .*

"Oh, yes I do," I told his still eyes.

Chapter 120

THIS TIME the newspapers had it right. *Chimera was dead.* The multiple-homicide case was closed.

There was no great joy in the final outcome, at least not for me. Homicide didn't get together and wipe the board clean. There were no toasts with the girls. Too many people had died. I was lucky not to have been among them. So were Claire and Cindy.

I took a few days off, to give my side and hand some time to heal, and the IA teams a chance to piece together what had happened at the shooting scenes. I hung out with Martha, took some long walks along the Marina Green and Fort Mason Park as the weather turned damp and cold.

Mostly, I replayed the events of the horrible case. It was the second time I'd had to fight a killer one-on-one. Why was that? What did it mean? What did it say about my life and what it had come to?

For a moment, I'd had an important piece of my own past given back, a father I never really knew. Then, that gift was taken away. My father had disappeared into the dark hole from which he had crept. I knew I might never see him again.

In those days, if I could have come up with one meaningful thing I wanted to do with my life, I might have said, *Let's give it a ride.* If I could paint, or had some secret urge to open a boutique, or the stick-to-itiveness to write a book . . . It was so hard to find even the thinnest slice of affirmation.

But by the end of the week, I just went back to work.

Late that first day, I got a buzz from Tracchio to come up to his office. As I walked in, the chief stood up and shook my hand. He told me how proud he was, and I almost believed him.

"Thanks." I nodded, and even smiled. "That what you wanted to say?"

Tracchio took off his glasses. He shot me a contrite smile. "No. Sit down, please, Lieutenant."

From the edge of his large walnut desk, he picked up a red folder. "Preliminary findings on the Coombs shooting. Coombs *Senior.*"

I regarded it tentatively. I didn't know if some IAB bureaucrat had found something suspicious.

"There's nothing to worry about," Tracchio assured me. "Everything checks out. A perfectly clean shooting."

I nodded. So what was this all about?

"There is one thing outstanding, though." The chief stood and leaned against his palms on the front of his desk. "The M.E. lifted nine rounds out of Coombs's body. Three belonged to Jacobi's nine millimeter. Two came from Cappy's. One from your Glock. Two twenties from Tom Perez out of Robbery. That's *eight.*"

He stared down at me. "The ninth bullet didn't match up."

"Didn't match?" I raised my eyes. It didn't make sense. The commission had every gun from every cop who was involved, including mine.

Tracchio reached into a desk drawer. He came back with a plastic baggie containing a flattened, slate gray round, about the same color as his eyes. He handed it to me. "Take a look. . . . Forty caliber."

A jolt of electricity surged through me. *Forty caliber . . .*

"Funny thing is" — his eyes bore in — "it *did* match up to *these*." He produced a second baggie containing four more rounds, nicked, flattened.

"We took these out of the garage and trees outside that house in South San Francisco where you followed Coombs." Tracchio kept his eyes fixed on me. "That make any sense to you?"

My jaw hung like a dead weight. It didn't make sense, except . . . I flashed back to the scene on the steps of the Hall.

Coombs rushing toward me, his arm extended; that frozen moment before I fixed on his face. From behind him, the thing I always remembered, couldn't put away: *a voice, someone shouting my name.*

In the melee there was a *pop*. . . . Then Coombs lurched.

The bullets didn't match up. Coombs had been shot with a .40 caliber handgun. . . . My father's gun . . .

I thought of Marty, his promise as he stood in my doorway that last time.

Lindsay, I'm not running anymore. . . . My father had shot Frank Coombs on those steps. He had been there for me.

"You didn't answer, Lieutenant. That make any sense to you?" Tracchio asked again.

My heart seemed to be bouncing side to side in my chest. I didn't know what Tracchio knew, but I was his hero cop. Catching Chimera would erase the "Acting" in front of his title. And like he said, it was a clean shooting.

"No, Chief," I answered. "It doesn't make any sense."

Tracchio fixed on me, weighing the file in his hand, then nodded, placing it at the bottom of a heavy pile of other reports.

"You did a good job, Lieutenant. Nobody could have done better."

Epilogue

I'LL FLY AWAY

FOUR MONTHS LATER . . .

It was a sparkling, clear March afternoon when we all went back to the La Salle Heights Church.

Almost five months after that first bloody attack, every chink in its exterior walls had been sanded and painted over with fresh white paint. The arched opening where the church's beautiful stained-glass window had shone was draped with a white curtain erected for today's event.

Inside, VIP's from the city government sat shoulder to shoulder with proud parishioners and families gathered for the occasion. News cameras rolled from the side aisles, recording the proceedings for the evening news.

The choir, dressed in white gowns, belted out "I'll Fly Away," and the chapel seemed to swell and resonate with the triumphant power of the raised voices.

Some people clapped with the music, others tearfully wiped their eyes.

I stood in the back with Claire and Jill and Cindy. My body tingled with awe.

As the choir concluded, Aaron Winslow stepped up to the pulpit, proud and handsome as ever in a black suit and dress shirt. He and Cindy were still together, and we all liked him, really liked *them*. The crowd quieted down. He looked around the packed house, smiling peacefully, and in a composed voice began. "Only a few months ago, the play of our children was rocked by a madman's nightmare. I watched as bullets desecrated this neighborhood. This choir that sings for you today was gripped with terror. We all wondered, *Why . . . ?* How was it possible that only the youngest and the most innocent of us was struck?"

Cries of "Amen" echoed from the rafters. Cindy whispered against my ear, "He's good, isn't he? Best of all, he means it."

"And the answer is . . . ," Winslow declared to the hushed room, "the only answer can be, so that she could pave the way for the rest of us to follow." His eyes scanned the room. "We are all linked. Everyone here, the families who have suffered loss, and those who have simply come to remember. Black or white, we are all diminished by hate. Yet somehow, we heal. We carry on. We *do* carry on."

At that moment, he nodded toward a group of young children dressed in their Sunday best, flanking the large white curtain. A girl in braids, no more than ten, tugged on a cord, and the canvas fell to the floor with a loud *whap.*

The church became awash in brilliant light. Heads turned, followed by a collective gasp. Where once shards of fallen glass had left a jagged hole, a stunning stained-glass window shone intact. Cries of acclamation rang out, then everyone began to clap. The choir started up softly in a hymn. It was so damn beautiful.

As I listened to the moving voices, something stirred inside me. I glanced at Cindy, Claire, and Jill, thinking, reliving just how much had happened since I'd last stood in this place, since Tasha Catchings had been killed.

Tears welled in my eyes, and I felt Claire's fingers at my side. She probed for my hand, squeezing me by the fingertips. Then Cindy cradled her arm through mine.

From behind, I felt Jill bracing my shoulder. "I was wrong," she whispered in my ear. "What I said when they were wheeling me into the OR. The bastards don't win. We do. We just have to wait to the end of the game."

The four of us stared at the beautiful stained-glass window. A sweet and gentle robed Jesus was motioning to disciples, a yellow nimbus around his head. Four or five followers were trailing behind. One of them, a woman, had turned to wait for someone else, her arm extended. . . .

She was reaching toward the outstretched hand of a young black girl.

The girl looked like Tasha Catchings.

TWO WEEKS LATER, a Friday night, I'd invited the girls over for dinner. Jill said she had big news that she wanted to share.

I was coming back from the market, grocery bags in hand. In the vestibule of my walk-up, I fumbled for the mail. The usual catalogs and bills. About to move on, I noticed a thin white envelope, the standard air mail variety with red and blue arrows, the kind they sell you at the post office.

My heart jumped as I recognized the script.

It was postmarked *Cabo San Lucas, Mexico.*

I put the grocery bags down, then I sat on the steps and split the envelope open. I lifted out a folded piece of lined paper. Inside, a small Polaroid photo.

"My beautiful daughter," the letter began in an edgy scrawl,

By now, you must know everything. I've come a long way down here, but I have stopped running.

You no doubt have some idea of what happened that day at the Hall. You modern cops have it all over old slugs like me. What I wanted you to know was that I wasn't afraid to have it come out. I hung around for a few days to see if the story broke. I even called you at the hospital once. *That was me* . . . I knew you didn't want to hear from me, but I wanted to hear that you were all right. And of course — *you are just fine.*

These words are not enough to let you know how sorry I am for having disappointed you again. I was wrong about a lot of things: one of them was, you can't leave everything behind. I knew that the moment I saw you again. Why has it taken me my whole life to let such a simple lesson sink in?

But I was right about one thing. And it's

more important than anything else. No one is ever so big not to need help every once in a while . . . even from their father.

The letter was signed, "Your stupid Dad," then below it, "who truly loves you . . ."

I sat reading the note a second time, holding back a rush of tears. So Marty had finally found a place where nothing would follow him. Where no one would know him. I choked with the sad realization that I might never see him again.

I flipped the grainy photograph.

There was Marty . . . in a ridiculous Hawaiian shirt, posing in front of some dilapidated fishing boat, raised on a scaffold, maybe twelve feet long. There was a little note on the bottom: *New start, new life. I bought this boat. Painted it myself. One day, I'll catch you a dream . . .*

At first, I laughed. . . . What a jerk, I thought, shaking my head. What the hell did he know about boats? Or fishing? The closest my father ever got to the ocean was when he was assigned to crowd control on Fisherman's Wharf.

Then something grabbed my eye.

In the background of the photo, past the proud countenance of my father, against the masts and hulls of the blue marina and the beautiful sky . . .

I squinted hard, trying to make out the lettering on the freshly painted hull of his new boat.

The single word scrawled there, in plain, white letters, in his own simple hand.

The name of the boat: *Buttercup.*